THE MANHUNTER

Ellen Anthony

LN Books Limited

THE MANHUNTER
A Syran Novel Book 1
Ellen Anthony

The characters and events portrayed in this book are fictitious. Any similarity to real persons, living or dead, is coincidental and not intended by the author except for those persons who begged to be used and abused in this book. No part of this book was created by an artificial intelligence program.

First Edition Copyright 1999 Ellen Anthony
Published by Hard Shell Word Factory
Award: Finalist, 2000 Epic Award (Science Fiction)

Second Edition Copyright © 2023 Ellen Anthony
Published by LN Books Limited

Published by LN Books Limited
4500 Cannon Avenue 63
Klamath Falls OR 97603

ISBN-13: 978-1-948168-07-6

DEDICATION

To all my friends and family who have
put
up with my writing for so long.
It ain't over yet.
To Imo and Carol, my late-night
companions,
and for Dave who listened to it all.
Many thanks!

Table of Contents

DEDICATION 3

TABLE OF CONTENTS 4

PROLOGUE 6

CHAPTER 1 - DATYL 7

CHAPTER 2 - *THE SEAWIND* 19

CHAPTER 3 - MISHAP 25

CHAPTER 4 –COAST 29

CHAPTER 5 - TEMPTATION 42

CHAPTER 6 - ALONE 49

CHAPTER 7 - BEES 55

CHAPTER 8 - PIGS 66

CHAPTER 9 - BOWER 75

CHAPTER 10 - SEFRON 88

CHAPTER 11 - MONAR 97

CHAPTER 12 - RAIDERS 107

CHAPTER 13 –HOLD 115

CHAPTER 14 - PROMISE 124

CHAPTER 15 - GARDON 132

CHAPTER 16 - TREES 139

CHAPTER 17 –TEMPLE 144

CHAPTER 18 - LYDA 151

CHAPTER 19 - EDAN 158

CHAPTER 20 - CHOICE 167

CHAPTER 21 - EDAN 178

CHAPTER 22 - PREPARATION 188

CHAPTER 23 - WOMEN'S DAY 196

CHAPTER 24 - WAITING 207

CHAPTER 25 - SCROLL 219

CHAPTER 26 - TURNABOUT 225

CHAPTER 27 - SYNDA 231

CHAPTER 28 - DRUNK 245

CHAPTER 29 - CHOICE 255

EPILOGUE 259

THE AUTHOR 261

Prologue

There comes an end to every civilization then a beginning. The Sunborn, a space-faring race, was nearly doomed by genetic problems and sterility. In an effort to save their race from extinction, they abandoned their starship for life on pastoral Syra and crafted a new society with the more fertile Kalryn.

Generations after the First Colonists, some of the desperate measures of their ancestors remained. A fertile woman is encouraged to bear a child. If she has no husband, she may hunt a man to father her child and keep him for three days and nights.

This is the story of one such manhunt and what happens when Synda of Datyl chooses a man who dares to love her.

Chapter 1 - Datyl

The midday sun beat hotly down on the port of Datyl, leaving few shadows in which to escape the heat. The normal activity of the busy port was quiet now as sailors and dockworkers took shelter until the summer day cooled. At the dock the ships stood alone at their moorings with not even a swell to keep them company during the hot part of the day.

One lone figure worked high in the rigging of a tall ship. After nearly a fortnight in port *The Seawind* would sail soon and preparations were underway.

One of the oldest ships on Syra, *The Seawind's* hull shone bright white without the scarring of weather or mark of barnacles on its stark whiteness. Neither metal nor wood, the hull had stood the test of time and hard use since the days of the colonists.

The upper works of *The Seawind* were a rich, contrasting black with only a wide red line around her unused stack to mark her from her sister ships. Her three masts scratched the sky with the furled sails looking like snow on her spars.

On the deck Davyd Yorkson was watching the sailor up in the rigging, his lean athletic body sprawled comfortably in a deck chair in a way that belied his alertness. He could see the sailor wore his tie-off even from thirty feet below but he didn't have as much faith in flimsy ropes as the sailors who trusted their lives to them. His brown eyes followed the trim sailor from spar to spar as he checked the lines.

Wishing he could climb the rigging himself, he had to be content with watching. Six weeks on *The Seawind* hadn't dulled his fear of heights or made him more nimble. No, he could only help out on the deck and even then he deferred to the ship's sailors. He was just a passenger with time on his hands—a trader with cargo below decks.

"Back aboard already?" the captain asked when he stopped beside his chair. "I thought you were still ashore."

"No sir." Davyd rose to his feet with all the grace of a fighter and smoothed his curly black hair back in a habitual gesture. "The wine is stowed and my business is done."

Picking up the sword and scabbard that lay beside his chair, he hooked it on his wide leather belt, the movement automatic after lifelong training.

"It's just as well," Captain Krayton replied with a faint smile. "There was a messenger from the Temple for you."

Davyd hesitated. "For me?" He tried to think what business he had with Datyl's temple.

"Yes. They heard you were in port, I think, and they knew your name."

"Not *my* name." Davyd was puzzled. "I've not been here before. Maybe they want Wydon or my father." Being a younger son he was used to the confusion.

"That could be," the captain said, "but it doesn't matter. They have another commission if you want it."

"Did they mention what it was?" Davyd was noncommittal. He already had two commissions. A third would mean another profit but he could afford to turn it down.

"Escorting a priestess to Gardon. Hardly a problem since you'll have that wine to transport."

Davyd hesitated then decided. "I'll listen to them at least. Where should I go?"

"The Temple. Ask for Priestess Libet."

Davyd nodded and thanked him before going below to his cabin. As he readied himself for another trip into town, he tried to think of a suitable price for such a duty. He didn't worry about charging too much—they could always bargain with him—but he would hear about it if he charged too little. Mother Rayna would learn of it and he'd feel the rough edge of her tongue and get yet another lesson in his family's worth.

Changing his tunic for a yellow one, he nearly hid it beneath a russet brown surcoat save for where the tunic could be seen through his elaborately slashed sleeves. After pulling his boots over brown hosen, Davyd adjusted his sword belt and brushed a bit of lint off. Brown and gold looked good on him and he was grateful they were the family colors. If he had to dress like a cock showing off his plumage, at least it wasn't red.

He had to make a good impression. After all his family was known in three cities for their excellent wares and guaranteed protection.

Touching the padded pouch he wore under his surcoat, he debated stashing his most valuable cargo before leaving the ship, then decided against it. He had no wish to explain *their* loss when he returned to Gardon. Checking to make sure the pouch didn't show, he let it be.

The afternoon heat was beginning to fade when he strode away from the docks and into the more orderly streets of Datyl. Here there were no horses to foul the streets or make it dangerous for passersby and the few oxen were prodded slowly along with their carts. Some people were abroad already and more appeared as the city bells rang the third hour of the afternoon and the stores reopened for the evening's business.

Striding quickly down the streets, he was longer surprised when people noticed his sword and gave way for him. After nearly a fortnight of walking Datyl's streets, he was used to the glances and ignored them.

Datyl was a city apart from the rest of Syra. Isolated by the seas surrounding it and low in population, the folk didn't worry about raiders or thieves. Instead they cultivated the arts and manufactured goods unknown anywhere else—and they frowned on those who carried swords.

Davyd tried to take no notice of the older men who scowled at him or the women who shied from his path. He wasn't welcome here—no swordsman was—but they liked his money well enough. Most even knew the name of York.

If the Temple hadn't sent for him, he wouldn't have bothered leaving the ship again. As much as he appreciated Datyl's beauty, he was tired of the stares. If it hadn't been for the pouch he wore, he would have been tempted to leave the sword behind.

It was his first royal commission. Like his father and brothers, he was pleased when Queen Fara sent for him on the eve of his trip and offered it to him. It was a simple task but the goods were valuable and the sum of money large. He'd agreed, more concerned about the safety of the money than what he now carried. She had entrusted him with two hundred solari, all in gold coins.

Well, the money was all but gone now. Instead he carried three precious crystals. Worth more than he could make in three years, he kept them safe and wore his sword to be certain they stayed that way. Rarely without it, he felt uneasy when he laid the sword aside. It was a part of him.

Pausing at the gate of the Temple, he looked for a guide.

"Pardon, my lady," he said, giving one a courteous bow. "I was sent for. Is the Priestess Libet close?"

"Libet?" The Temple guide looked blank for just a moment then smiled. "Let me help."

With a graceful hand, she beckoned him to follow and led him through several courts to his destination. "Your name is?" she asked as they paused before a door.

"Davyd Yorkson of Cam Gardon."

"Wait," the priestess said and slipped into a large gallery. She quickly returned and led him into a long sunlit room and past several groups of Temple folk busy with their own affairs.

"This way." She led him to an older woman by a window. "Priestess Libet."

He bowed again and got an impression of light brown hair streaked with gray and a pleasant smile. Standing with feet slightly apart, he waited for her to speak.

"You aren't the Yorkson I remember." The priestess looked him over. "Which one are you and what is the order of your birth?"

"Davyd Yorkson." Smiling to show he took no offense. "I'm the third son of six."

"Ah, I didn't know York was so busy," the priestess said. "I've yet to meet most of you—I've only met Monar and Wydon. Have you sisters too?"

"Four of them," Davyd answered. "All of them still at home."

"I see." The priestess paused. "Well, I've no doubt of your skill or your family. Would you be willing to escort a lady and her companion to Gardon?"

"For the right price, my lady," Davyd replied. "Would you be one of them?"

"No, my traveling days are done. The lady is named Synda and she's a very talented artist. This will be her first trip from Datyl and we all want to make sure she gets to Gardon safely."

"Captain Krayton assures me you are responsible. I assume you'll be hiring guards when you reach Sefron?"

"No ma'am," Davyd said then continued quickly. "My brothers have guards ready. I'll join Wydon there with a caravan for Gardon."

"Better than I thought." She looked pleased. "I'm to offer you one hundred solaris for their delivery safe to Gardon."

"One hundred?" Davyd was stunned—it was more than twice the figure he had decided on. Trying not to accept too quickly, he delayed. "I would like to meet the ladies first."

"Of course."

The priestess held up her hand and he offered her his, helping her to her feet. He didn't keep the contact long, mindful that priestesses disliked touch and some could even sense thoughts. She gave him an approving smile then beckoned to two ladies waiting nearby.

Davyd glanced that way then stopped and stared.

A manhunter! He gawked at the red robes, the hooded face, and tensed. She was hunting, looking for a man to father her child, and he reacted like any man, aroused and wary in the presence of a hunter.

He could tell nothing of what she looked like—whether she was slender or fat, young or old. The robes hid her figure from view and not even her face could be seen.

Reason caught up with him and he knew she was trouble. This woman was seeking a man and declaring it to the world. Every man who saw her would be panting after her, hoping she would choose him—and they wanted *him* to guard her.

"A manhunter?" He frowned at the priestess. "You want me to escort someone on a manhunt?" He would have to double the guard and watch her closely even on the ship. No, he wanted no part of a manhunt.

"Yes," the priestess answered. "Lady Synda, come here and meet your escort."

The red-robed woman drifted toward them, her face still shadowed by her hood.

Davyd hesitated, looking for a way to say no, when two shapely hands appeared from the depths of the robe and pushed the hood back and he was looking into the most beautiful face he'd ever seen.

Her hair was silky gold and stirred on her shoulders as she lowered her hood, her eyes downcast with maidenly shyness. The static of the hood made strands float on the air and gave her a halo of golden hair. Her skin was golden too and even the green eyes she raised to his had flecks of gold in their depths.

Those eyes locked innocently on his and held his gaze. Her lips parted and he wondered how she kissed. Heat filled his loins and he wondered what she looked like beneath those robes. He swallowed hard.

"My lady, I can't imagine *you* need to go on a manhunt," he said and was fascinated when she blushed, her skin turning a light pink. She lowered her eyes with sudden shyness.

"Synda, I think he approves," the priestess told her. "Now go doff those robes and prepare to leave. *The Seawind* sails tomorrow."

"Priestess, I've not said I'll take this commission." Davyd hardened his heart, refusing to look at the lady again. "As lovely as Lady Synda is, I'm leery of taking a manhunter. She'll distract the sailors and the problems of guarding a hunter are more than my brothers are prepared for. Surely she can find a man to father her child here."

"I won't!" The girl glared at him, her eyes full of fire. "It's my right to choose. If you don't want to escort me, I'll find another."

"Children," the priestess interrupted. "Synda, he's right. You've already agreed not to wear the red robes again until you reach Gardon and you won't tell anyone else you hunt. Do you give your word on that?"

"I do." The young lady set her lips in a determined line. "I have no intention of telling every man I meet what I want."

Davyd hesitated, wondering how he could get out of this commission. Thinking of the hundred solaris, he knew it would be hard to explain to his mothers.

A manhunt? Surely that was reason enough. That custom was left over from the ancients and allowed a woman of means to hunt a father for her child if she were too closely related to those available.

She could choose almost anyone and demand his services for three days and nights before leaving him forever.

The problem lay in the hunt. Shrouded in red, the woman remained a mystery to all but the man she chose—and every man dreamed of being the one to receive her favor. She could cross marriage lines in her quest or hunt her family's enemy and nothing would be said. It was her right to have a child and her right to hunt.

He didn't want the commission. He especially didn't want it with this beautiful temptation.

"Have you decided?" the priestess asked. "The price is one hundred twenty solaris—half in advance and the other half credited to you here in Datyl."

Davyd had to think again, torn by the new price. He could hire more guards—and she wouldn't hunt him. No one could compel someone in their employ. That law was strictly enforced, especially among the Sunborn and this lady was more definitely Sunborn.

"She'll not wear those robes until Gardon?" he asked "If she'll abide by that, I'll take the commission."

"I agree," the girl spoke quickly, her face as happy as a child's. "Thank you. I'm so looking forward to seeing Gardon."

"We're a long way from there," Davyd cautioned but his warning didn't seem to dash her spirits.

Making her goodbyes quickly, she even curtsied low to him before dashing off to her packing. Her companion followed at a more stately pace.

"She's a bit young," the priestess said, "but Lady Alva will keep her in check. You won't have to worry about her."

"I will though." Davyd watched her disappear. "She's too pretty for a manhunt."

"Too pretty?" The priestess smiled. "You think all the ladies who choose to hunt are ugly?"

Davyd bit his tongue, knowing he must look a fool.

"Let me assure you, Yorkson, that Synda is no prettier than most," the priestess gently rebuked him. "It's only the robes that make you think so."

"Yes, priestess," he stiffly responded. "I must return to *The Seawind*. Will Lady Synda require my escort there?"

"No, I'm sure she'll be fine." The priestess got back to business. "You'll find fifty solaris in here." She produced a small pouch. "Here is another ten. I'll see Synda writes a draft for the rest before she boards the ship."

"Thank you, lady." Davyd took the pouch and added the ten gold coins she counted out for him. Knowing how much value the Sunborn put on honor, he didn't count it. "May your wine be sweet and all your friends healthy." He bowed before following his guide out.

What was he doing? That lady even looked like trouble. If it wasn't for the gold… He hefted the pouch in his hand, then tucked it into his tunic and out of sight. It lay heavy against his stomach.

If anyone discovered what she was, what she wanted, it would make the voyage damned difficult. There wasn't nearly enough room on a ship. Thinking of those green eyes and those sweet lips, he wished he didn't know what she was after. At least he was safe from her choosing. Until he delivered her to Gardon and was discharged from her service, she could do nothing to him.

If only he had time to put those solaris into a cargo. Maybe when he reached Sefron he could buy one. Knowing his parents would be more pleased with solaris used than the coins themselves, he planned to do the best that he could. When they found out he escorted a manhunter — he brushed that thought quickly away and strode back to the harbor.

"DID YOU SEE HIM?" Synda shed her robes and turned happily to her companion. Standing in her short white shift, every soft curve of her slender body could be seen. "Goddess, I want to sketch him. Such muscles and those colors!'

Grabbing the pale green dress that lay waiting, she slipped it quickly over her head as she talked. "Did you see his eyes?" She sighed, happy with the man who was to guard her.

"Synda, you'll have all the time you need if you make that ship." Alva was critical. "And I'm sure he'll agree to be sketched or even painted. Let's get you ready."

"I nearly am. I just need the skirt." She picked up a skirt of darker green and slid it over her head, settling it quickly on her hips. It was the height of summer in Datyl and she followed practical custom in wearing a lightweight dress over her shift and a thicker skirt. During the winter she'd return to heavier clothes.

Slipping her feet into low-cut boots, she brushed her hair quickly and was ready to go.

"Synda, no." Her companion stopped her. "Wear your hair braided. By the looks he gave you I think that guardsman finds loose hair offensive. I've heard women wear it bound in Gardon."

"Oh, dolfyns. I'm not going to wear it up every day."

"No, just until we leave port," her companion said. "Then he can live with it until we reach Sefron and see the styles there."

"All right." Letting her companion braid her golden locks, she dreamed of the adventure ahead.

"HERE SHE COMES." Davyd pointed the girl out to the captain. "The one in green." His jaw set and his lips tightened as he saw she was just a wee thing and slender as a sapling.

"I see." The captain waved to some of his crew. "You there. Help with those trunks."

Davyd's eyes went over the baggage on the ox cart and he nearly groaned. Five, no, six trunks. He would have to add those to the caravan in Sefron. Why did she need so many? Didn't she know Gardon had dressmakers?

"Lady Synda? I'm Krayton, captain of *The Seawind*. Welcome aboard."

"Thank you, Captain." She smiled and gave him a curtsy. "It looks a wonderful ship. May I paint her?"

"We would be honored," the captain responded. "My crew will see your trunks stowed. Which ones do you need in your quarters?"

She turned and looked. "The blue one. The others are for Gardon. Alva, do you need any?"

"No, my things are also in the blue one." Her companion smiled at the captain. "I remember how tight some ships are."

The captain smiled. "You'll find *The Seawind's* cabins are larger than most. You'll have a closet instead of a cupboard."

Davyd listened, relieved her companion had sailed before.

"Tell me, lady, have you sailed on one of the exploration ships before?" The captain rolled the ancient word off his tongue easily. "If not, I must give you the tour."

"Tour?" The girl brightened and Davyd knew exactly what she was thinking. Like most girls she had an insatiable curiosity to see where men lived and worked.

"Yes, lady," the captain replied. "There is something I must show you. Every person who boards this ship for a night must be shown its greatest danger."

Synda sobered at the captain's seriousness.

"I've not traveled on any of the ancient ships, captain, and Synda is new to sailing," Lady Alva smoothly replied. "Please lead on."

The captain offered her his hand. "Davyd?" He looked at him and Davyd stepped up, offering his own to his charge. He wanted to see her reaction to the room.

Most folks knew *The Seawind* was a very old ship and a few knew the unused stack near the stern was a sign of ancient power, but only those who traveled on her or her sister ships knew about the ancient room beneath her decks—a room full of death.

It was there the captain took them. Located in the middle of the aft hold, there were narrow walkways around the white cube and a ridge behind it that extended to the very end of the ship, splitting the hold behind it.

Krayton paused before the room and let them take a long look at the metal bands that crossed its door and encircled the cube. An ancient warning sign lay on top of those. He said nothing as Synda curiously walked around the cube-shaped structure, her hand finally coming to rest on the sealed door.

"What is it?" the girl asked. "And why is it sealed so tightly?"

"It's death, Lady Synda.."

She jerked her hand away from the door.

"I can only tell you what was told to me when I first came aboard *The Seawind*. Do you see the radiation sign?" He pointed to the triangle as he said the ancient word. "Do you know what it means?"

"Yes." Synda stepped back further. "We were taught to beware and report this sign. It warns of a sickness the Temple can't cure. Why is there one here?"

"These ships were powered by something that sign guards," the captain explained. "They could move faster than the wind and come into dock with no help from oars. The technology which built this ship was mighty beyond any we have today."

"But there was an accident aboard the largest of our ancestors' ships. The death that powered the ship got loose and killed many before they found out it was no longer captive. They had to catch it all up again and seal the room but it was too late. Everyone on board the ship died."

"I remember that tale," Synda murmured.

"The ship was taken to a barren island and left to rot," Krayton continued, "by order of King Arden. It was the last order he gave before he died of the sickness too. He also ordered that all the power sources be silenced and the rooms sealed. So they've been for nearly five hundred years."

"And no one?" Synda stared at the door. " — no one has been in one since?"

"Only once. *The Harmony's* room was breached and the ship had to be destroyed. The man who did it died within days and so did its captain. I show you this room and tell you the story so you know what could happen. If you were to enter that room, within a day your bowels would be weak and your hair would start falling out. You wouldn't be able to eat or drink and the pain is something the Temple can't ease. No one would be able to touch you or help you in any way. You couldn't even be given cremation. The whole ship would have to be sailed to the northern ice and left for your tomb. That's what happened to *The Harmony*."

"Gods." She breathed the word and backed away from the door. The grisly tale had its effect on her companion too. She looked pale and uncomfortable.

"No one comes down to this hold alone," the captain warned them. "And your trunks will be in the forward hold. I'll show you where in a moment but first I need your word that you'll not touch that door again."

"You have it," Lady Alva quickly replied. "I've no wish to see that kind of death, much less have it."

"And you, Lady Synda? I should warn you that you'll not leave port on this ship if you don't give your word."

"Never!" Synda tore her gaze from the door. "I'll never come down here again." Her face was pale in the ship's light. "I want to leave."

Davyd was mildly surprised at her reaction. He'd heard the same tale when he boarded *The Seawind* in Sefron but it had only reinforced his decision to obey the rules aboard ship. There were always secrets he wasn't supposed to know and this was just another. He hadn't thought about it since except to wonder if the crew were trustworthy. It was just another rule to obey and he'd given his word to do so.

Wondering if the girl's curiosity was stronger than her word, he followed her back on deck.

The Seawind would sail on the morning tide and he would be on his way to Sefron. He looked at the spires of Datyl and smiled. He had always wanted to see it and knew he would come back again but right now he was happy to let it go. Gardon was his home.

Chapter 2 - *The Seawind*

7 Galtos 850

IT wasn't quite dawn when *The Seawind* weighed anchor and slipped away from the wharf on the outgoing tide but everyone was up for the leave-taking. The crew slipped around like the ship like ghosts, almost silent as they went about their assigned tasks.

Occasionally the captain would give an order in the predawn light but they'd done this many times before and little needed to be said.

Synda watched, fascinated as the first sails were unfurled and the ship turned into the wind. No longer carried out by the tide and longboats, *The Seawind* seemed to quicken and come alive as the wind caught her sails.

Synda thought all were white but one sail seemed nearly black. Thinking that curious, she looked around to ask why it was but none of the crew were near.

"What sail is that?" she asked her guardsman and pointed to the dark sail on the bow. "Why isn't it white?"

"The jib?" Davyd Yorkson answered her. "It's red. You can't tell it in this light. *The Seawind* has a red sail to mark her from her sisters. I saw *The Dolfyn* on the way here and she sports a blue sail."

"I never noticed that before." She chewed her lip then asked another question. "Why that one and not one of the others? It looks odd."

"Don't ask me," Davyd said. "Like you, I'm just a passenger." He yawned. "You might want to go back to bed, lady. There won't be much to see until we come to Midway."

"Not much to see?" She wondered if he was daft. "How can you say that? There's the dawn." She pointed to the lightening sky. "And you can still see some of the stars and one of the moons."

"Alva, I'm going to get my sketch pad," she said to her companion. "If you want to go back to bed…"

"Oh, I am," her companion assured her. "I'm not as young as you. Remember the captain's warnings though"

"I will. No climbing aloft but I do want to capture the sunrise." She headed for her cabin.

"You'll keep an eye on her?" her companion asked the guardsman. "If not, I'll stay."

"No, I'll stay," Davyd said with regret for his bed. "Until she learns how the ship moves I'd better be close by."

"Thank you," Alva said. "I think you'll be good for her. She needs someone she can't order around."

Davyd rubbed his eyes after the lady departed and decided it was time to leave his sword below. Now that they were out of port it was more cumbersome than helpful. Having learned on the outgoing trip to keep it stowed, he took it back to his quarters then collided with his charge.

"You!" Synda was neatly pinned against the wall in the narrow companionway, her arms filled with a sketchpad and colors. "Let me pass."

"At once my lady." Davyd stepped back into his quarters with irritated promptness. She'd yet to call him by name. The ship rolled to port and he was caught off-guard, ending up beside her again, both arms braced to keep from crushing her. She stared up at him with startled green eyes and he smiled reassuringly. When the ship rolled back he straightened up, letting his arms drop so she could pass.

Following her up on deck, he nearly cursed. She was too pretty and too tempting. What was he thinking when he said yes? He needed to keep his distance. He was her guardsman and nothing more.

The captain joined them as Synda picked a spot on the deck from which to watch the sunrise.

"Staying up, lady?" he greeted her then motioned to the sketchpad. "I see you are."

"Yes sir." She smiled warmly at him. "The sunrise is so wonderful."

"I understand." He followed her gaze. "I forget that some people are seeing it for the first time."

After a moment he continued. "Lady Synda, you'll get a better view of it from the poop deck and the roll is not quite so bad. If you wish, I'll have the cook bring your breakfast there."

"Oh, yes." She looked pleased at the prospect and shut her sketchpad again.

Davyd followed them up to the short deck and waited as a crewman hurriedly set out chairs and a small table. Once she was settled the captain joined him.

"I'm sending half my crew back to quarters for more sleep. When they come back on…"

"No." Davyd barely shook his head. "She's my responsibility. I'll not add work for your crew."

"As you wish."

After the captain left Davyd took his first vigil at watching the fool girl.

THAT first morning set the pattern for the days that followed. When Synda was on deck Davyd was always close by. Sometimes he busied himself with ship's work and other times he did exercises to keep himself trim but always he kept an eye on the girl.

In the afternoons she escaped the heat in the privacy of the captain's cabin, keeping only her companion for company. Davyd took advantage of that respite to sleep or work on his trade journals. Like his brothers he could write well and dutifully recorded what he learned for his family's benefit.

He also took the time to look over Wydon's notes about Midway. Thinking of the solaris he carried, he looked for a way to put some of them to use at that island port.

Just when the trip was getting long and tempers short *The Seawind* put in at Midway and her captain announced they would stay four days before making the final leg of the voyage to Sefron.

Lady Synda and her companion asked leave to reside at the Temple for three nights and Davyd donned his sword once more. Like Datyl Midway had little violent crime but he took no chances. Until the Temple's gates were closed on them and he had their promise to remain there, he put that duty first.

Finding trade items proved to be easy. A grower was willing to part with a dozen grafted saplings for fifty solaris and another coin bought him six barrels of fresh water to keep the Tyran apple trees alive. It was risky taking the trees but Davyd wasn't worried. Hiring one of the grower's journeymen for a year, he gladly paid him another solari to tend the precious trees. With luck he'd sell them in Gardon for three times what he paid for them.

The captain said nothing when the journeyman came aboard with his charges, having already heard Davyd's plans and accepted pay for their passage. The new forest was installed on one of the raised hatch covers and lashed tight with their barrels and pots. A new hammock was strung in the quarters Davyd shared with the ship's Second. A likable fellow, the journeyman saw to his charges and helped in the ship's galley to fill his time.

The evenings proved to be the longest. In the hours after sunset not much could be done without wasting precious lamp oil. That was when the ship's company brought out their pipes and drums and everyone was encouraged to sing or tell a story.

Being the only one from Gardon, Davyd found himself telling stories of his city and its queen. More familiar than most with Gardon's early history, he enjoyed telling stories he'd learned at his father's knee.

Everyone knew his father was a trader but none aboard *The Seawind* knew of York's journey into the Flamyn lands to visit a city ruled by a legendary race of women. He told the tale then had to remember details as Krayton and his crew shot questions at him. Too late he recalled the crews of the ancient ships were not just seamen but explorers. Serving aboard ships like *The Seawind* was considered a choice post since it allowed them to visit continents not settled by men.

When the sleep bells sounded and the crew started to disperse, Davyd knelt by his precious apple trees. Feeling the dirt of their pots and touching it to his lips, he tried to decide whether it was too salty from the sea spray.

"Are you going to water them?"

He looked up to see Synda standing in the moonlight, her light-colored dress making her a spectral figure. Behind her shone Luna, first of Syra's moons, outlining her head and turning her hair silver as it drifted on the light breeze. Her face was shadowed. He couldn't remember seeing anything so eerie and yet so beautiful.

"My lady?"

"Are you going to water them?" she repeated. "You shouldn't if they're in Hop's charge."

"No, I'm not going to water them." Davyd rose to his feet, irritated by her attitude. Who did she think she was? He squelched his reaction with an effort, keeping his voice even. She was his charge and a noblewoman too. "I was checking for salt."

"You should let Hop do that. You wouldn't know if they were swimming in it."

"Not true." Davyd's lips tightened. "I *have* farmed. I was fostered on a hold for three years."

"That doesn't make you a holder," Synda insisted. "Besides apple trees are different. They die easily. They can't be grown at all without grafting them to Syran roots."

"That's why I got four-year-old trees." Davyd struggled to hold his temper. "And that's why Hop is here. I do know my trade, lady."

She looked like he'd just slapped her, her eyes wide and hurt. Davyd instantly regretted his tone but she had it coming. For the past three weeks she'd been telling him what to do and he'd catered to her, only refusing to take off his tunic so she could sketch his muscles.

She was always sketching and, when she ran out of other things to sketch, she chose him. He let her do it since they were always together but looked forward to her finding new subjects. At least she didn't bother the crew very often, keeping mostly to him and the captain.

"Lady, I'm sorry," Davyd apologized. "This voyage has been too long and I want dirt beneath my feet again."

"My name is Synda," she snapped at him. "Why don't you ever say it?"

"My name is Davyd," he retorted. "I'm not sure you know it."

"Why, of course I...." She flushed. "I guess I haven't. I'm sorry, Davyd. Why didn't you say something sooner?"

"I waited. Lady Synda, you'd best go below. I'm sure Lady Alva is waiting for you."

"Oh, let her wait." Synda abruptly turned to look at the moon and its light fell on her upraised face and made her look even more ethereal. Davyd wished he could sketch her like that but he could only appreciate her beauty. "Luna is full and the captain said Systa is too."

"She's not in the sky yet." Davyd automatically glanced at the eastern horizon for the smaller moon. "You could be up all night waiting."

"And you think it's foolish." Synda turned on him. "I will see both moons at the full. I want to sketch them over the ocean."

"Systa rises near dawn. If you want to sleep all day tomorrow…"

She looked vexed as he pointed out the problem. They were hours from dawn. The crew wasn't even up for the midnight watch. Synda gazed again at Luna's bright glow then abruptly gave in. "I think I'll ask the watch to wake me when it rises," she began then caught her breath as her guardsman abruptly turned, his face set and cold in the radiance of the moon.

"As you wish." His polite words belied his anger. "If you want, I'll tell them."

"No," Synda quickly said, her pulse quickening. "No, I've changed my mind. Lady Alva is waiting and…" Without further argument she headed for the companionway.

Davyd followed her, unsure she really meant to go to bed but hoping she would. Two more days to Sefron. Gods, he was ready to be quit of this ship.

Chapter 3 - Mishap

1 Tyras 850

SYNDA looked over the sketch she'd hurriedly drawn last night of the guardsman standing in the darkness, his dark hair and set expression made even colder by the light of the moon. Not quite pleased with her effort, she set to work refining it by darkening the background and adding detail to his profile.

So interesting. She loved the way her guardsman looked. He seemed so dangerous even when he didn't wear his sword. Her pulse quickened as she studied the final product. Never had she spent so much time with one model. If he would only…

"Another one?"

She started guiltily as Alva peered over her shoulder at the sketch.

"My, he looks angry. What did you say to him?"

"I don't know." Synda shrugged it off and closed her book. "But it was such an interesting look I had to sketch it."

"Synda, you spend far too much time drawing him. Why don't you try something else today? I'll sit for you if you want."

"It's just he's so interesting the way he moves." Synda tried to explain it. "It's like he's wearing that sword of his even when he's not. I think it should be in every sketch."

"He's a swordsman and he only seems interesting because you haven't known any others. Wait until we get to Gardon. I understand most men wear swords there—even the Sunborn. It's violent too. It must be or merchants wouldn't be swordsmen too."

"It sounds exciting." Synda smiled, thinking of all the things she wanted to do and all the subjects she would have to paint. "So different from Datyl."

"Different, yes. Exciting maybe." Alva picked up her embroidery. "Let's stay out of his way today. I'm sure he has other things he must get done."

"Yes, aunt," Synda obediently replied, swallowing her irritation. "But I can't wait until we get to Sefron. I want to paint again." She thought of all the trunks filled with canvases in the forward hold and the paints stashed with them. Unsure whether she could get such supplies in isolated Gardon, she'd brought her own. Clothing she could buy but the canvasses had to be the best and properly prepared. She needed her own.

She wanted to commit so many sketches to canvas. Painting *The Seawind* under sail was one and she wanted to paint her captain as he gave orders from the poop deck. Another she thought had promise was a trio of sailors, one of them a woman, as they cleaned fish. She hadn't known there were women on the crew before.

They dressed like the men in short breeches and shirts and worked at the same hard tasks, keeping the ship in trim and the sails mended. The only concession to their sex was a separate crew cabin not fat from the captain's own. Nine of *The Seawind's* crew were women.

Still it was a sketch of her guardsman that thrilled her the most. She flipped to the page in her sketchbook and studied it again. She'd caught him when he was relaxed and laughing at something Alva had said. His brown eyes were merry and his face — she liked the way he smiled. He had such a warm smile.

She wanted to paint him. Flipping to another sketch of him doing the Prime, his arms outstretched in a striking motion and one leg lifted in the air, she could feel the power of the move. If only she could get him to shed his tunic. She wanted to sketch his wide shoulders as they really were and the muscles of his chest and stomach. She'd asked him but he had told her it wasn't proper. The sailors obliged when she asked them but her guardsman wouldn't.

He really was the most irritating man. He followed her everywhere on deck and, if she hadn't found him such a good subject, she would have had words with him before now.

Following Alva to the captain's cabin, she set her easel and prepared to work. It was so nice of Captain Krayton to offer them his cabin during the day. She'd even sketched him at the big desk he used. Today, though, she wanted to do something different.

A loud knock made them both start.

Her guardsman was there, one shoulder braced against the door frame as the ship rolled. "Good morning, ladies. I bring good news." He nodded toward the big windows.

Synda looked and saw a smudge of coastline on the horizon. "Is that Sefron?"

"No, just the coast. Tomorrow evening we should tie up at the dock in Sefron. The captain thought you would like to know."

"Oh yes," Alva said. "I'll be so glad to see something besides sea."

"We're within sight of the coast, my lady. Maybe you'd like to come up on deck for a while?"

"Not me. I think I'll go see nothing's lost instead. You never know what's rolled where on a ship."

"True," Davyd replied. "Lady Synda?" he asked like he'd forgotten she was there.

"Yes!" She hid her annoyance and grabbed up her sketch pad. Today was almost their last day on ship. She looked forward to something besides the sameness of ship and ocean.

Following her guardsman up on deck, she was surprised to see the coast so close. When it failed to grow any closer though, she looked around for another subject to sketch. There were no crew members on deck. Looking up, she saw a team furling a sail. She couldn't get the detail she needed there so she looked for something else to draw.

The guardsman was watching her but trying not to look like he was as he stretched his arms and legs. Suddenly decided as to what she would sketch, Synda sat next to the rail and made herself comfortable. Pretending to be intent on a coil of rope, she waited until the guardsman had started the rhythmic movements of the Prime before turning to her real subject. He looked so good.

Drawing quickly, she sketched in the lines of his body first and added detail as he repeated movements. Clothed in an odd combination of bulky tunic and loose breeks, he looked wrong to her and she wished again that he'd take off the tunic and let her sketch the lean body she knew had to be underneath.

She paid special attention to his bare feet and the expanse of bare leg showing below his breeks. The dark hair on his leg looked almost like fur and she wondered if his chest was that way too.

If only he'd take off that tunic. It was even held in place by the wide belt he always wore. Vexed, she got up and sat on the rail, one shapely foot stuck between the railings to protect her from the gentle rolling of the ship.

DAVYD pushed against an imaginary foe and spun in a movement, his attention focused on the moves of his body.

He knew the girl was sketching him but let that concern go. She would stay put as long as she was drawing and he would not neglect his exercises. In truth he needed them after nine weeks on the ocean. Gods, he longed to feel a strong horse between his legs and smell fresh forests instead of this salt brine.

Turning again he saw where the girl was sitting but didn't pause. Finishing the movement, he abruptly spun and opened his mouth to order her off the rail.

He didn't get a chance. Suddenly the ship changed direction and the whole deck rolled to starboard as the sails lost the wind then caught. He lost his balance in the sharp roll and jumped up as the ship rolled back to port.

Gone! He stared at the spot where the girl just was and yelled. Hoping one of the crewmen heard him, he didn't stop to think. Leaping over the rail, he dove cleanly into the water and pushed upward with all his might. He had to find the girl!

Chapter 4 – Coast

1 Tyras 850

STRUGGLING to the surface, Davyd frantically pushed himself out of the water. Not seeing the girl, he did it again and caught a glimpse of something green. Diving for it, he missed.

Propelling himself out of the water, he spotted it again. This time his hand caught a piece of her skirt. He pulled her to him.

"Let go!" Synda pushed him away. "I can swim."

"No." He sputtered water and pulled her close again until their legs were touching as they trod water. "You stay close." He was sharp, his relief at finding her turning to anger. When he got her back aboard ship…

Her wet hair was plastered to her face and her skirts floated as she trod water beside him. Thank Kala she hadn't been wearing shoes when she went over.

"The ship isn't slowing," she suddenly said, the first tinge of panic in her voice.

Davyd turned in the water to look. Studying the ship, he realized she was right. No sails were being lowered and there were no cries of alarm. Already *The Seawind* was too far away to hear their shouts.

Keep calm. He remembered his father saying that and concentrated. *There's always a way out. Just keep your head.* Not willing to let the girl know their danger, he forced a smile.

"They'll be back. It takes time to stop a ship that size."

"They aren't losing sails," Synda screamed at him. "They don't even know we're gone."

"Be quiet," Davyd snapped back. "Save your strength for swimming." He made it an order.

She obeyed, her face pale.

"We were near the coast." David propelled himself out of the water and came back down with a splash. "There." He pointed toward it. "We stay together and swim for the coast. *The Seawind* will be back."

"How far?" Synda tried his trick of shooting up out of the water but her skirts dragged her back down. She went under and came up sputtering beside him.

"Those skirts will make it harder," David said. He wasn't going to tell her to lose them. Who knew how long it would be before the ship came back? "Hold on."

Grabbing the floating fabric, he rolled it like a tent, using his legs to keep above water.

She gasped and tried to push him away, then caught his idea and rolled up one side herself.

Tying the gathered fabric in a knot, Davyd hoped it would hold. *The Seawind* was nearly out of sight now.

"Let's go."

They struck out in a smooth swimmer's stroke, using it to speed their progress to the coast. He kept his eyes on her, afraid she would tire and wondering if he could get them both to shore. No longer counting on the ship returning, he knew they had to make it to shore.

Synda kept pace with him, ignoring the water-bloated donut she pulled with her. How could he be so calm? She wished the ship would return. She wished for dolfyns—anything. Yet this infuriating guardsman just acted like he did this every day. Determined not to lag behind, she matched his strokes and kept her face above the swells.

Tempted to get it done quicker, she wanted to go to a faster stroke but she followed his lead and lay on her side in the water, her legs kicking in a motion she'd been taught for long swims. After a while they got leaden and her arms ached but she still kept pace with him only stopping to float when he leapt out of the water to get his bearings again.

"Almost there."

She wanted to call him a liar. She resumed her stroke with an effort.

Sometime later she heard him say to float and she rolled obediently on to her back, only struggling when his arm went around her neck. So tired. Suddenly feeling safe in his grip, she let go.

Davyd felt her give up and swam grimly on. He was close. He knew he was close. Pulling the exhausted girl behind him, he kept moving and resisted the urge to rest. Afraid they'd be swept back out to sea, he moved his free arm and kicked leaden legs. He wasn't going to lose her.

Appealing to the Protector in a silent prayer, he felt the answer almost at once. Caught up in a current he was too tired to see if it would lead him to shore. He rode the surf until it started to recede then found the strength to fight his way through to the sand, the girl still with him.

Half carrying and half dragging the girl, he got her up beyond the tide line then collapsed beside her. He should guard he thought but closed his eyes and knew no more.

ON BOARD *The Seawind* Captain Krayton shaded his eyes with his hand and debated taking another sail down. They were traveling up the coast now but it was tricky keeping enough sea room with the wind so strong. Twice they had to tack to clear a headland and, even though he knew these waters well, he knew there would be more harrowing moments. Nearly all his crew were above deck and working to keep the ship safe.

"Captain Krayton."

He turned to Lady Alva and was surprised to see the tree tender behind her. The lady looked pale.

"Captain, we can't find Synda or Davyd."

"Where were they last?" he demanded. "And when?"

"On deck more than four hours ago," Alva replied. "I'm sorry. I can't find her." She wrung her hands.

In sudden decision Krayton rang the ship's bell loud and hard. His crew stopped where they were to listen.

"Haul down those sheets," he yelled at the crew in the rigging.

"Bring us about," he shouted at the helmsman.

Crewmen leapt into action, rapidly climbing the rigging to help furl the sails. He waited till the last sail was down and half a dozen crewmen dropped to the deck.

"Ship search," he bellowed and his crew froze. "Lady Synda is missing—the merchant too. Find them." No more needed to be said to send his people running. They knew what it meant.

"Tory, take Hop and check the aft hold. Make sure the doors are secure," he ordered his Second.

"She wouldn't go there," Alva said. "She had nightmares for days about what you said."

"Check it," Krayton told his Second. "Better there than in the water."

He noted the time and took a reading on the compass and another on his starfinder. Going to his charts, he made quick marks and cursed.

"Gods." He never hated making good time before. Figuring the ship's speed for the distance covered, he saw they'd been averaging nearly fifteen knots—almost a record. That meant they had a lot of coast to cover.

"When did you last see them?" he asked the lady again.

"Not an hour after breakfast," Alva replied, her face pasty white. "I've been looking for nearly half an hour."

"Well, I talked to Davyd when I made this reading," he said, pointing to a spot on the map. "And we're here now." He traced their position on the coastline and thought the woman would faint. "I haven't seen Synda at all today. If they've gone over…"

"And no dolfyns today." He grimly remembered that. The sea shepherds often played around the ship and could be counted on to rescue swimmers and even retrieve what they lost.

Going to a locked cabinet near the wheel, he fitted in the small key he always wore. If the search turned up nothing he would have to use the dolfyn call. He took out the flat box on its rope and waited, hoping they would be found.

THE SUN WAS sinking low when Davyd finally stirred and felt the rough sand beneath his hands. Rolling over, he sat up.

The girl lay quietly where he'd left her and he nearly panicked when he couldn't see her breathing. Cupping his hand over her mouth, he felt her warm, soft breath and relaxed.

Her slender legs were long and pale almost down to the ankle where they suddenly turned tan from weeks barefoot. Her sparse golden hair enhanced their color and he wanted to stroke one, to feel the soft length of it.

Quickly he averted his gaze. Telling himself he was only looking for injury, he still felt ashamed of his weakness. He needed to think about survival.

Feeling the pouch around his waist, he made sure the crystals were there and safe. Longing for the sword he left in his cabin, he took quick inventory of what he did have. His knife was still secure in its sheath. Taking it out, he wiped it dry, then heard a soft gasp behind him.

"You're awake."

He turned toward the girl, then away again when he saw her front was still wet from lying on the sand and her clothing clung to her, showing him what he didn't want to notice. He had no business seeing her as a woman.

"Lady, I'm going to get wood." He kept his voice even with an effort. "I'll hear if you call. You may want to straighten your… hair." Heading for the trees, he was glad she didn't protest.

Shoving those thoughts to the back of his mind, he concentrated on his task. He found wood, including a straight sapling that would made a decent spear, then scouted for food. Not familiar with the shoreline vegetation, he had to go further inland than he wanted and was disappointed to find only sweet roots.

Digging up enough for a meal, he marked the spot and hurried back to the beach with his wood. Noting with relief the girl had untied her skirts and put them back in order, he relaxed. If only they had blankets.

"I have wood and some sweet roots. I'll try to catch some fish. Can you build a fire?"

"Me?" Her voice squeaked. She looked like she'd never seen wood before. "I've never built one."

Reminded of her rank, Davyd just nodded and started building it himself. "It's easy. You just pile wood here and here then another layer." He built a rough square two layers high then topped it with smaller pieces he broke to size. Scraping tinder off one branch, he tucked it in the crannies then automatically reached for his hunting kit and swore.

"Gods." He stared out at the empty sea and swore again. He didn't have his hunting kit. It was still in his cabin with his sword.

"What's wrong?" Synda asked.

"I can't light the fire. My flint, my snares, everything is back on the ship."

"Well, there's no need to make a fuss." Touching one slender hand to the tinder, a large spark jumped from her finger and the tinder burst into flame. "I can light fires any time."

He jerked her hand back as the tinder caught then felt foolish as he remembered. She was Sunborn. He didn't need flint. She could cast off sparks like that and even heal with the inborn talents all Sunborn had.

"You haven't traveled with many Sunborn, have you?" She sounded smug. "I thought you knew."

"I forgot," he admitted. "Well we don't need the flint." He caught his breath. He had to stay in control. She looked to him for protection and he couldn't be weak. "Thank you."

"You're welcome."

She settled down to watch the fire, its light brightening her face and hair.

"I'll go find us some fish," Davyd muttered, "in the tide pools."

How were they going to survive? He'd hoped *The Seawind* would return quicker than this. They had no supplies and only the one weapon—and no shoes. He needed shoes. *She* needed shoes. She'd probably never gone barefoot before her arrival on ship. If they were to go far, they had to have some.

Finding a large tide pool, he waded into the grayish water and felt a fish brush his leg. Grabbing, he missed it. Trying again he realized how futile it was. He couldn't really see the fish in the fading light and his reflexes were too slow. He gave it up to search under the rocks for shellfish, finally peeling some mussels off a rock and grabbing a crab that snapped at his fingers. It wasn't much but it would have to do. Tomorrow he would do better.

She was still sitting at the fire when he got back and he squelched his irritation when he saw she hadn't moved. "Lady?"

She turned desperate eyes to him. "We can't stay here. There's something moving in there."

"Where?" He set his catch down and studied the trees, outwardly calm but his pulse raced. "Stay here. I'll be right back."

Could there be a hold? He hadn't seen one. An animal? He tried to think what predators he should watch for. Not gapaks. They were too far east for them. Kranaws were fierce but only attacked men when cornered.

Going quickly down the list, he knew Tyran wolves were the worst. The others he would face in daylight. In the dark, though. He jumped when he heard a snort and ducked behind a tree just as the animals spooked and went crashing through the underbrush. One dashed out onto the beach before veering back into the woods and the firelight shone on his black antlers.

Deer! A herd of them. Davyd wished he had his spear made or, better yet, a bow. Just one of those Tyran deer would feed them for days. Walking back to the fire, he guessed they came to feed on the seaweed littering the beach.

"Did you see him?" Synda was standing by the fire, her eyes searching the woods for another glimpse of the buck. "He was gorgeous. The fire light made his eyes red and—"

"—And he could have been supper." Davyd finished for her. "Admire beauty another time, lady, when your belly is full and you have a sketchpad."

She looked shocked then hurt as he roughly reminded her where they were. Regretting his words he still didn't apologize for them. If they were going to survive, she needed to think about survival. He couldn't have her wandering around with her mind on sketching.

On the ship he could afford to cater to her, galling as it was sometimes, but he couldn't now. There was no one else to help and no one to watch her while he found food. She had to take his orders Sunborn or not.

"Tomorrow I'll have a spear," he reported as he cleared a spot in the fire and put the shellfish in. Looking for the crab, he decided it had gotten away. He should have killed it before he left it with her. A dozen shells and some sweet roots was all they had. It was a poor meal for two.

The girl watched, fascinated, as the shellfish popped and sizzled in the heat. The acrid smell of burning shell made her move out of the smoke but she watched Davyd fish them out with a stick and let them cool on the sands.

"Why do they do that?" Synda asked as the last one abruptly popped its shell. "I've never seen them do that before."

"The fire kills them," Davyd casually replied. "The shells pop when it gets too hot inside and they die. That makes it easier for us." He was glad his brother's wife had shown him that trick.

"They were *alive?*" She stared at him in horror. "You put them in the fire alive?"

"Yes." Davyd wondered why she was upset. "You mean you didn't know that shellfish were cooked that way? Haven't you ever eaten crab?"

"Yes, I—" She looked sick and turned away. It took a while for her to look at him again and when she did it was with such unnatural calm that he knew she'd done a Temple exercise. "I never saw them cooked before. I'm not hungry."

Davyd hesitated. "You will be, lady. I only found sweet roots in the trees. Tomorrow I'm sure I can find more but this is all we have tonight."

"Sweet roots? What are they?"

Davyd fished them out from his tunic and laid them in the firelight. Finger-thick at the top, they had hairy tendrils sprouting off them and looked an unappetizing brown. The girl sniffed.

Deliberately he picked one up and brushed the dirt off before biting into it. They were tough but the sweet flavor was good and the fiber more filling than anything. "Children eat these all the time," he explained. "Sweet and they'll take the edge off your hunger."

Reluctantly she took one and brushed it off. She took her time examining it before she put it to her shapely lips. He watched as she took her first bite, half expecting her to spit it out but she didn't. She chewed the root then managed to give a weak smile. "It's good."

"Better than nothing," he told her. "I'm surprised you haven't had them before."

"Oh, I might have. Seasonings in a dessert or something."

"But you never saw the raw root before?" Davyd divided up the shellfish into two even piles. "Those and kivaks are a child's favorite treats."

"I've had kivak." She brightened. "Mother gave it to me when I was young. She hated it when I caught cold."

"Me too." Davyd smiled. "Except there was always someone in the family with a cold and it usually spread anyway. I don't know how many times Mother Nan split us up and tried to stop it."

"Were there lots of you?" Synda looked interested and even picked up one of the shellfish as they talked, then looked at it blankly.

"If you eat that, I'll answer." Davyd dared her and fished the meat out of the one he had. Deliberately he chewed it, hating the leathery texture. He swallowed it down and reached for another. "If not, you'll go to bed hungry."

She looked torn as she stared at the shellfish, her face showing her distaste.

"The Temple says not to waste life. That mussel gave his life so you might live. Would you throw his gift away?"

She shuddered. "No."

He could barely hear her.

Gamely she fished the creature out and chewed. She had courage.

"There's ten of us." He answered her question. "I'm the third son. My brothers, Monar and Wydon, are older. They're waiting for me in Sefron. The others are still a jumble. Donal is my youngest brother and still at home. He's fourteen."

"And you're twenty-seven?" She asked before she thought, then grimaced as he pointed to the shells. She took another.

Davyd waited until the meat was in her mouth before he answered. "Twenty-one. I've been traveling for my family since I was seventeen. I started trading in the store when I was seven."

Synda looked amazed then giggled. "I'm older than you are. If Alva knew…"

"But you're Sunborn. A Sunborn woman takes longer to grow up—that's why the gods gave you more time."

"How old are you?" he asked. "You never said."

"It's not important."

When Davyd deliberately took a shellfish, she capitulated.

"All right, I'm twenty-six."

"Twenty-six?" he repeated, shocked. Looking over her slender, girlish figure, he found it hard to credit—and she was such an innocent.

"You said it yourself. Sunborn age slower and I've only been fertile for two months. It's not all that odd."

"No, it isn't," Davyd conceded. "You're right, my lady." He knew Sunborn women aged slower and their fertility was often delayed but she seemed so innocent. The few he knew were more worldly. Why Lady Lyda had shocked his mother when she was but twelve with the news she would marry Prince Valdyn and share his bed. It looked like she finally would. Their intention to marry this fall had been announced before he left Gardon and he suspected the crystals he carried were wedding gifts.

He ate his last shellfish then picked up a sweet root to fill the gaps in his belly. Thinking of the problems facing them, his frown deepened.

"Don't look so glum. *The Seawind* will come back."

"Probably," he answered. "If not, my brothers will be combing the shores themselves. Father too. Do you have family?"

"Only me and my mother and she's in retreat on Kala. She won't miss me until that's done."

"How long?" Davyd asked. "And where's Kala?"

"Three years," Synda replied with a mischievous look. "And I can't tell you where Kala is. You're a man and men can't go there."

"I don't know why any man would want to." Davyd shot back but now he remembered why there were women on the crew of *The Seawind*. They could set foot on the women's island but no one else. The captain wouldn't even break that taboo. Created as a place of sisterhood, that small island was sacred to women. It was a place apart. "Three years? You won't see your mother for three years?"

"Yes, but it's all right. We've lived apart for nearly ten already and I have my painting. Alva runs my household."

"That doesn't make up for family," Davyd abruptly said. "As much as I wanted to be alone as a child, I can't wait to go back at journey's end. I wish we were there now."

Gods. He stared out at the surf and wished his father were here or any of his brothers. He had no illusions how hard it was going to be to survive with no weapons or supplies. If *The Seawind* didn't come back, they would have to make their own way to Sefron and they just weren't prepared.

And he had his duty. He had to keep this tempting woman—this hunter—safe. His mouth set in a grim line as he thought what he might have to do and knowing there was a line he couldn't cross. If he compromised her, gave her what she sought, she could be exiled or executed. What his family would do to him he didn't want to think about.

Seeing she was watching him, he shook off his mood. Drawing his knife, he jammed it into the sand between them.

"That's our only weapon. I can make others tomorrow but right now that's all we have except for our clothing and these." He pulled out a coiled wire, three sets of earrings, and a handful of coins.

"Why these?" Synda picked up a set of earrings and turned them toward the firelight. A 'Y' was engraved inside an inverted triangle on each disk and a safyr stone twinkled from between its arms.

"For my sisters," Davyd explained. "Three of them like such baubles. Glynda asked for the harp wire. She plays."

"And they are all the same? I wouldn't like that."

"Each set has a different stone," Davyd brusquely said. "In any case they won't get them now. I need the hooks to catch fish." He twisted one apart and took the medallion off. "I can use the wire for a snare."

"We have two knives." Synda dug in her waist pouch and laid down a little knife. "See? I use it to sharpen my pencils."

"Two knives." Davyd struggled not to smile. "I'm glad you have it. We might need it to clean fish."

"Clean a fish?" She cocked her head and gave him a puzzled frown. "Why do fish need to be cleaned? They aren't dirty."

Thunderstruck, he stared at her. Was she really that naïve? Seeing her little smile, he knew she was joking.

"You sketched sailors cleaning fish," he accused her and she giggled. He watched her laugh and couldn't remember any woman who looked so beautiful. All too soon she stopped and he brought her back to the business of surviving.

They had precious little. Synda had no money — something that didn't surprise him — and only her little knife and drawing sticks. She mourned her sketch pad but there was nothing that could be done about that. Surely it was adrift somewhere or at the bottom of the sea.

Even more than his sword, he longed for blankets as the night turned chill. Building up the fire one more time, he hollowed out a nest in the sand. Escorting her into the cover of the trees just once before bed, he waited until she was asleep before scouting the area one more time and seeing to his own needs.

Finally he could put it off no more and settled next to her in the sand. With a silent prayer for *The Seawind's* return, he fell asleep.

ON board *The Seawind* Captain Krayton looking at the gathering darkness and cursed. Not on board. Somehow both passengers had fallen over and no one had seen it.

There were dolfyns about the ship now. Nearly a half dozen pods had answered his call and watched as he pointed to signs that meant they were searching for men. The intelligent creatures had responded quickly, covering more miles of sea than the ship could do but the results were disappointing. They found no sign of them.

The only thing that tempered his concern was the knowledge that dolfyns would also report bodies. They'd found neither. Somehow the missing pair had gotten to shore.

Tomorrow he would send boats ashore here and further south to where he thought they might be. If they weren't so close to the treacherous waters of the coast, he would be tempted to sail *The Seawind* down and look for a fire but that couldn't be done. He couldn't risk his ship for two people.

The ship was at anchor for the night, her sails furled and waiting for the first morning light. In the darkness a few crew were preparing provisions for the longboats and stowing gear they would need for the morning's search. Tonight there was no singing and Lady Alva had retired to her quarters. Most of his crew were in their hammocks. Until the two were found there would be no more shifts and his crew knew it.

"Captain?"

He turned to look at his Second standing shadowed in the darkness. "Yes Tory?"

"Another pod reports no sign," Tory reported. "They've been rewarded but I think they're staying too."

"They'll do that. They don't like failing any more than we do." Often a dolfyn pod would work days on a search before losing interest and returning to their feeding grounds. In return for their efforts they were paid with things they couldn't make. In this case he'd given them large colored balls from the ship's special store. The pods would herd the things for days and play with their new toys. It was small payment by his standards but something the dolfyns enjoyed. Except for the rare times they needed medical attention, it was what they requested.

Searching for men was but one task the dolfyns performed. Taught originally to herd the thousands of Tyran fish the Ancients planted in the oceans of Syra, the dolfyns followed the school and showed the fishermen where they were.

They also reported die-offs when they happened and had saved more than one species from extinction in Syran waters. Not able to speak, the dolfyns could recognize pictures on a board and used it to report what they'd seen. The language was limited but worked well enough with these shepherds of the sea.

Looking down onto a silvered back, he admired its sleek beauty. Yes, the Ancestors were wise. They'd brought dolfyns to partner those who sailed the seas.

"Sir?" Tory was still waiting. "One of the longboats is ready. Some of the crew would like to leave tonight and row down the coast."

"Tell them no," Krayton said. "We wait until first light. There are too many rocks and I'll not risk it. Besides I want to drop the boat further south. *The Seawind* can put her into position faster than they could row tonight."

"Yes sir. I'll tell them." He saluted and turned to leave.

"Tory?" Krayton stopped him. "Trust the merchant to keep her safe. The sons of York are a resourceful lot."

"Yes sir." His Second went on his way.

Krayton stared at the dark shore and hoped he was right.

Chapter 5 - Temptation

2 Tyras 850

SO COLD. Davyd frowned in his sleep as he tried to figure out how his front could be so warm and his back so cold. His bare feet felt like ice in the cold dawn air.

He thought about reaching for the covers then sleepily remembered there weren't any. Gradually he puzzled it out until he suddenly recalled the girl.

He was holding her. His eyes popped open and he took a sharp breath when he found his face buried in her golden hair.

She had one of his arms trapped beneath all that hair and was using it for a pillow. His other arm was draped over her side, his hand cupping one breast with forbidden familiarity. Their bodies fit together like two spoons, her sweet bottom nestled against his manhood, his legs drawn up to fit behind her skirted legs.

Suppressing a groan, he tried to ignore the growing warmth in his loins. Slowly moving his hand from her breast, he inched away from her.

She murmured a protest when he took her pillow away but didn't wake.

Gods, he hadn't meant to hold her like that. Thanking Kala she was unaware of his behavior, he quit the sand couch and headed for the trees, only stopping when he was safe from her sight.

He should never have lain beside her. Thinking to share his warmth by sleeping back to back, he must have turned in the night. Gods, he was stupid. He shouldn't have slept with her at all. Cursing his stupidity, he did what had to be done and walked back to the beach to check his charge.

She looked so innocent. Her golden lashes rested on her cheeks and her skirt was in disarray from her movements during the night. One tanned foot was peeking out and he gently tugged the fabric down to cover it then turned away.

There was no sign of the ship. Looking out over the surf he couldn't see anything made by man. A fish leapt up in the air far out in the water and he longed to catch it but it was no use. He had to make weapons and they had to find water.

Aware of his nagging thirst, he knew she'd feel it too. He had nothing to carry water in either. Maybe he could find some fruit. Leaving her there on the shore, he strode quickly back into the woods, only slowing when he set a foot wrong. He had to take more care with his bare feet.

Stopping often, Davyd listened for the sound of running water among the forest sounds. A cacophony of bird calls made him change direction once and he followed, hoping they were guarding a precious stream.

A rugur tree. He looked disgusted at the greenish yellow fruits and knew he didn't dare use them to quench his thirst. Not yet ripe, the juice of the long fruits had bad effects on men and women alike. He passed it by, hoping for a safer source.

His persistence was rewarded by a redfruit tree, its boughs heavy with luscious red and purple globes. Picking as many as his tunic would hold, he took another route back to the beach, still hoping to find a stream.

"Davyd!"

Hearing her shrill yell, he quickened his steps. Hearing her call again, desperation in her voice, he wanted to run to her. What happened? His heart thumped but he still stopped just inside the trees. Looking to see what danger she was in, he saw nothing but the girl walking up the beach, her eyes on the trees.

"Davyd, answer me," she shrieked.

She was scared. She woke up alone. Well, he couldn't take her with him. Her feet…

"Over here." He stepped from the trees.

She turned on him, her fright immediately going to irrational rage. "Where were you? I've been calling for hours!"

"You weren't awake hours ago," Davyd told her. "I wasn't awake. I thought you'd be thirsty so I brought these." He started pulling redfruit from his tunic.

"You left me alone." She didn't even glance at the fruit. "I thought you'd gone."

"Me?" He looked at her in honest surprise. "Why did you think I'd go?"

"I don't know," she wailed then burst into tears.

"Lady, don't," he begged her. "Please, Synda, no tears." He wanted to hold her but didn't dare. "I'm sorry. I thought I'd be back before you woke. I'll never leave you."

She spun away from him, fists clenched as she tried to stop crying.

He was reminded again how young she looked. For all that she was older and Sunborn, she was still a protected little girl. He hadn't expected her to panic.

"Please," he softly said and pressed a redfruit in her hand. "I couldn't find water. These will have to do until *The Seawind* comes back."

"It's not coming back. Don't you see? They should have been here by now."

"Not at all," Davyd glibly lied. "I've been on it longer than you. Krayton doesn't sail at night when he's this close to a coast. I'm sure he's coming back along the coast. Just wait."

"But you won't be here." She looked hopeless. "I saw you at a hold."

His heart stopped. "You had a Foreseeing?" He understood her panic now. "When? Do you feel all right? Are you prone to them?" He grabbed her wrist, turning it over to feel her pulse.

"Don't be silly." She yanked her hand away. "I'm hungry and thirsty and cold but I am not going to die on you." She bit into the fruit and glared at him.

Davyd studied her, trying to decide what to do. A Foreseeing was nothing to toy with—he knew that from stories his mother had told him. Half-expecting Synda to be ravenously hungry or, worse yet, to faint, he didn't understand her reaction. Even when she picked up another redfruit and started on it, he waited.

"Would you like to talk about this Foreseeing?" he finally asked and picked a redfruit up. "We should both know what it shows. I may need to protect you from it."

"It wasn't that kind," Synda said. "You were in a hold talking to a holder. He gave you a sword and you gave him something else—I couldn't see what. You were happy."

"And where were you? I wouldn't go without you."

"I don't know." She studied the fruit in her hand. "That's why I thought—" She looked at him with frightened eyes. "Davyd, please don't leave me. I don't know anything."

"I know," Davyd answered. "Synda, I would never leave you. I took an oath to protect you and I will never break that oath. We'll reach that hold together or neither of us will be there."

"You didn't take an oath," she said. "Just the commission."

Davyd stared at her, suddenly aware she was right. He'd neglected that. Of course, she'd not asked for one and neither had the priestess. Why had he forgotten it?

"You're right but I'll swear to you now—by the Flame and Galton."

"You believe?" She looked amazed. "What do you know of the Flame?"

"The Flame is life eternal," he returned the ritual answer, "and the energy of all."

She looked stunned that he would know but Davyd had been raised with that. His mother was a believer and he'd learned it from her. There were no gods in the Flame but the power behind it was real.

Holding out his hand, he waited for her to place hers over it and accept the oath he offered. Slowly she did it.

"I, Davyd Yorkson, pledge to protect you, Synda of Datyl, until you enter the gates of the Temple at Gardon. I swear this by Galton, Protector of All, and the Eternal Flame. May the Pit have me if I fail."

"I accept your oath and cherish it, taking your protection until such time as I must dismiss you," Synda solemnly replied. "May Galton protect us both."

Davyd let his hand drop, bothered by the wording of her oath. She had fumbled it. Surely she knew he wouldn't accept dismissal. He couldn't. No, she was inexperienced or just didn't know.

"Do we leave?" Synda asked.

"Not today," Davyd said. "We need shoes and I won't leave this beach without weapons. I'll make those today."

"But we don't have anything to make shoes with." She looked perplexed. "Surely we can go without."

"Not you and I won't. If we have to run anywhere, it's a poor time to catch a thorn in your foot."

She seemed to accept that and picked up another redfruit. Sitting down on the sand, she bit into it and juices spurted, running down her chin before she could stop them.

Davyd watched her wipe the juices away, thinking how he'd like to help. She was so innocent. It was just as well, he decided. It was hard enough for him to restrain his passion without worrying about hers.

Removing the broad sword belt he always wore, he measured the tanned leather against his hand before he decided it would do. "Your foot, my lady."

She looked blank.

"Your foot." He motioned for her to stand. "For soles."

"From your belt? You shouldn't give up your belt."

"Yours is too narrow and I'll get another. Just stand on it please."

She obeyed then looked rebellious when he asked for one of her drawing sticks. With a deliberate hand he marked the outline of one foot, then the other. Within minutes he was sacrificing his belt to shoe a lady.

There were other things that needed to be done too. He wanted to make a sign for *The Seawind* to find because he had no doubt either Krayton or his brothers would come this way. If they didn't need water, he would choose to wait here and prove her Foreseeing false.

Surely she was with him at that hold. Remembering his mother's explanation of Foreseeings, he knew the one having it could rarely see himself. Yes, that must be it. He couldn't be alive and smiling at a hold without her. That wouldn't happen.

Synda watched her guardsman work, wishing she had her sketchpad to capture it as he cut soles for her shoes. He was always so different. One moment he ignored her and left her alone on the beach and the next he swore he'd never leave her again—and last night he even smiled at her.

She wanted to see that smile again. Convinced her sketchpad was ruined, she knew she had to reach Gardon to get another. She wanted to catch his likeness for all time.

Wondering what she could do to help him, she suddenly recalled her underskirt. She could do without that. No one would know.

"Davyd, I have to…" She pointed toward the trees. "No, don't get up. I'll scream if anything—please." She felt foolish but the guardsman stayed where he was.

She came back a few minutes later with her morning needs taken care of and most of her underskirt in her hands. "Here. I think we might need this."

"Yes." Davyd smiled at her and her heart sang. So easy. Settling back in her spot, she watched as he worked the soles. Finally her patience wore out and she broke the silence.

"Do all people in Gardon wear swords?"

The question caught Davyd by surprise but he didn't laugh. One glance told him she was serious.

"Not at all." He smoothed the edges of the leather against the flat of his knife blade. "Guardsmen, holders, traders—those who make their living giving protection or needing it wear swords. You won't see a baker wearing one."

She looked thoughtful. "I've heard Gardon is so dangerous with people being killed on the streets every day."

He grinned at her. "And I heard Datyl is paved with gold."

"Really?"

"Really," Davyd said. "And the people are soft." Privately he agreed with that. He hadn't met any man he'd hesitate to cross swords with.

"We aren't that soft. Just because we don't go about with swords and fight all the time."

"That wasn't what I meant," Davyd denied. "Datyl is like a ripe berry waiting to be eaten. If someone *could* attack it, the city would fall. No defenses."

"It doesn't need defenses. We have the ocean."

"Right." Davyd knew she had the same mindset of all those in Datyl. Their city was impregnable because of the ocean. "But some day there might be ships out there with raiders aboard. The city should be prepared."

She just looked stubborn.

Davyd braided some strips of her underskirt and pushed the ends through the tough leather soles. She was pouting now.

"Look, Gardon has been attacked before. When it happened it was an army and it took everyone with a sword to win that war. It could happen again so Gardon needs to be prepared. Besides that, there are raiders."

"But you don't have to live like that. You don't have to live in Gardon."

Not live in Gardon? That's where his family was! Shaking his head, he dismissed that idea.

"I live where my family is." He gave her a quick smile.

She opened her mouth again but he'd had enough. "You'll be going back to Datyl where you won't have to worry about swords and fights in the streets. That's good for a lady but Gardon is my home."

Finishing the first sandal, he motioned for her to stand up and try it on.

Where he lived was no concern of hers.

Chapter 6 - Alone

2 Tyras 850

IT WASN'T even noon before Davyd changed his mind about moving on. They needed water. Setting the sword-shaped sign he'd made upright in the sand for *The Seawind* to find, he gathered up the few items he'd made.

There wasn't much. The extra leather from his belt provided some snares and a sling and the lady's underskirt made a gather bag. A spear with a fire-hardened point was his only real weapon. His shoes would have to wait until he found hides to make them.

The walk along the beach wasn't hard but the sun was hot. The shade underneath the trees beckoned but he didn't suggest they take their shelter. They needed to be seen. Surely Krayton was searching the beaches by now.

Twice he thought he saw dolfyns in the distance but said nothing to his charge to give her false hope. They couldn't help them. No matter what the stories said, dolfyns were just happy creatures of the sea. They had no tongues and couldn't fetch *The Seawind* to them. It was worthless to think otherwise.

There were times when the shore got rocky and they had to pick their way carefully but it soon turned back to sand. Not once did they have to leave sight of the sea.

"Look," Synda said and pointed excitedly. "Is that a stream?" She turned to him, licking her dry lips.

He studied it, seeing the indentation in the beach and the verdant growth on the rise above it. Rushes, bushes, even trees marked the edge of the bluff. Below there were only a hardy rushes but that bluff looked promising. They would have to climb. He didn't like the idea of camping where a ship couldn't see them.

"I think you're right but let's be careful. If it is a stream, there might be animals drinking."

"Good. I'm starved."

He frowned. "Where there are animals, there are also hunters—maybe even wolves. We go slowly, lady."

She lost her smile and let him lead.

He hated to do that but knew she was ill-prepared to catch even a buck deer unawares. He doubted she had even seen animals outside of the marketplace. Certainly she didn't know what they could do.

His caution was wasted. Approaching the stream, he saw there was a small waterfall cascading into a deep indentation in the shore. It was only a dozen feet high but any animals would be up above where the water was fresh and the tide couldn't foul it.

"It's salty." Synda made a face as she tasted the water in the pool. "We can't drink this."

"The falls isn't," Davyd said. "Come over here and drink from it."

He showed her how, cupping his hands to take in the very edge of the waterfall and lifting hands to his face. He was getting wet from the spray but even that felt good.

Timidly picking her way across the rocks, she planted her feet next to his and leaned out into the spray to catch some water. The next instant her foot slipped on the wet rocks and he grabbed her, barely saving her from a tumble into the water.

"Do it now."

Wrapping his arm more securely around her slender waist, he waited until she'd drunk her fill before pulling her back and out of harm's way.

She was smiling when she turned to him. Her golden hair shone from the water drops trapped in its web. His jaw clenched as he brushed her hair back with a quick hand then let her go. She looked hurt at his sudden rejection.

"We camp here," he said. "On the beach. I'll find wood."

He left her standing there and scrambled up the bank at its lowest point.

Gods! He prayed to Galton to rescue him from her charms. Never had a woman so entranced him and it had to be the one he couldn't have. Desperate for company, he hoped *The Seawind* would return. He didn't look forward to another night with a tempting child.

Child. She was just a child. It made no difference that she was older. She was Sunborn and just a protected child for all that. He had to remember—and he was sworn.

He couldn't touch her. It was against the law for any Sunborn to seduce someone in their employ. Knowing the penalty for her would be severe, he regained his control as he gathered up the wood he promised.

"Build a fire," he yelled as he tossed the wood onto the beach. "I'll look for food."

Turning back to the forest, he was rewarded with more sweet roots, then spied a large tuber plant. Digging the tuber out, he grimaced. Last year's growth. It was large and woody and tough. If there had been any others, he would have passed it by as not worth cooking but there weren't.

There were signs of deer and gak here and he guessed they had feasted on the tubers long ago. Sometimes the animals wiped out a patch with their digging or it could be that a lone seed had flourished in a pile of dung. It was no use looking for more.

Setting his snares for the morning, he paused long enough to carve a burl from a tree. That he could turn into a cup.

"Did I do it right?" The girl asked when he returned to the beach. She had a pile of wood ready for his approval.

"You did fine." He reached over and took two crosspieces off before he smiled. "We'll be warm tonight."

She seemed to glow under his praise. Reaching out one hand, she touched the waiting tinder. A bright spark fell into it and caught. He was always amazed by that ability and wished he had enough Sunborn blood to do it. Starfire was a real talent to have.

"What did you find?" Synda asked. "Any meat?"

"No," he responded. "Tomorrow we'll have something besides fish."

Laying out his small pile of booty, he saw her disappointed face. "Or I can check the snares before the sun sets."

"No, we can have fish," she hastily told him. "Even mussels. I do like mussels." She looked so determined to like them that he almost laughed at the lie.

"I don't like mussels that much," he told her with a wide grin. "If we can find something else, we'll pass on them."

"Can I help? Please, I'd like to help."

"Then come on." Washing the tuber in the brackish water, he laid it in the fire pit before waving to the ocean. "Let's see what the tide brought in."

They spent a happy hour looking at and discarding sea creatures. Twice he tried to spear a fish but the little ones were too small and quick for his skill. It wasn't until he found a large bomar in a tide pool that he had any luck.

The Syran fish fought on the end of his spear, its jaws snapping in rage as he flipped it high on the sand. The girl watched, wide-eyed, as it flopped around. It seemed a long time before it quit moving.

"Don't touch it yet," he warned. "Sometimes they aren't dead."

Poking it with his spear, he still jumped when the open jaws clamped shut and the fish flopped again. Pinning it with his spear, he stabbed it with his knife until it lay still.

Cutting off its head first, he tossed it aside then split the fish with practiced skill. The girl watched with wide eyes as he pulled out one of the earring wires and tied a piece of leather to it. Baiting it with offal, he cast it into the water. One of the fish that had eluded him promptly snapped at it.

A wordless sound of disgust made him look at the girl but she had already turned away and was walking back to the fire. Noting her hurried walk, he almost followed then thought better of it.

SYNDA nearly gagged when the guardsman baited the hook with the guts of the savage fish then had to turn away when another fish took the bait. How could they? They were eating each other.

She'd never seen such a horrid thing. She'd never seen such a horrid fish. She would have remembered those snapping jaws if she had. Trying to shake that memory from her mind, she settled into a meditation pose beside the fire and tried to remember more pleasant days.

It was hard. She never dreamed fish were so savage or so maltreated when she dined on them in her own home. They were just there, headless and perfectly cooked by her own cook. She longed to be back there in her sheltered life. Remembering the savageness of the fish, she felt no desire to sketch it, much less eat it.

Hearing the guardsman's feet crunching on the sand, her eyes flew open and she managed a brave smile. He looked grim as he silently dropped two cleaned fish by the fire. Moments later he had them wrapped in wet seaweed and sitting in the fire. Neither one was the savage fish.

"What happened to the other one? Aren't we going to eat it?"

"The bomar?" He looked surprised. "No, lady. They aren't worth eating when we have these. Besides I didn't think you'd care to."

"He gave his life. We should use it and be thankful."

"We are. We took a killer out of the water and fed him to the ones he would kill. His life was not wasted in their eyes or mine."

She thought of those savage jaws and shuddered before she let the subject drop. She didn't want to eat him. She didn't want to eat any of them.

It was nearing sunset when her guardsman fished the food out of the fire and handed it to her on a trencher of tree bark. She ignored the fish but ate the tough tuber he gave her without a qualm and chewed on a sweet root to fill her emptiness.

"You have to eat the fish too," he told her. "Neither of us can skimp on meat. We've still got a long way to go."

"I'll eat it later." Taking a look at his set jaw, she knew she wouldn't win that argument and picked up a piece with her fingers. "Do they have fish in Gardon?"

He blinked. "Of course."

"But not like these," he continued. "River fish are smaller and have a lot of bones you have to watch out for. These are easier to eat." He gestured toward her plate. "Eat it."

She took a small bite and was surprised to find it was good. She took another bite before asking another question. "Did you learn to fish there?"

"Not for these." He sat down to his own trencher. "My brother's wife is from Sefron and she insisted I go shore fishing with them. Since I've always tried to know what is edible and how to catch it, I went along."

"Oh. Why would a merchant need to know how to hunt? Don't you usually have food with you?" She asked the question before she thought about where they were and why he was hunting. Goddess, she sounded stupid.

"It's not my fault the ship rolled," she stiffly denied. "And you didn't have to come after me."

"You shouldn't have sat on the rail," he said, his smile gone. "And who else is going to show you how to survive? You need me."

"I hate you when you're right." She conceded in a tight, angry voice. "Thank you for coming with me." She set her trencher down then walked away.

"Synda, wait."

She ignored him.

"I said wait!" He grabbed her shoulders then quickly let them go. "Damn it, I'm supposed to protect you. If you go charging off when you're angry, you're likely to spook some animal that will fight back." He spoke in angry clipped tones. "You stop when I tell you to."

"You're my guardsman. I don't have to listen to you."

"You do." He looked so angry she stepped back. "It's my job and, as you recently reminded me, you should never second-guess someone you've hired to do the work."

She stared, shocked to have her own words flung back at her.

"Now you'll allow me to escort you and I'll scare up the animals," he grimly continued. "And if we meet something that decides to fight, I want you up a tree. You can climb trees, I hope."

She didn't know what to say. Slowly she nodded.

"Good." Satisfied, he stepped ahead of her, his hand reaching automatically for a sword hilt that wasn't there.

Synda followed him into the darkening woods and wished she was back home in Datyl where you didn't need a guard to answer nature's call.

Chapter 7 - Bees

3 Tyras 850

DAVYD watched the sun rise over the restless sea with bleary eyes, cold and cramped in the sitting position he'd taken hours ago to keep warm. His feet were warmer now, buried as they were in the sand, but the fire was out. Having no more wood to feed it, he'd let it die rather than leave the girl.

She looked cozy enough. Knowing he shouldn't sleep next to her again, he'd half-buried her in sand to keep her warm. She'd objected, of course, but he'd told her he was just going to tend the fire before doing it himself. Waiting until she quit protesting and finally went to sleep, he built up the fire as high as he dared and slept by its warmth.

Where was the ship? He knew if it didn't appear soon they would have to leave the beach. There was no way around the fall's pool without swimming and he was loath to do that. The girl had no spare clothes and she looked too attractive when wet. Besides she could catch cold. No, they would have to go upstream to find a crossing place.

Deciding it was time, he unburied his feet and ankles and stretched, brushing sand off his skin as he went. Wondering whether he should wake the girl before checking his snares, he paused to study her angelic sleeping face.

Her hair was dirty now and there were smudges on her face but she was still beautiful. Her full lips were slightly parted and he ached to cover them with his own. Suddenly aware where his thoughts were taking him, he turned away.

Gods, he must be as dirty as she was. Davyd rubbed his hand over the stubble on his chin and grimaced. He hated having a beard. He especially hated growing one.

Rubbing his hand through his dark curly hair, he could feel the oily dirt there too. Maybe they should both wash. He imagined guarding her while she bathed in the cold stream and cringed. No, that would be foolish. Better to press on and hope for rescue before they got too rank.

Well, he had to let her know he was going after the snares. Thinking hard, he finally fished out one of his sisters' earrings and laid it in her hand. Wondering what she would think of that little token, he smiled and touched her hair with the lightest of touches before going after his snares.

SYNDA waited, her breathing quiet and regular until she was sure he was gone then opened her eyes to see what he'd put in her hand. An earring? She didn't understand at first then she remembered the medallion. It was the sign of his house.

Clutching it close, she studied the Y inside the triangle, her heart strangely happy as she looked at the little piece of gold. He'd be back. He had to come back.

She closed her eyes then found she had to move. All the water she drank yesterday was making itself known. Brushing the weight of sand away from her legs, she found a spot where her guardsman couldn't see her from above to do what had to be done. She was quick, knowing he would return in a rush if he saw her gone. Kicking sand over her leavings, she returned to her spot.

He was such a puzzle. One moment he was so nice to her and the next he was so vexing. No doubt he'd yell at her again when he came back just to keep it in balance. She didn't know guardsmen could talk like that to one who paid them.

And he looked so rough. Unwashed and bearded, she could picture him as a villain. He looked like the very worst of men now but still she wanted him around. She wondered if she dared sketch him that way.

He was so strong. Making her way to the falls, she remembered when he caught her. His arms had felt so good around her waist, so strong and warm. She wanted him to do that again and was embarrassed by the thought. He'd only done it to keep her from slipping.

If only they were somewhere else. It was hard to look good for anyone when you had only one dress to wear for days and days— and it was so light it showed all the dirt. Having slaked her thirst in the falls, she abruptly sat down on the rocks and tried to scrub some of the dirt off.

One thing led to another and she washed as best she could, finally taking a deep breath and plunging her whole head underwater.

"WHAT?" Davyd caught sight of her just as the fool girl looked ready to pitch headfirst in to the pool. Before he could reach her her head was underwater. Grabbing a fistful of her hair in his panic, he yanked her back.

She sputtered and spat water then turned on him. "You're not supposed to be here!" She glared at him. Brushing soaking wet hair out of her way, she howled. "I was trying to get clean!"

"I'm sorry." He backed up, retreating from her fury. "I thought you were falling in."

"Falling in? How could I fall in when I was *kneeling?* I look a mess and I want to be *clean,*" she screamed at him, her voice rising to a wail.

"You look beautiful."

She stopped in shock.

"I mean," he stammered. "I'll go."

He beat a hasty retreat, cursing what he'd said. Climbing back up the bluff in a rush, he headed for the clear pool he'd found, throwing off clothes as he went. Not thinking of the padded pouch he wore, he jumped in and let nature cool his ardor.

"Gods," he spat and dove under again, scrubbing at his hair.

"Pitfire," he shouted when he came up again.

Why did she have to be so beautiful? So aggravating? He wanted to spank that pretty bottom of hers and tell her exactly what she did to him.

No, he wanted to do other things. He wanted to give her the child she hunted for and feel her around him. He finally admitted his lust and knew he was going to be in pain until he could finally deliver her to Gardon.

He went under again, wishing he could wash his desire free, wishing he didn't know what she sought. If only someone was here. If only it had been Lady Alva. He couldn't imagine having such wicked thoughts about her. No, she was a sensible woman.

She must be worried sick about her charge. Thinking that, his blood finally cooled and he climbed from the pool to shake off as much water as he could. He was a guardsman—a protector. He'd better start acting like one.

Grabbing his breeches, he scrubbed more water from his skin with their fabric before donning them. His tunic came next but not before he opened his pouch and checked the treasure there. Satisfied the crystals had taken no hurt, he put them back and donned his tunic.

He had to get to Gardon. He had to get *her* to Gardon. If the ship didn't find them today, he resolved to start walking and looking for that hold she'd foreseen. They couldn't be more than a week from Sefron even at the pace they were going. If they found a hold, there would be horses. Yes, if they could just get some horses. He felt the pouch around his waist. He had money. The crystals couldn't be parted from him but there were still seven solaris in the pouch. He could use those.

His composure restored, he walked back to the beach, his eyes scanning the sea for the ship. Today there weren't even dolfyns in sight.

The girl was sitting by the firepit, glaring at him as she ran her fingers through her hair. He looked away from the sweet sight.

"We go inland today to cross the stream," he said as he gathered up the catch from his snares. Sitting down with his back to the girl, he busied himself skinning the rabbit and slicing the meat. He needed to rebuild the fire to cook it. They still had a couple of pieces of redfruit to go with it. He needed to find more.

"What about *The Seawind?*" the girl asked, her tone still snappish. "I thought you wanted to stay on the beach."

"I do." He glanced at her and looked away. "But we can't cross the stream here. There are spots up above where we can. We'll come back to the beach as soon as we cross."

"We should cross here," she insisted.

He scowled. "We'll cross upstream. That's the end of it."

She set her lips but made no more protests. Instead she busied herself spreading out that glorious mane of hers to dry.

Gods, he wanted to wrap it around his hands and pull her close and—he looked away again and concentrated on his task until he could think clearly again.

"I want you to braid your hair today," he told her. "It'll catch in the bushes and you might get hurt. It's not safe running around with it free."

"I won't," she snapped. "You're just mad at me for washing it. It was filthy and you didn't even care except I did it without waiting for your permission." She bounced to her feet and stalked down to the shore, her shoulders hunched over her anger.

Davyd let her go. The first time she snarled it, she'd see why and he wouldn't even have to mention how distracting it was. No, he'd better let it go.

Collecting some rocks from the beach, he made a marker that pointed inland for those that followed then got busy cooking the rabbit meat on flat stones he added to the fire. He could see the girl and wasn't too concerned with her getting out of sight. Besides she'd have no time to sulk later and should get it out of her system now.

Finally he was ready and could delay no longer. Filling the rough cup he carved from the tree burl with cool water, he carried it to the girl.

She didn't look at him, her eyes scanning the sea for the ship.

"Lady Synda, it's time to leave." He kept his words formal as he held the cup for her. "One last drink of water."

"There are no dolfyns today," she said, her voice full of misery. "I thought...I thought they'd bring *The Seawind* here."

"I hoped they would too," Davyd told her. "But they can't talk. No doubt they were hunting for themselves."

"I wish..." She turned to him and he wasn't surprised to see she'd been crying. "Can't we stay here one more day?"

He shuddered. Another day with her here? He knew his control wouldn't last. No, they had to keep moving.

"We'll come back to the beach as quick as we can," he promised her, "but I think it's unwise to count on the ship. The gods help those who work for what they want."

She nodded then drained the cup he held and handed it back. "I'm ready."

He wanted her to smile but took her compliance instead. Grabbing his spear and the gather bag, he led her to the easiest climb.

AFTER midday Captain Krayton stood on the deck of *The Seawind* and carefully scanned the beaches for any sign of the missing. His crew had already searched more than thirty miles of beach and found nothing. Now he was expanding the search to lands further south. If he had no results soon, he would have to appeal for help in Sefron.

Spying a waterfall on the beach, he told his Second to mark its location. If they ever needed fresh water, there would be a good source. It was too bad the folks he searched for weren't there.

The Seawind passed it by and continued on down the shore, unseen by those they sought.

TWO HOURS later Davyd was still looking for a place to cross the stream. It had gotten wider as they went upstream and more treacherous with pockets of sinking mud to trap the unwary. The bugs increased too. There hadn't been any down by the shore but the marshy swamp bred them and soon he was covered with bites.

They didn't seem to like the girl. She walked along with blissful unconcern, once nearly tripping into what looked like smooth ground. He pulled her back and showed her it was just a thin layer of dirt over thick mud. After that she stayed beside him and walked where he walked.

"That's enough." He looked at the sky and saw it was after midday. "I don't think we're going to find a better place."

"But it's too wide," she protested. "And there are snakes."

"I know." He looked over the greenish water and judged it was more than fifteen feet to the other bank. Handing her the gather bag, he looked over what was at hand.

"Eat some more of that rabbit. It will take a while to drop that tree." He motioned toward a dead tree by the stream. "We'll cross on that."

She looked doubtful but obeyed him, chewing on cooked strips of rabbit while he attacked the tree, first with his weight then his knife. It didn't give easily but neither did he. Finally the tree fell toward the stream. A cloud of insects flew up at it bounced on the other bank, then settled.

"I think that's a hive," Davyd told her. "We'd better have a torch to keep them off us."

"A hive?" She looked curious. "What's a hive?"

"Gods, you've never heard of a hive?" He couldn't believe her. "That's where bees store their honey."

"Honey?" She perked up. "Can we get honey from a tree? I've never had—"

"Of course we can. *If* you want to get stung a hundred times or more. Lady, those are *wild* bees and they will *not* give up their honey for your asking."

"Oh." She studied the tree. "Well, I don't think I'd like wild honey anyway. Mussels are much better."

He stared at her in disbelief then his lips twitched as annoyance gave way to the absurd. Finally he smiled and she smiled back. Somewhere inside him a knot loosened. He hadn't wanted to fight with her all day.

"We'll get across that bridge and head back to shore," he promised her. "You'll have mussels tonight if you want them."

"Oh, I think I can live on this." She handed him a strip of rabbit. "I didn't know rabbit could taste so good."

"It is good," he acknowledged as he bit into it. "I'll try to catch more when we camp."

She watched him eat then dug into their gather sack for their wooden cup. "It just needs some water." She started to get to her feet but he waved her back down.

"Not here," he told her. "You see that green on the water?"

"Yes. It's pretty."

"It's also bad. The water flows very slowly through here and sickness grows in such places. Let's wait until we find a place where the water flows fast and clear."

"Like the waterfall?"

"Like the waterfall. We never touch standing water. Remember that."

"Yes sir," she meekly replied.

"Ready?" He raised an eyebrow.

"Yes sir," she repeated.

"I hope you can keep your balance." He picked up a dead tree branch and shredded the end with his knife, then stuffed brown moss in. "Light it, please."

She obeyed. Gathering up the energy inside her, she pushed it down to her fingertip and out. A fat spark flew to the head of the torch and the moss caught and sputtered, giving off heavy smoke.

Davyd grabbed the sack and heaved it across the stream. It opened and the cup flew out but it was out of the way. He sent his spear over the same way, neatly pinning the sack.

"Now you."

Wondering wildly if he would throw her too, Synda hesitated before taking the hand he offered. He guided her to the log and she followed, placing her feet where he did and inching out across it.

"Just keep your eyes on me," Davyd told her in a smooth voice. "And hold on to my arm. If you fall, we'll go together. Don't fall though. You wouldn't want to get that green slime in your golden hair."

She listened, amazed, as he kept talking. The only fright she felt was when the bees boiled out of their hive and he waved the torch around. The wood beneath her feet cracked under her weight and she felt bees around her legs. Biting her lip as she got stung, she retaliated with a sting of her own. The bees swerved from her as they felt the power of the stars. Some probably died but she didn't care.

"We're across," he told her and she realized they were. Surprised to find herself back on solid ground, she reluctantly let go of his arm.

"I got stung," she reported. "I think I did anyway."

"You'd know if you did. I know I did." He tossed the torch into the stream then turned to show her where an angry bee was still stuck to his neck. She gasper. There were other stings too. She pulled the bee off but wasn't sure what to do.

"Pull the stingers out," he told her in a matter-of-fact voice. "Then put mud on them. They'll be all right."

"Mud?" She was scandalized. "You don't put mud on anything."

"You do on bee stings. It draws the poison out. My mother taught me that."

"Your mother isn't a healer." She was disgusted at the thought. "The Temple says to clean wounds then heal them. You never dirty them."

He gave her a black look and spoke in a voice deceptively calm. "My mother *is* a healer. Do it."

She wanted to explain but didn't dare. How had she gotten on his bad side again? It seemed nothing she said was right.

Pulling out the tiny stinger on his neck, she searched for more. "Did they sting under your tunic? I should check there." She started to lift it up but he pushed it back down.

"Lady, you don't need to tend those stings," he told her in a flat voice. "*I'll* care for those."

"Why? You can't tend those on your back and I am not interested in what you carry here." She made a grab for the pouch and he reacted, catching her hand.

He let her go so quickly she got mad.

"You think I didn't know? All that time on the ship you were carrying that thing around your waist. It makes you look paunchy! And I could see it when you came back this morning. You think I'm some kind of fool?"

He didn't answer her but abruptly pulled his tunic over his head. Without a word, he presented his back for her examination.

Synda glared at him, tempted not to help, but her common sense returned. She wouldn't have him in pain. Trained in healing she had a responsibility to help others and she wouldn't betray that not even for Davyd Yorkson.

Her hands were cool as she lightly quartered his back, looking for more of the angry red dots that signaled stings. Her hands slowed as she went, feeling the strong muscles, caressing his shoulder blades, and tracing the line of his spine. Such muscles! Guessing this might be her only chance to see him this way, she took a long time to finish.

"Three stings," she said and scooped up some mud to plaster on that fine back. It looked so black against his pale skin. He hadn't discarded his tunic in a long time.

"Let me see your front."

"No." He dropped the tunic over his shoulders so quick she was startled. He turned to her, his face set. "I've already checked for stings there. Let me see yours."

"Mine?" She abruptly remembered the sting she'd felt and reddened as she recalled where it was. "No, I'll tend my own stings. I'm a healer and you're not."

He looked ready to argue.

"Besides, it's on my leg," she finished in a rush, her face flaming. "Please let me tend it."

He was grinning now and she wanted to wipe that smirk off his face. Turning away, she abruptly sat down and waited for him to leave. Infuriating man. She wished she'd let his stings go.

Looking around to see where he was, she raised her skirt to expose the sting. It was on the back of her thigh but she could reach it. Thanking Kala for small favors, she pulled the stinger out and plastered it with mud, surprised when it felt good against the soreness of the sting.

She found another sting even higher on her leg and treated it the same way. Satisfied she'd found them all, she looked around for her guardsman.

"Ready?" He seemed to appear out of nowhere with their gather sack and spear. "Let's go. I want to be back at the beach before dark."

"Yes sir." She followed, not surprised when he left the bank of the stream and led her deeper into the woods. Relieved to be away from the bugs, she just followed.

DAVYD grinned, remembering her blush. She deserved it. She'd tortured him with her cool hands on his back forever and strained his control. He thought it just that she got back some of the embarrassment she gave him. It almost made up for her finding out about the pouch.

He should have thought about that skirt. Thinking how many bees could have gone up it, he shuddered. As angry as they were and with no way out, it was a wonder she got off so lightly. Well, maybe bees didn't like the Sunborn either. None of the other insects seemed to touch her.

Leading her on to more solid ground, he quickened the pace. If they were to make it by nightfall, they had to move fast. Ignoring the pain when he put a bare foot wrong, he kept going.

"Wait. Davyd, I think I see a fruit tree."

"A fruit tree?" He looked where she pointed and shook his head. "We can't eat rugur—not at this season."

"Why not? It's good."

"Lady, it's not good now. In a few weeks it will be. Right now they aren't ripe. Redfruit we can have but not rugur."

He saw the stubborn set of her chin but refused to give in. Like most boys he'd tried unripened rugur once and knew exactly what it would do to him. He would rather starve than let her see him like that.

"Let's go." He started walking again and was relieved when she followed. Someday someone might tell her what rugur did but he wouldn't do it. The Temple *should* have told her. It was probably used in the manhunt.

They walked for another hour before he spotted a redfruit tree. The boughs were so heavy with fruit they nearly touched the ground. With a cry of delight, the girl started past him.

"Wait!" Davyd grabbed her.

He heard another low grunt and nearly froze with fright. "Back."

Pulling her with him, he hoped she wouldn't scream as a wild pig raised her head and looked straight at them. The ugly sow stared at them then went on eating.

He started to relax.

A loud grunting to his right warned him and he propelled the girl toward the nearest tree. "Up!"

Dropping the gather sack, he shifted the spear in his hand. Jabbing at the boar who made a tentative charge, he made it change direction. Settling back into a trot, the boar headed back to the redfruit tree.

"Up the tree," Davyd hissed. "Now."

She moved as a third pig grunted a warning. Scrambling up, she gasped as a huge boar charged right for them.

Davyd jabbed at its eyes and the boar tuned with a squeal of pain. Seeing the girl was safe, he jumped aside as the wounded boar charged again with a bellow of rage. Scrambling up the tree, he barely got out of the boar's reach. Putting his feet against the rough trunk, he felt his skin tear but kept climbing, dragging the girl to the higher branches as he went.

Below him the boar's squeals propelled all the pigs into motion.

The pigs charged, hitting the tree with such force it shook. More charges followed. He clung to the girl. Hoping the tree would hold, he held her tight and prayed.

Chapter 8 - Pigs

3 Tyras 850

DAVYD held on through the attacks, clutching Synda and the tree's trunk against the shaking. The enraged squeals of the wounded boar egged the others on until finally the pigs tired.

Some of the hairy pigs lost interest and drifted back to the redfruit tree. More followed until only the tusked boar he'd scratched still hammered away at his tree. Finally even he left and took out his frustration on a smaller target. Charging a half-grown male, he sent him squealing into the woods then thrust his bearded face into one of the low-hanging branches and rattled it, sending fruit raining down.

Davyd watched from his perch, then slowly relaxed his grip on the girl. She clung to the bole of the tree, her face pasty white. The boar saw him move and charged their tree once more but none of the others made more than a half-hearted attempt to join him.

"Up in the fork," he whispered to the girl. "It's safest there."

She nodded and slowly climbed up another three feet, freezing every time the boar looked toward the tree. She stood in the crotch and waited for him, her arms wrapped securely around one of the trunks.

He joined her then helped her sit down against him.

"Keep quiet. They'll go when they've had enough," he murmured.

They were jammed tightly into the fork and couldn't fall without the entire tree going with them. Still he wrapped his arms around her waist and could feel her rapid breathing.

"Relax," he whispered again. "They can't get us. Do a Temple charm."

She nodded and her golden hair brushed against his cheek.

His arms tightened and he closed his eyes as he suddenly became aware of his position.

Gods. He couldn't get closer than this. With grim determination, he set to doing his own charm, slowly repeating old lessons in his mind with that didn't work.

She was more relaxed now, her breathing slower, as she used some discipline of her own.

"How long will they stay?" She looked up at him with those wondrous green eyes, her head tilted back against his shoulder so she could see him.

"Until they've eaten as much as they can hold," he told her. "Then they'll go for water. That's when we can leave."

She seemed reassured by that.

He watched the pigs and tried not to think about her.

The old boar found their gather sack and tossed it. Davyd watched silently while the pig ripped their sack and spilled his few tools across the clearing. Other pigs joined in and he knew they could smell the rabbit. He grimly witnessed the destruction of everything he'd accomplished, helpless to save any of it.

"I'll find the snares later," he whispered reassuringly. "And I still have my knife."

She looked worried anyway and he didn't blame her. The few possessions they had were needed if they were going to survive—only the spear and cup could be easily replaced.

They were more than twenty feet off the ground. He hadn't realized they'd climbed so high or so fast. Finding the view unsettling and not wanting to watch the pigs' destruction any longer, he focused on the girl.

She'd shifted.

"Forget them." His arms tightened around her. "We'll get by."

"Oh, I wasn't—" She denied then her eyes flew to his. "You're bleeding. I knew there was something wrong."

"It's just my foot." Now he was aware it hurt. He must have scrapped half the skin off in the scramble up the tree.

"Let me see it. You can't sit up here and bleed—" Her words cut off as several pigs left the remains of the gather sack to charge the tree.

Davyd clutched her tightly against him as the tree shook. When the charge abated, he gave in, pulling his injured foot up and resting it on the other trunk. It was an awkward position but let her see the long tear. It was ugly, stretching from his toes to his instep and still oozed blood.

Gritting his teeth as her cool hands touched it, he let examine the tear. Thinking she would let it be, he gasped as a tingle of Starfire raced along his sole and disappeared, taking the pain away.

She leaned back against him.

"It's healed," she said. "The skin is still tender and will be, but… it's done."

Staring at his foot, he saw the gash was gone except for a thin line of newly healed skin. She'd used her healing skill. That was another inborn ability of the Sunborn. They could tell a wound to close and heal. They couldn't heal every wound, but this one wasn't beyond Synda's skill.

Not all Sunborn could use that ability even though the Temple encouraged them to learn it. Glad that his lady could heal, he smiled at her upturned face and planted a light kiss on her forehead. "Thank you."

She just closed her eyes and rested against him, accepting the kiss as her due.

Knowing such healing took its toll, he wasn't surprised when her breathing slowed and deepened. Carefully moving his foot back down, he shifted into a more comfortable position and surrendered to the inevitable. She was asleep.

He tried not to think of her sleeping so close but he enjoyed the feel of her. Her waist was slender and easy to hold. Her breasts rested softly on his arms and he wanted to touch them, tease her nipples. Her legs, though, were the most tempting. Her hips rested against his own in the narrow fork and her skirts were pulled up to reveal one sweet knee and a good expanse of the other.

He leaned his head back against the tree and prayed for strength. Somehow, some way he would get her out of this tree. He couldn't stand having such a luscious package so close to him. Even her hair drove him wild.

Keeping an eye on the pigs below, he held her safe. Then the weight of his own fatigue began to be felt and he laid his chin on her shoulder, thinking he would just rest his eyes. He liked the feel of her clean hair against his unshaven cheek. He closed his eyes.

SYNDA felt so comfortable. Her waist was warm and felt wonderfully secure with the guardsman's strong arms about her. She had no fear of sleeping, even in a tree, with Davyd holding her.

Some tired part of her brain told her she should worry but she couldn't. She felt too safe.

Her neck was warm too. She could feel his slow, even breath on her neck and some dim part of her mind told her he was sleeping. That nudged her toward wakefulness. She didn't move though but let him hold her.

Remembering how tired he looked that morning, she resolved to let him sleep. She would keep an eye on those ugly pigs.

She could see some of them without turning her head and felt a little alarm for they'd quit eating. Most were stretched out on their sides and sleeping as soundly as her guardsman. She almost giggled at the comparison, imagining Davyd asleep on his side with them.

She was really too comfortable. His strong arms held her close and his chest made a wonderful backrest. Even his head seemed to be exactly where she wanted it. It was like they fit together. She couldn't even complain about the rough tree between her legs. It felt good. She imagined it was a man for just an instant and shied away from the thought. No, not that. She would think about that when she got to Gardon.

Not wanting to spoil the beauty of this moment, she closed her eyes to savor it. He felt so good to her.

She suddenly stiffened as his lips moved against her neck. He nuzzled her, his rough beard sending shivers down her body and a warmth to her middle. Biting her lip to keep from calling out, she heard him mumble something against her tender skin. He was still sleeping!

Blushing, she realized he was dreaming of her. When his arms tightened even more about her waist, she took a deep, shuddering breath.

He was instantly awake. His head lifted from her shoulder and his arms loosened so much she grabbed for them. She didn't look at him though, afraid of what she might see.

"Gods, I didn't mean to go to sleep."

"You needed it," she generously told him. "And I just woke up. I think some of the pigs are gone."

Brushing her hair out of the way, he peered down. "Yes, about half."

He scrubbed his face with his free hand. "We should be able to go soon."

"I'm glad. Sleeping in a tree is not that comfortable. My legs are getting cold."

"I'm sorry," he responded and she felt guilty.

"Don't be." She looked up at him. "It's just that I want to get back to the beach. I didn't think sand was comfortable before but..."

"I know. You can stretch out in it."

"I'm trying not to be a pain, Davyd, really I am. If we have to stay here, I'll be quiet."

"We *aren't* staying here," he muttered in such a fierce tone that she felt rejected. Her face must have shown it because he added, "I hate heights."

"You hate heights?" Synda squeaked, her eyes getting wider as she looked down and realized how far they'd climbed. "But you got us up here."

"Getting *up* is not the problem," he grumbled. "And we will get down but we will *not* stay up here."

She grinned, amused that her strong guardsman had such a silly fault. Before she thought, she reached up and stroked his rough beard then snatched her hand away as his eyes darkened and his jaw set.

"I'm sorry. I just wanted to see what it felt like. I won't do it again."

"Good."

Looking down they saw only three, no, four pigs remained. Even as they watched, one got up and started walking in the general direction of the stream. An old sow grunted and rose to her feet to follow, stirring the last ones with her passage.

"Now?" Synda asked.

"Now." Motioning for her to hold onto a trunk, Davyd reached for the one in back of him and edged his way up so he was kneeling. He started down, stopping when he was just able to touch her bare legs.

"Come on and don't look down," he said. "Swing your leg over and kneel like I did and I'll guide your feet." He tapped her foot.

"Wait a moment. You've got too much skirt. Can you grab the back and tuck it in your belt? No, the *front* of your belt."

Synda nearly laughed as she understood what he wanted. Knotting it through her belt, she realized it made her skirt almost into breeches. More confident with her dignity covered, she let him guide her down the tree.

It took a long time to get down and she wondered how they had gotten so high in such a short time. When they finally touched ground, she couldn't resist giving him a quick hug to show her thanks.

He stiffened. Remembering his dream, she backed away with sudden shyness.

"Let's go." He scowled at her and picked up the remains of the gather sack. Finding two of his snares and the cup, he didn't stop to look for more. Scooping up fruit the pigs had missed, he hurried her away.

THE nightly quiet of Sefron's port was abruptly disturbed as *The Seawind* was rowed into dock. Unlike most ships she didn't drop anchor and wait until the light of day to dock but her own crew manned her long boats and rowed her in.

Her sister ship, *The Dolfyn*, noticed and added another boat to hers before the Dockmaster roused his own men. For a ship to demand docking at such an hour meant they had problems.

"What news?" the Dockmaster asked Captain Krayton as soon as the lines were tied and the gangplank lowered. "Why sail at night?"

"I lost two people overboard—a merchant and a Sunborn lady," Krayton tersely explained. "They made it to shore but I need search parties and a messenger to go to York's."

"York's? You lost that merchant?"

"One of his sons. You have someone?"

The Dockmaster pointed to a likely boy. "You. Go stir up the Yorks."

"Wait." Krayton stopped him. "Tell them Davyd needs them. Come tonight."

"Yes sir." The boy took off.

"And who was the lady?" the Dockmaster asked. "And who is this lady?" He bowed to the woman in Krayton's shadow.

"Lady Alva of Datyl." Krayton introduced her. She hadn't been far from him these past three days. "Her charge, Lady Synda, was the one who went over. I'm sure Davyd followed her. The ship was under sail and no one saw."

"And the dolfyns? Did they report?"

"They didn't find anything," Krayton told him, "but Davyd left a sign. They're walking this way. I need horsemen and he asked for his brothers."

The captain of *The Dolfyn* stepped up, clasping his hand and bowing to Lady Alva. "I just brought horses from Farpoint, Krayton. If you want the stalls…"

"Thanks. Yes, I'll take them. As soon as *The Seawind* is offloaded and we have the searchers, we'll be off again."

"In that case, I'll open a warehouse tonight. What cargo do you have?" the Dockmaster asked.

They fell to discussing the cargo until the Yorks arrived.

The brothers arrived together, grim and ready for trouble. Two guardsmen were at their backs but Krayton doubted anyone would tangle with the York brothers tonight. They scanned the dock and then the ship for their brother.

"Where is he?" the older demanded. Only twenty-seven, Monar Yorkson was already a man of note. Like his father he was an outstanding merchant and swordsman. His shoulder-length black hair was in a merchant's style but there was no doubt he could use the sword at his hip.

The other brother was younger and wore his hair short in a swordsman's style but Krayton knew Wydon was as sharp as the others when it came to trade. He'd sailed with him before.

"He's south of here about eighty miles," Krayton reported. "But alive as of three days ago. Come aboard."

He led them down to his cabin and handed them the bark chip Davyd had written his message on.

"Synda safe. Walking north. Get brothers. Davyd Yorkson." Monar read the message out loud then handed it to his brother. "That sounds like him. Who is this Synda?"

"She's one of the premier artists of Datyl," Krayton said. "Davyd was hired to escort her to Gardon. If she's lost…"

"Davyd won't lose her," Monar replied. "None of us would. Why was she going to Gardon? No, never mind. There had to be a good reason."

He glanced at his brother.

"What about his cargo?" Monar asked. "Is it safe?"

"Of course." Krayton thought of the wine and trees and was surprised by the question. "I'd like to unload at first light. The wine is still stowed and I need to clear those trees of his to get to the hatch."

"Trees?" Wydon broke his silence. "He bought trees?"

"Apple trees," Krayton explained. "But there's a man hired to care for them. He'll go with them to Gardon."

"I didn't mean wine and trees." Monar waved that away. "He had a royal commission. Can I see his cabin?"

"Monar, he's probably wearing them," Wydon said, one hand on his brother's arm. "I know he made a pouch to carry them around his waist. He showed it to me."

"Carrying what?" Krayton was confused. "If they were messages, I'm sure they got fouled by the water."

"Not messages. Please let me see his cabin."

Frowning Krayton led them to the small cabin Davyd had shared with his Second and the tree tender. The small trunk Davyd used was there and had only been opened to stow his things once it was certain he'd gone over. He watched as Monar went through it then popped open a compartment he hadn't known was there. It held journals and a few trinkets but not what the merchant searched for.

Handing a journal to Wydon, Monar turned back to him. "He must still have them. I can have a score of men ready to go at tomorrow noon."

"It will take longer than that to ready *The Seawind.* The next morn. I left two men with supplies where he landed. If they find them, Davyd will wait for us."

He wondered what Davyd was supposed to be carrying. The merchant hadn't breathed a word to him. He suddenly remembered the artist's complaints.

"If Davyd was carrying something under his tunic, it would explain. The lady thought Davyd her best subject for sketching. She complained to me that he wouldn't take his tunic off—even suggested I order him to. I couldn't, of course."

He smiled at their stunned expressions. "You'll have to meet the lady. Her art comes first in her life and she thinks it should come first for others too. I think your brother was the first to refuse her something."

Wydon held out the journal to his brother and pointed out a page for him to read. His older brother nodded.

"Yes, he's got the crystals with him."

Krayton wondered if he meant to say that out loud. Crystals? Meditation crystals? More than one? Aware of the price of those things, he suddenly understood Monar's concern and his respect for Davyd grew. He hadn't said one word about them nor shown them even to him.

"I'll take charge of the cargo." Wydon abruptly closed the journal and folded his hands around it. "It was to be my task anyway. Monar, do you want the guards I had for the caravan?"

"Yes, brother," Monar agreed. "You can delay. Captain, how much to hire *The Seawind?*"

"For passage, two solaris," he named an incredibly low figure. "Twenty men and twenty horses. More than that, four sols each. You provide feed for the animals and provisions."

"Done," Monar quickly agreed. "And thank you."

"No thanks needed," Krayton said. "My crew nearly deserted when they found the sign to go look for them. They won't be happy until they know they're safe."

He fished in his pouch and found the other thing Davyd had left. "Your brother also left this. I know your family will want it." He handed the gold medallion to Monar.

The older Yorkson took it and showed it to his brother before wrapping it up and slipping it into his own pouch. "I'll send it on to Mother Nan. She needs to know." His face was less grim than before but Krayton doubted he'd sleep tonight.

Remembering how the Yorks talking about their family, he doubted any would rest easy until Davyd was found again. And if he died…

Chapter 9 - Bower

SYNDA stretched in her leafy bower, more comfortable than she'd been in days. Looking up through the bent branches of her sturdy cage, she smiled and brushed her hand across her lips as she remembered a lovely dream. Turning over, she looked around for her guardsman but didn't see him. She stayed in her little cage as she had promised and waited for him to come back.

It was impossible to return to the beach last night and Davyd finally suggested this solution. Making her a strong bower in case more pigs appeared, he had tied it shut and made a nest for himself on the other side of the fire. That was still burning and had been every time Synda woke.

She'd been comfortable enough with her leafy roof and a bed made of springy boughs and now she knew why he didn't sleep with her. Pleased, she stretched again. He wanted her.

Alva would be shocked. She knew that but it didn't bother her. After all she was on a manhunt and the normal rules didn't apply. If she wanted she could even ask the favors of a married man without upsetting tradition. If she chose to hunt a Kalryn, was it so bad?

She lay in her bower and continued examining her sleepy thoughts from last night. She wasn't sure why she had chosen Davyd above all others to sketch but she had. In her eyes he was both perfect and dangerous. Now she knew she was safe with him. No matter how he might bluster and snap, he'd never hurt her. No, he just wanted her to obey him so he could keep her safe.

He wanted her. She still couldn't get over that. Her cheeks grew warm as she imagined what it would be like to have *him* in her bed. Her insides tightened and a rush of warmth told her she shouldn't be thinking such thoughts. Not now. It felt so good knowing he wanted her.

Sitting up in her bower, she took the tattered gather sack off her feet and looked around before she lifted her skirt and checked the bee stings she got yesterday. Peeling the last of the mud off, she saw they were nearly healed and didn't waste any power on them. That done, she rearranged her skirts and started raking her hands through her hair.

She'd had lots of time to think last night. First he'd made her sit in another tree while he set his snares. After that she helped him with the fire and weaving her little bower. She hadn't helped with cooking the meat but she had paid attention when he showed her how it was done.

She knew the ship wasn't coming back. It had been foolish to think it would but she had held on to that hope as long as she could. Last night, though, she'd agreed with Davyd that the best solution was to walk north until they came to Sefron. That hold—she remembered her dream and knew they would come to one. Confident of that, she hummed as she worked on her hair.

DAVYD stopped just outside the clearing and listened, hearing a noise he couldn't immediately identify. Stepping behind a tree he scanned the clearing and listened, puzzled, before he realized it was the girl.

She was sitting cross-legged in her little cage and he was mesmerized as she combed her fingers through that glorious mane of hers. She was humming. She looked like the Goddess herself as she tended her hair, a contented smile on her face.

He groaned and turned away, wishing once again someone—anyone—was with them. She was too tantalizing. Last night she'd insisted on checking his foot again and her gentle touch had nearly proved his undoing. Even asleep in that damned cage she managed to tempt him. He wanted to keep her there and out of his reach.

The humming stopped.

"Davyd?" Her pleasant voice called and this time there was no panic, no alarm in it. She just seemed curious where he was.

He cupped his hands, not wanting her to know he was watching, and used them to make his voice seem further away. "Coming."

Retreating on silent feet, he approached the clearing from another direction with his gatherings in hand.

"Good morning, my lady." He dropped his haul beside the fire and flashed her a smile as he undid the stout door of her cage. "Well rested?"

"Yes."

His heart skipped a beat at her smile.

"It was the best night yet."

"Good. We'll try to do the same tonight." He followed her into the trees then turned away as she tended to her needs. "I've found a deer path leading north. I think that's out best route now."

She rejoined him with an even sunnier smile. "Oh, I agree. I'm sure we'll find a hold."

He didn't know what to make of her. Today she seemed so confident, so secure, that it unnerved him. He wondered if it was a Temple exercise or whether she knew they were close to safety. Maybe she was just making the best of their situation.

Suspicious of her good humor, he returned to the fire. She joined him and even watched as he skinned a rabbit and laid out its meat to cook. Beside it he had a small bird and she looked away when he chopped off its head and skinned it too.

"You've hunted these a lot."

He looked at her, seeing her face was pale and eyes enormous as she stared at them.

"Yes. My father started taking us hunting when we were seven. Then I was fostered on a hold when I was eleven. He wanted us to learn how to survive."

"Did he know you'd be a merchant? I mean merchants don't usually leave their shops."

"I'm a trader, not a merchant," Davyd corrected. "I don't sit in a store. With my father's store in Gardon and my brother's in Sefron, we need to buy wares and move them from city to city. Wydon and I do that. Sometimes we guard things for others. That's how I came to Datyl. I was to buy wine for my father's store and guard something else."

"What you wear around your waist? What is it that you have to wear all the time?"

"Ask me something else, lady. You shouldn't even know about those."

"Those?" She seized on the word triumphantly. "I thought I felt three. And they were round." She stopped and looked at him suspiciously, then abruptly got up and walked back to her bower.

She knew. Deciding it was no use to hide it any longer, he followed her. Pulling up his tunic he showed her what she suspected.

The black belt around his middle was padded to give him a paunch but the padding had compressed in the water and lost its shape. Now it showed three even orbs through the fabric. Unlacing the leather thong that held the cloth closed, he spilled the three globes into his hand.

Three perfect palm-sized crystals, one a little smaller than the other two, caught the light. As he shifted them, they seemed to glow in their depths.

Looking at him for permission, Synda picked out the small one and looked through its clear crystal. It was flawless. They all were.

"Someone puts a lot of trust in you," she said with awe. "These—I only own one meditation crystal."

"I don't own these." He put the pair back and watched her face as she examined the third. "Queen Fara does. She just trusted me to get them home safely."

"Did you buy them too? I mean these are worth more than any of my paintings."

"I know."

Davyd watched as she smoothly rolled the ball from one hand to the other, then it seemed to take on a life of its own as she rolled it up her arm and walked it through the air on the backs of her hands. He gasped when it abruptly disappeared and grabbed the hand that held it.

"Here." Smiling, she offered her other hand. The crystal rested in her palm. "Davyd, you honor me by letting me see these. I will never tell. I swear that by Kala."

He grabbed her fingers, pressing the crystal into her palm as she kissed them. "And you've shown me something beautiful." For a long moment he looked into her eyes then took the orb and put it back in its place. "Promise me something."

"Anything."

"If something should happen to me, see these get to Gardon. I won't have my family indebted by their loss."

She was silent and he saw the fear in her eyes.

"Please."

"Yes," she whispered then her voice got louder. "But *nothing* is going to happen to you. I need you."

With a groan, he took her in his arms and pushed her head down against his shoulder. "Nothing will happen. Nothing will part us. I swear I won't leave you."

He rocked her, needing to feel his warmth, her soft curves against his lean body. She clung to him, her arms going up to encircle his neck and draw his head down to hers.

Before he knew what she was doing, she ran her fingers lightly along his unshaven jaw. Then she stroked his stubbled cheek and laid her fingers on his lips.

Davyd groaned at the feather-light touch. He wanted to take her, kiss her full lips. When she stood on tiptoe to kiss his nose in a child's kiss, he broke.

Cradling her head in his hands, he tilted it back and plundered her lips. His were hot and hungry as they met her tender mouth but he couldn't be gentle. Forcing her lips apart, his hot tongue flicked against hers.

She responded. Her mouth opened wider and her body melted against his. Soon he was bearing her entire weight in his arms. Pressing one knee between her thighs, he kissed the hollow of her neck with hot lips and started to lay her down.

What was he doing? He stiffened, shocked by his actions, and abruptly stood her up again. Tearing himself away, he groaned as he felt the stiff, throbbing heat of his need. Knowing he'd gone too far, he grabbed his spear and ran.

GIVING a wordless cry of protest, Synda sank to her knees, her breath heavy and mind dazed by his passion. She felt hot and confused, certain she had disgusted him but wondering how. And she ached.

Goddess! She felt the empty ache in her loins, the tenderness of her breasts, and wanted more. Was this love? Was this passion? She didn't know which was which but she knew she wanted more.

Not knowing what else to do, she climbed back into her leafy bower and pulled the door closed. Her mind was all aflutter with confused thoughts of him and she reveled in it one moment and was terrified the next. What if he didn't return?

He had to come back. He had to!

DAVYD shuddered, his passion finally spent. He stared at the wreck of a tree in front of him, the victim of his frustration. Unable to run as he wanted to, he had taken it out on the tree.

His laugh was shaky. He must have scared all the game for a mile around with his cursing. Gods, how did he get into this mess? Why did he have to love her?

That kiss—he groaned and hid his face—that kiss was his undoing. She had responded to him. Remembering her hot willingness, he felt his manhood harden again. No!

He couldn't have her. It made no difference whether she hunted or no. When he gave her his oath, he entered her service and it was forbidden that any Sunborn—no, any master—compel that kind of obedience from one who served them. He knew it could mean exile for her, even death, if the courts decided she flouted that law.

She was Sunborn. He was Kalryn and only a trader besides. If his family knew he was having such thoughts, they'd disown him. Worse, they might forgive him and suggest he take up a hold far from the cities. Banishment.

He had to go back. He had to control his passion and convince her it was wrong to even remember it. They must behave properly. Vowing to never hold her—even touch her—again, he rose to his feet and found his spear.

Retracing his steps to the clearing, he wondered if she was keeping watch. Remembering the pigs, he hurried along.

He needn't have worried. She was sitting in her bower looking utterly contented as she ate. Didn't she know? Suddenly irritated with her composure, he clamped his jaw shut and thrust his spear into the ground. Not looking at her, he took some of the meat and ate himself, noting some was singed and tasted of ashes.

"It was burning," the girl said. "I saved what I could."

"You did well. I shouldn't have left."

"I was all right. Only a deer stepped out to look at me. I don't think she knew I was here until she nibbled at my leaves." Her voice was full of laughter. "You should have seen her. I tried not to make a sound but she was so startled."

He slowly smiled at the picture she presented. "That must have been a sight."

"Oh, it was," she said, her face radiant. "I've never been so close to a deer. I could have touched her."

"I'm glad you were safe in there. Deer can attack, you know. They usually run but the bucks can turn on you."

"Her hooves looked sharp. And I promised to stay in here."

"Yes." He looked at the cage and wished he could just keep her in there and safe from him. "Thank you. I wasn't thinking when I left."

There was an awkward silence before he gathered the nerve to say what had to be said. "Synda, I'm sorry. I've behaved poorly toward you and I want you to know it will *not* happen again."

She looked disappointed.

"I'm your guardsman and I've sworn to get you to Gardon," he continued. "I should never have held you and I beg you will forget that kiss. It was my fault."

"I share the blame." She was solemn. "Davyd, I wanted you to kiss me. I thought..."

"You thought?" he suddenly exploded, his anger released by her admission. Pacing up and down, he spat words at her. "You didn't think! What is the penalty for Sunborn who love their servants?"

She turned pale. "I'm on a manhunt."

"That wouldn't excuse you and you aren't hunting now. You aren't in the robes and you don't have the scroll. I doubt the courts would agree you're under that protection."

"Then I dismiss you from my service."

He barely heard the words. When they registered, his heart froze. She couldn't! She wouldn't. His shock gave way to anger.

"You can't. I remember you fumbled your oath but I didn't. I'm sworn to deliver you to the Temple at Gardon and *I will do it*."

She looked rebellious.

"You *will* remember I'm your guardsman," he continued, determined to end this. "And you will hunt some other. I am *not* for your pleasure."

She gasped as if he'd thrown water on her.

"And you'll keep your hair braided too," he ordered. "Every man who looks at you is entranced by that hair. If you don't braid it, cover it."

"I don't want to." That broke her trance and one lovely hand went up into her tresses. "I've never bound it. Don't you like it?"

He glared at her then abruptly changed tactics. "Like it? I love it." He dropped his voice to a soft husky tone and crouched to look at her in the cage. "It's so fine it floats on the slightest breeze and looks like a nimbus of power around you. You look like the sun."

She listened, her cheeks going pink.

"And when I see it like that, I want to touch it and smooth it down and wrap its soft gold around my hands." Davyd saw her blush, then changed, his voice suddenly harsh. "And so does every man you meet and not all will remember you're Sunborn!"

He abruptly stood up and flung one of his snares at her. "Keep it covered or keep it tied if you still want to hunt when we reach Gardon."

She gasped but he didn't care. Ignoring her sulk, he started breaking camp.

Gods he wanted her. If only once he could have her, teach her how to be a woman —

He dropped that thought abruptly, recognizing it for the trap it was. He *had* to remember what she was. Vowing to treat her with every courtesy, he was still relieved to see she'd listened to reason and braided that wonderful hair back. She even folded it up and wrapped the snare as a headband around her head.

His lips twitched as he realized she'd deliberately overdone it but he let it go. They had lots of miles to go and the day seemed half-done already.

For the first time he handed her the gather bag to carry and preceded her, ready to guard against attack. This was how it *should* be done. He would bend no more rules for the lady.

THE deer trail led them to another stream, its banks firm instead of marshy but wide enough he hesitated in asking Synda to jump it. Looking for a tree to fell, he knew he'd just have to take the time to make another bridge.

"What are you doing?" She looked at him with cool eyes and a haughtiness he was getting used to. Very much the Sunborn lady now, she was letting him know it.

"Looking for a bridge tree, my lady. It's too wide for you to jump."

"Nonsense. Just give me the spear."

He did and watched as she planted it butt-first on the ground and leaned on it to test its strength. Then, before he knew what she would do, she planted it in the stream and vaulted over, neatly landing on the other bank without showing more than an ankle.

"Your turn." She tossed the spear back at him and walked away.

Recovering from his surprise, he took a run at the stream and landed on the other side.

"Where did you learn to do that?" He caught up with her in a rush. "I've never seen anything like that."

She was smiling a smug little smile. "It's a child's trick. Anyone from Datyl knows it."

Distracted by her stunt, he followed her. Everyone knew it? He doubted that. Yet how did she know? She did it so neatly she must have done it before. Vowing to cut her a spear of her own, he led the way.

They had gone some distance before he saw the first hoof print and stopped to examine it. Made by a horse, it was large and oval and he could see the nail marks in its shoe. It wasn't a wild horse running with deer. This horse was shod.

"Be careful, Synda. Horsemen."

"The hold," she stated, her smile flashing again. "I told you we'd find a hold."

"It may not be a hold. It could be a hunting party or even raiders. It's better to be cautious."

He didn't relish the idea of coming up on horsemen in the woods. Dirty as they were, they could be mistaken for raiders or holdless. A sensible man would have them pinned and helpless before asking questions. He didn't want to think what raiders would do.

As the number of hoofprints grew, he would see some were older and some newer and that looked good. Someone traveled this route frequently enough to make it a trail. He doubted raiders would do that.

The trail abruptly stopped at the edge of wide fields. The girl gave a glad cry and tried to step out ahead of him.

"Stop," he commanded and grabbed her arm. "Synda, listen to me. You wait. We both wait until the men in the fields can reach the hold," he spoke rapidly. "If you go rushing up there, they'll think you're a raider or, worse yet, you are escaping from me. You walk and stay beside me."

Turning to the fields, he saw at least one man had spotted them. The man behaved as he expected, taking his hoe and walking toward the hold. He shouted to his fellows and motioned toward him and the girl.

Waiting until a bell sounded from the hold, he wondered if this Sunborn lady knew anything about how to act when approaching a strange hold. He doubted it.

"Can we go now? Or do we have to wait for them to come to us?"

"No, we can go now. Synda, do you know the guesting formula? We'll have to do it when we get there."

"I know there is one." She started walking, her steps too quick, and he pulled her back to a more sedate pace.

"Do we have to take all day?" she wailed.

"No. But we do have to give them time to prepare and decide whether to give us shelter. Face it, Synda. It's not every day a lone man and a woman walk out of the forest covered in dirt. How would you treat someone dressed like us?"

That got her thinking.

Davyd reviewed the guesting formula in his mind and hoped they would accept it from him and not Synda. It was custom that the leader give it but he couldn't remember any time when a lady was involved. He would have to try.

The hold was a prosperous one. Besides the fields, he could see an orchard of fruit trees. There were irrigation ditches too—a sure sign the hold was long established.

More than a score of men stood at the hold's gates before they reached it. One woman, her hair gray and figure portly, was there and Davyd knew she must be lady of the hold. Beside her was her lord and Davyd was relieved to see he looked fit and used to the sword at his hip.

Gods, he wished he had a sword. They were coming to this hold defenseless. The grim faces of the men didn't bode well either.

"Take the spear," Davyd suddenly said.

"What?" She looked at him like he was daft.

"They may think I stole you. Take the spear."

She obediently took it and gave him the gather bag.

The effect was worth it. The men at the gate seemed to relax and spread out more as he approached. Some even wore smiles as he stopped in front of their lord. They looked him over.

The holder was old and gray-bearded but fit. Davyd thought him between fifty and sixty. Beside him were two that could only be his sons. Others in the group bore a strong resemblance to him too. A large family.

The lady was eyeing Synda but she didn't look upset to find herself facing a woman in such disrepair. If anything, she looked like she might take her in and wash her. He hoped so.

"It's not often we get seamen walking out of the woods," the holder finally said and motioned to the short breeks Davyd wore. "You are a seaman?"

"We fell off a ship but I am a guardsman and trader from Gardon. This lady is my charge until we reach there."

"I see." The holder looked her over with interest. "I would be interested in your tale. I offer the guesting."

Davyd smiled with relief. "I am Davyd Yorkson and this is Synda of Datyl," he began and noticed his name created a stir. "We crave shelter. It has been long and there are many tales to tell and weary feet to rest."

"Then there be meat and drink within and beds for weary bones for the payment of your tale." The holder glanced at his wife for her consent. "So Hold Alwyn honors the guesting."

His lady held the guesting cup while one of his sons poured wine into it, then handed it carefully to the holder. Alwyn smiled and saluted him. "In the name of Galton!" He drank deep.

Davyd took the cup without hesitation. "In the names of Kal and Kala." He lifted the cup and drank himself until it was dry. Turning it over in a ritual gesture, he handed it back.

He watched at the lady holder gestured for more wine.

"Be welcome to my hold, Lady Synda," she said and drank a portion of it, then handed it to her with a warm smile. "I am Janas."

"Thank you." Synda drained it dry as Davyd had done, even copying his gesture. "It looks wonderful!"

The lady laughed and took the cup from her. "Come with me."

"She'll be fine," the holder told Davyd.

The gates were opened and he could see the number of women and children who watched them. He was impressed again how prosperous the hold was. The stable yard seemed full too.

"I know she will. But I'm glad we came on your hold and not another."

Many of the men were leaving, going back to the fields.

"We've walked three, no, four days now."

"Yes, you look it. Since my lady cares for your charge, I'll see to you. I would know how a man with the name of York came to fall off a ship."

He stressed the name and Davyd wasn't surprised he knew it. The man probably had dealings in Sefron and might know his brother. Now he appreciated his mother's strategy of keeping the same name on each store.

"I'm the third son," Davyd said. "Monar is the oldest."

"I thought so. Let's see to your needs first then talk."

THE SUN was setting and the hold gates closed for the night before he saw Synda again but he'd put the time to good use. Freshly shaved and bathed, he'd accepted the clothing the holder generously offered and was pleased to try on good used boots. Feeling like a proper guardsman again, he needed only a sword to complete it and regretted again that his sword was still in his cabin on *The Seawind*.

He was allowed to trade during a guesting. Transferring six solaris to his belt pouch, he hoped to use those to buy more than horses and weapons. With so many men on the hold, surely Alwyn could spare a couple to escort them to Sefron.

When he rejoined Synda, he saw she'd also been given the best hospitality of the hold. Her gown was a plain one of yellow linen but the bodice she wore over it was brown embroidered with flowers of yellow and green. She even wore a new purse at her belt and new shoes on her feet. Only her drawing sticks remained in the same leather holder as before. The yellow of the gown almost matched her hair and he was glad she'd braided it in a more becoming style. No doubt the lady holder had suggested it.

She made a lovely picture but he steeled himself to treat her properly. She was Sunborn and he had to remember that.

"My lady." He greeted her with a warm smile. "Hold Alwyn treats you well."

The holder's lady beamed when he said the words and he knew she approved of Synda's change almost as much as he did. "My thanks to the lady for such a lovely sight."

"You're more than welcome, sir." She bobbed a curtsy and he could swear her wrinkled cheeks were rosy. "It's not often we have company here and Lady Synda is such a change. She's already told us about wild pigs and climbing a hundred feet into a tree."

"Climbed is not exactly what happened. I think one tossed me up there."

The lady laughed. "I would like to hear the full tale." Touching the hand he offered, she didn't take it but preceded them into the great hall, leaving him to escort Synda.

The hall was large, nearly forty feet long, and filled with tables in a u-shape. One, the head table, was set on a dais that also served as a makeshift stage. The walls were white-washed to reflect more light from the oil lamps on the walls and hanging from hooks on the massive beams. A huge fireplace dominated one wall but no fire was set. The night was too warm for it.

The room was like many he'd seen in his travels and he knew the tables could be broken down and stored to make room for other activities. They would even put the children to bed here if the nights got too warm or too cold. During the winter most of the hold's crafting would be done here.

Tonight though the tables were set up and he knew the hold expected to hear news of Datyl and how they came to be off their ship. He prepared to embroider the tale.

Chapter 10 - Sefron

5 Tyras 850

IN the early morning hours *The Seawind* unfurled her sails and headed for the open sea leaving Sefron's spacious harbor behind. The wind caught her canvas and the ship swung about as her sails flapped overhead.

Down on the deck a score of horses flattened their ears and tried to get away from the alarming sound but were held in place by narrow stalls and leather slings. Pawing the deck with bandaged legs, they lathered and rolled wild eyes at the riders who worked to keep them calm.

"Healer!" Monar called out to the man who walked from horse to horse. The horse tender got to him just as his bay stallion tried to rear again. Helping Monar get him back down, the healer wasted no time in putting the horse into a deep sleep.

It was over so quick Monar had no time to worry about it. The healer just put his hand on his stallion's head and murmured a word to him. The horse's neck went limp and his body relaxed in the sling.

Monar grabbed his halter before his head could bang on his stall and cupped his hand over his nostrils. The warm moist air of his breathing was steady and he quit worrying. He knew the healer had just touched the part of the horse's brain to trigger a sleep set but he was still unused to that Sunborn talent. Having no more defense than his horse did against a sleep set, it bothered him.

Around him his men were following his lead and the fright among the horses was less as the worst ones were plunged into sleep.

Seeing his horse was fine, he went to check his brother's buckskin stallion. Confident he would find Davyd, he'd brought his horse and a tractable mare for the Sunborn lady. The stallion was asleep like his own but the mare had calmed down. She was nearly a match for the stallion being the same color in her body but with mane and tail as white as the stallion's was dark. They made a good pair and he hated to use them for packhorses until his brother was found.

He tried to remember all the training his little brother had but it was hard to convince himself that Davyd could take care of himself and his charge. After all he was six years younger and this had been his first sea voyage.

He knew Wydon was just as worried but they couldn't both leave the caravan preparing to leave Sefron. No, they had obligations to others and only one needed to find their errant brother. Since Wydon's assignment was already given, this search had fallen to him.

He hoped his brother had kept his head.

GRABBING another goat by her hind legs, Davyd pulled her over his bucket. As he squeezed her teats, it was almost like his trip to Datyl had been a dream and he'd been here on a hold all this time. Only the meditation crystals around his waist and the unfamiliar faces told him he was wrong.

It would be easy to stay here for a couple more days but he knew he had to leave. His family would be worried and there was the girl. No, they had to be on their way tomorrow. By tradition the guesting only protected the traveler for three nights and he wasn't willing to push it by staying that long. It was better to trade for the things he needed and hire more men, then head north.

As the bucket filled with sweet goat's milk, he tallied up what he needed. Two horses, clothing, supplies, and weapons — preferably an arming sword. Although he could use a saber or a tuck sword, he found the arming sword more suited to his style of fighting. Being able to cut or thrust from on foot was more important than on horseback and a tuck sword was just too short for his tastes. No, an arming sword was what he wanted.

The holder had been pleased last night with his tales and even more pleased with Synda's quick sketches. Davyd had to admit the girl had talent. Even on board ship he had found it impressive. She captured detail in her work that he never noticed until he saw it in her work. If she wasn't *always* sketching.

He let the last goat go and smiled at the girl waiting to take his bucket. Like most holds this one had only two milk cows and over a dozen of the easier to keep goats. The other livestock, with the exception of some riding horses, were also essential to the hold. Tyran chickens, rykas, gaks, tame pigs, and rabbits supplied the hold with meat and eggs.

Their crops were the usual ones. They grew more emar than some but he supposed that was for market in Sefron. Emar made the best flour and was always in demand. If they milled it here, it would be easy to transport too.

He should see what industries they had. Every hold had some craft they practiced during the cold winter months. Well, they knew he was a trader and the reputation of his family. Mindful of his trade, he hoped to find something to bring better fortune to Hold Alwyn and the House of York.

He was still thinking along those lines when Alwyn sought him out. The man was smiling when he stopped beside him, a lead rope in one hand.

"You work too hard, merchant." He motioned toward the straw he was forking into the stalls. "And I thought you were interested in horses."

"I am." Davyd finished the stall with one last forkful, then set the long-tined pitchfork against the wall. "I'm just not good at sitting when there's honest work to be done."

"It's appreciated but consider the guesting paid. Your tales last night and the lady's sketches are rich payment for what we've given you."

"Thank you. I would be a merchant now and not a guest. Agreed?"

"Agreed.. And I've got a couple of horses to show. I think your road would be easier and I'll accept a writ on your brother's store in trade."

"That won't be necessary. I have some coin with me."

"Good." The holder gestured toward the horse stalls. "Let's go."

Davyd followed and watched as the holder and a young boy led out not two, but four horses for him to look over. Mindful that a good choice would gain the holder's respect, he judged them carefully, going over conformation and paces first then manners and disposition. When he couldn't choose between the two evenly matched mares, he sent for Synda to make the choice for him.

"Fine horses," he told the holder, satisfied with the gelding he'd already chosen. The bay gelding wasn't the same quality as his stallion but he had fire and enough training to make a good trail horse. The one he rejected was younger and still uncut but he felt the holder had included him only as a courtesy. No doubt he would be gelded soon.

"You pick well too." The holder grinned. "Some would have chosen the stallion."

"Not on the trail. I'd just as soon not fight a green horse while I'm guarding."

"Understood. I'll include saddles and tack with them of course."

"There's another matter too. Have you two men I can hire for a ten day? Lady Synda needs more guards and I'm not vain enough to go it alone."

The holder seemed relieved by the question. "I can spare two. You may not need them for a full ten days though. You're only three days away from the North Road and four from Sefron."

"I wasn't sure. I thought you must be close to Sefron because you trade there but I didn't know where we landed or how far it was."

"Not far." Alwyn smiled as Lady Synda crossed the court to look curiously at the horses.

"My lady." Davyd greeted her formally. She looked so good today in a clean dress of bluish gray and a surcoat of true blue. Her hair was braided with ribbons of blue and her eyes seemed more blue than green when she looked at him.

"My guardsman. Holder Alwyn." She had smiles for them both.

"My lady, Alwyn offers a choice between these mares." Davyd claimed her attention, suddenly irritated by the sunny smile she gave the holder. "I can't choose which is better. Since it will be your mount, I give the choice to you."

"I see." Gazing thoughtfully at the mares, Synda approached them slowly. The black one shifted slightly and she touched the brown first, lightly stroking its neck and murmuring to it. The mare responded, turning her ears to listen to what she had to say.

When she went to the black mare, Davyd was surprised to see it flatten its ears and pull back. The boy holding her stopped her so

Synda could examine her. His lady brushed her fingertips lightly over the black neck then turned.

"This one," she said, picking the brown. "That one doesn't care for women."

"True." Alwyn was grinning. "Kola will go well for any man but my daughters have complained about her before. You made a good choice."

"And this one's name?" Synda stroked the brown mare. "She has a sweet face."

"Sweet?" Davyd looked at her in surprise. To him it looked like she had breeding but he would never call her sweet.

"You come close, lady. I think my daughter named her Honey for her color and not her face."

"If she's your daughter's horse..." Synda hesitated in mid-stroke.

"Lady, you don't know the way of the hold." The holder patiently explained. "Horses are owned by the hold, not the trainer. If the hold needed money, I would even sell my stallion for it."

"My daughters are good at raising foals and gentling them so they care for them. My Rosa trains them for riding. Honey isn't the only one they've named. Besides horses must be sold and Honey is ready for that. You won't break their hearts by giving her a good home."

Synda still looked uncertain so Davyd added to his argument.

"Lady, on the hold where I was fostered, it was the same. The hold's women were happy when one was sold. They used the money to buy things they couldn't make."

"That's true," the holder confirmed. "I sold two horses in Sefron last fall and my lady made a long list of the things she wanted. I nearly had to buy them back to pack everything home."

That made her laugh.

"Please, lady. I know Rosa would be pleased to see you ride her."

"I will." Synda gave in and stroked the mare's neck again. "But I would like to thank Rosa for such a fine horse."

"Then you must ride north to Hold Farkon. You'll rest there tomorrow night if you want. Two of my sons and Rosa are there."

Synda looked to him and he nodded. Staying at another hold would make their trip easier.

"As for guardsmen, I can offer you one with ten years' experience in Sefron's Third Guard. Bradon came to me with his wife and children nearly five years ago. He's a good man in a fight."

"I met him last night. I'll take him. And the other?"

"The other isn't so experienced," the holder admitted. "But Tras is skilled with a sword and he's a good tracker. I would like him to get experience if you'll take him. He's my youngest son."

"Understood." Davyd remembered being paired up the same way. One good man always went with him until he gained enough experience to offset his youth. He was proud to be included in trades on his own merit when he was just seventeen. "How old is he?"

"Sixteen."

"I would like to meet him first but he's probably ready. If he's like I was at that age, he's more than ready."

"True enough. They'll have their own horses, of course."

"Agreed." Davyd got down to the business of the trade. "I can only offer a half-solari for seven-day hire of both men," he proposed and saw the holder nod in agreement. "But I can offer two and a half solaris for the horses, their tack, and provisions for a seven day."

"Four."

"Three," Davyd countered. "And one riding dress for the lady."

"Three and a half," Synda interrupted. "And I want two dresses and an extra tunic for Davyd." She stopped when they looked at her but held her ground. "And a sword."

"Not the sword," the holder rejected. "We deal that separately. I accept three and a half for the horses, tack, provisions, and clothing."

"Done," Davyd quickly answered with a sharp glance at the lady. Didn't she know not to break in? Even though the price was what he intended to settle on, he was irritated. He didn't tell her how to sketch and she should leave the trading to him.

"Let's put the horses away," the holder suggested. "And then I'll show you what I have in the way of swords. There aren't many without owners."

Davyd agreed then waited until the holder led the horses away before he turned to his charge. "Let *me* deal for my sword. Is there anything else you need?"

She looked hurt by his rebuke but it passed quickly. "I want a healing kit. Alva always told me if you had one you wouldn't need it so I want one. I'll deal with Lady Janas for that. You wouldn't know what to put in one."

"I know but I'll leave it to you. Just don't go buying swords when you don't know what kind to buy."

"Yes Davyd," she responded with sudden meekness. "I'm sorry."

Unable to argue with that, he followed the mares back to their stalls and unsaddled the brown, letting the boy take care of the black. He wasn't surprised by Alwyn's choices for him to check, but he had slipped up on the black. The brown one was definitely better suited for Synda. She looked fast but well mannered.

Following Alwyn into the inner hold, he wasn't surprised when his lady joined them but looked askance at an older woman who followed. It was Lady Janas who unlatched a hidden door to a narrow armory barely a foot wide and five feet long. Inside five swords and a handful of daggers filled the tiny space.

A proof against raiders, the hidden closet was designed to foil a search by being nearly on the floor and held weapons not in use every day. If this hold was like the one he was fostered on, this wasn't the only cache of weapons. He had given his childhood sword to a stash like this.

Like that one, two of the swords she handed to her lord were short and made for youths—weapons boys had outgrown. A third was a saber and looked well used. He'd have to remember that one. A fourth was an arming sword but he mistrusted the guard. It was big and could keep his hand from turning properly.

The fifth sword caught his eye. As well used as the saber, its guard was the kind he favored and he knew this was the one he wanted. Put off only when she handed it to the woman instead of Alwyn, he suddenly knew why it lay here instead of at some man's belt.

"I am Marta Nys, merchant, but I was once wed to the man who wore this sword. His name was Rykar Salson. I had no sons by him and have only one son by Nys to inherit his sword. I'm willing to sell my Rykar's last possession."

"Thank you. May I hold it?"

When she surrendered it, he drew it and checked the blade, finding it clean of rust and unchipped. The well-worn hilt told him it was old but the blade didn't show the wear. He wasn't surprised when he found the maker's mark.

"This is from Datyl and steel as well." He looked at the holder. "Are you sure you want it to leave your hold?"

"I'm sure," Alwyn told him. "But only for a good price. I know the value of the sword."

Davyd knew too. A sword like this cost at least three solaris new and used it wasn't worth much less. Wishing he had one more solari, he looked at the woman. "I can offer you two solaris for the sword. It's worth more but…"

"I'll take it," she answered before the holder could. "Rykar would like it in your hands. I can see you'll treasure it too and care for it as well as he did."

"Thank you, Mistress Marta." He bowed to her. "This is a far better weapon that I hoped to get."

"Use it well and always in Galton's name."

"I will," Davyd replied. "I swear I'll not dishonor it."

"Then I'm pleased." She smiled then excused herself, forgetting to even take the solaris in her haste.

"You made a good deal," the holder told him. "I would have held out for four."

"I know," Davyd replied. "But I didn't have four — not after the horses." He knew he would have to use writs when they reached the North Road.

"Alwyn, she's pleased with two," Janas said as she began replacing the other swords. "And she could have sold it for more at Sefron but refused. Let it be."

"Yes, I'll let it be. I can't fault her for wanting to know the man who would wield it. Even though I never met Rykar, I've heard enough to know he was a fair man and a good captain."

"Yes, just like you." Janas smiled at her lord then took his hand to rise. "Davyd, I think you're of the same quality. Choose your lady wisely because I'm sure you'll have the pick of many."

"Yes ma'am," he replied automatically but his thoughts swerved to the one lady he couldn't have. Why did Synda interest him so? As she said, he had the pick of many. There were several in Gardon alone who would be happy to marry him and not just because of his family.

He should look at them and not the lady he couldn't have.

Chapter 11 - Monar

6 Tyras 850

"LOOK OUT BELOW!"

Monar heard the warning and looked up to see the hanging legs of his bay stallion as the horse was swung free of the ship. The horse was tossing his head but helpless as he dangled from the ship's crane.

"Guide him over here," Tory barked as the crewmen who held the lines. When the horse touched water he tried to buck free of the sling in a wild burst of activity.

"Easy fella." Monar got hold of his head and steadied him as the sling was removed and he was left with a float harness. "We'll be on shore soon."

"That's it for this lot," Tory called up to his captain. Slowly to match the horses' swimming speed, they rowed the long boat toward shore.

It was difficult getting the horses ashore with no dock but *The Seawind's* crew came prepared to swim the horses the last distance. With the float harnesses as insurance against drowning, the horses were simply led to shore by the boats.

"It's a good thing these aren't going back by sea," Tory said with a grin. "I doubt they'll willingly set hoof on a deck again."

"I'm sure *he* won't." Monar motioned toward his stallion. "He's never had a liking for water." Sure enough his ears were flat against his head as he swam.

"Well he'll not get any more like this." He checked the other horses for fatigue then turned back to him. "The horse tender says you should wash them in fresh water. They'll feel better and it will take the salt out of their hides."

"I heard." Monar looked ahead to where half his men waited. Each one had come with his horse and they were tending the animals and sorting out the supplies the longboats had brought over with the dawn. With luck they'd be on their way before noon and would catch up with Davyd soon. "Can you show me where that marker was?"

"It was several miles that way." The Second pointed south of where they were landing. "There was no fresh water there so our crew made camp by the waterfall. We know Davyd went inland from there."

"And I'll follow." Monar glanced toward the pool then back to his horse as the lead abruptly went slack. His stallion snorted as he found ground under his feet and bolted.

"Hold, Flash," he barked and tried to pull his head close but it was no use. With ground under his feet and floats banging on his sides, the stallion wouldn't listen. He yanked back and Monar sensibly let go the lead and shouted a warning to the men in the boat.

The stallion reached shore and started to run. One of the mounted men headed him off and grabbed his lead rope to bring him back. The stallion lashed out with a vicious kick, furious.

"I'm glad he didn't try to climb in the boat," Tory said.

"Climb in the boat?"

"Yes. I've only heard of it happening once but the horse had to be killed. He nearly toppled the boat and gashed a leg on an oarlock. Now the rule is any horse who tries is to be killed if the horse tender isn't here to put them to sleep."

"But you can't get a sleeping horse to shore," Monar said and suddenly understood why the horse tender wasn't in any of the boats. "I see."

"It's quicker to kill them than let them drown," Tory explained. "But I've not had to do it. I hope I never have to do it to one like him." He nodded toward the stallion.

As soon as the longboat beached, Monar reclaimed his stallion. Stripping off the cumbersome wood floats, he handed them to the nearest sailor and swung up on the stallion's bare back. The stallion tried to throw him but he held on and proved he could master the horse through one of his worst fits. Cantering down the beach, he finally turned him to rejoin the others.

They had to get moving. Impatient to go after his brother, he was still forced to consider the needs of men and horses first. Wondering if the sense of urgency he felt was due to some trace of his mother's Sunborn blood, he wanted to be gone. They'd go as soon as the last horse was ashore and ready.

UNAWARE his brother was to the south, Davyd continued leading his people north. They'd gotten off to a good start shortly after dawn and were riding on a well-worn trail between Alwyn Hold and its new sister-hold. They should be there before nightfall.

Tras proved to be a very grim sixteen-year-old who took his duties seriously and rarely even looked at the lady. Instead he took turns riding ahead or behind with Bradon.

Davyd knew he was simply trying to prove his worth but Synda was put off by his attitude. She couldn't even get a smile from him.

When they stopped at the nooning to rest the horses, she tried again.

"Tras, join me," she commanded but the youth looked first to Bradon then Davyd before he reluctantly obeyed.

Davyd had to hide his grin. The boy looked uncomfortable and Synda vexed. He could see it in the way she pursed her lips. At least the boy wasn't jumping to her every wish. If he did, he'd make no guardsman.

"Sit with me a while."

"Synda, he has duties. We all do," Davyd said. "Would you have him neglect those so you can sketch him?"

"Sketch him? I wasn't going to sketch him. I wanted to talk."

"Tonight," Davyd said. "My lady, the horses need watering and that takes two. Since Bradon watches over you, Tras and I will water the horses. With your leave?"

She looked ready to scream. Tight-lipped, she motioned Tras to follow him and looked even more irritated by the boy's relief.

"Thank you sir."

"Don't mention it," Davyd said with a grin. "She's young and more foolish than most women. Don't be surprised if she asks other fool things."

"Yes sir. I just didn't want to neglect the horses."

"I know. It's hard to keep your mind on work when someone as pretty as she is tries to distract you."

When they reached the stream Davyd left off talking and turned to watch the woods properly. Mindful of the boy's training as well as his duty, he followed the rules he had learned. Always have one man watching the woods and one with the horses. Keeping under cover, he listened and watched for any alarm not caused by their appearance.

Rejoining Tras as they walked the horses back, he reassured him he was doing well then froze when he saw the veteran guardsman talking to Synda. Irritated to catch him off guard, he picked up a stone and flung it into the woods behind the girl.

The guardsman reacted, flinging himself on the girl and down in a lightning move. They fell heavily then the guardsman sprang up, his sword drawn. His shout was loud and clear.

"Peace, Bradon. I threw a stone." Davyd was mollified by his quick response.

"You threw?"

The guardsman looked at the lady he'd put in the dirt and his jaw set as he helped her up. "Pardon lady. I thought it was an attack."

"So did I." She glared at Davyd as she brushed dirt off her knee-length split skirt and breeches. "Davyd, why? I wasn't distracting him."

"You were or I would have seen the stone fly," Bradon corrected. "If I'd caught Tras talking to you, I would have done more than throw a stone. Davyd, she's your charge." He walked stiffly away.

"I wasn't trying to distract him," she started before Davyd could. "Honestly. I only asked him two questions."

"That's two too many," he snapped, then took a deep breath. "Synda, they're doing their best to guard you but you keep breaking the rules. You may *not* talk to the one on watch. The rest of us you can. You may not interrupt duties that must be done."

"And you keep embarrassing Tras. He's trying hard to show he can do the job but you keep demanding his attention. I remember what I was like at that age and I'm telling you to stop."

"All I wanted to do was talk to him. He's so serious. Why can't I just talk to him for a moment?"

"You can tonight. We'll be within walls again and he won't be guarding. Don't distract him on the trail."

She looked rebellious, her lip sticking out in a pout. He ached to kiss her, cover those lips with his and give her something else to think about.

"Synda, he's not a man yet but he wants to be." He hastened to distract his thoughts from those lips. "He can't do his job well if he's forced to ignore what he's been taught to be polite to you. Don't make it hard for him. I think he wants a career in the guard."

"How would you feel if someone insisted on interrupting your painting and you couldn't say no?" he demanded and knew he'd struck the right note when she suddenly looked thoughtful. "That's what you're doing to him. You're stopping him from his work."

"I didn't think of it that way." She looked contrite. "I'm sorry. I *hate* being interrupted and I hated it most when I was young." She hesitated. "But doesn't he get any free time on the trail?"

"Not until nightfall. Even then someone must watch and another tends the fire and cooking. We're too small a group to have much leisure."

"I think I liked it better when it was just you and me," Synda said. "At least I could talk to you when I wanted to."

"But it was dangerous. If we had met raiders, we wouldn't have had a chance. As it was those pigs nearly got us."

"We didn't meet any raiders and I don't think we will," Synda said, then stopped with her eyes wide. She grabbed his arm. "Davyd, something's going to happen. I felt it."

He felt a chill go up his spine. "What did you see?"

"I didn't." Her voice was barely above a whisper. "It's just a feeling we should beware. Davyd, I'm scared."

"Let's get on to that hold. We stay in shelter tonight."

She nodded and he called the others.

THEY PUSHED their horses to reach the safety of Hold Farkon. Davyd's unease communicated to the others and they increased their alertness.

Once, not long before they reached the hold's fields, Bradon called a halt to look over a campfire's ashes. The old guardsman studied the clearing and ashes before asking Davyd his opinion.

"What's wrong?" He saw signs that several men had camped there but they were old. The piles of horse droppings were dry and breaking up.

"This wasn't here the last time we rode this way," Bradon said. "And it's too close to the hold for them to do it."

"And they were here more than a day?" Davyd motioned to the piles. "There's too many for one day and they didn't clear them away."

"Yes and that bothers me too. They know better."

"These campers weren't long out of Sefron. Look here — they shelled parlans." Davyd pointed out the scattered nut shells. "And it's too early for this year's harvest. They had to buy them."

Bradon grunted.

"How many are at the hold?"

"Six men, two teen boys, and four women. Nearly all are kin to us at Alwyn Hold. One of my sons came with Farkon and his brother."

"Nearly all?" Davyd caught that admission. "Who wasn't?"

"Two men from Sefron that Farkon knew. One was in the Second Guard and I trust him. The other I don't know. He seemed trustworthy and brought a wife of his own so he has a stake in the hold succeeding."

"These could be hunters who decided not to approach the hold." Davyd tried to dismiss their suspicions but Synda was still looking uneasy. Even her horse seemed to catch her nervousness. She chomped her bit and snorted, her muscles taut. "If they weren't, we should warn the hold."

"Aye. Let's warn the hold."

They mounted again. Davyd spoke quickly to Tras and the lady. "We go to the hold but keep your eyes out for anything amiss. This campfire shouldn't be here."

"It wasn't last time," Tras said. "I would remember it."

"That's what Bradon said too. More than a dozen men were here. It may have been a hunting party but let's be careful."

"Farkon should know," Tras muttered as they formed a loose diamond with Synda riding beside Davyd and Bradon in front. Tras brought up the rear.

Riding out on the hold's fields, Davyd wasn't surprised to see men stop and look at them. When they shouted and ran for the hold, he tensed. They didn't recognize Bradon or Tras?

Bradon kept his horse to a walk so the rest did too. When four horsemen burst from the hold's gates, he reined his horse around.

"Back!"

Davyd didn't need the warning. Seeing swords out, he drew his own. Ducking the first blow, he stabbed his attacker. The man fell.

"Davyd!" Synda screamed.

A man had hold of her horse's bridle. Guessing what he was after, he threw his sword and skewered him.

"To the trees!"

More men were pouring from the hold.

Bradon killed his attacker and slapped Synda's mare on the rear to send her bolting, then turned to help the boy. The teenager stood his ground but wasn't winning. Bradon cut his attacker's horse and it leapt forward, giving Tras the opening he needed.

Davyd swung low in the saddle and grabbed his sword then galloped after the girl. His heart pounded as he guessed what had happened. Raiders had taken the hold.

He swallowed the lump in his throat and urged the big gelding close to the girl's horse. She was clinging to the saddle, head bent low against the mare's neck as she ran through trees. Grabbing the mare's lead off the saddle, Davyd pulled her close to his gelding. Instead of slowing he kept them at a breakneck run.

Keeping close behind him were Bradon and the boy. Twice he knew they fell away and caught up again and he guessed they were taking out pursuers. Grimly he kept on until he judged the mare was nearly done.

Jumping them across a stream and taking a sharp right turn on the other side, he jumped them back across a little further down.

"Off," he ordered the white-faced girl and she slid off, ducking into bushes.

Jumping the horses back across the stream, he rejoined the trail where he'd left it, not surprised to find Bradon and Tras ahead of him now. They were waiting on either side of the trail and barely held their swords when they recognized him.

"She's hidden. How many?"

"Four there and two following," Bradon tersely reported. "Three more on our trail."

"We can handle three. Let's surprise them."

Tras had his bow strung and Davyd wondered how the boy had managed that while they were riding flat out. Telling him to have arrows ready, he tethered the girl's horse and started back down the trail.

They were nearly at the stream when two men rode into sight. Before they could recover from their surprise Tras downed one with an arrow. The other fled, shouting.

Davyd pushed the gelding as hard as he could but the horse was too worn. Cursing he went to collect the girl.

"There should have been three," Bradon said when he returned. "I saw three."

"So did I," Tras said, his face grim and tear-streaked. "Snake, where are the men of the hold?" he asked the man he'd unhorsed, his hands wrapped in his tunic. The arrow stuck out the man's back and Davyd knew it was fatal. "Tell me or go unburied."

"Dead." The man spat in his face then coughed. "All dead."

"Why did you want the girl?" Bradon demanded.

"Women dead," the man gasped and coughed again. "Bitch killed 'em." He went into a spasm, his breath coming in great gasps until his rough face went slack and his lifeless head rolled back.

"Bastard," Tras cursed as he tried to shake life back into him. "Pit fodder!" His words dissolved into a stream of curses as he wreaked vengeance on the lifeless body.

"Tras, he can't hear you." Bradon spoke sharply. "And they'll bring more."

"He killed Farkon!" Tras turned haunted eyes on him. "And Rosa and…"

"Come. We can't give justice if we're caught here. We're too few and we have the lady to protect."

Those words got through and his eyes flew to Synda's pale face.

Davyd couldn't see her behind him on the gelding but he could feel her fear in her tight hold on his waist. He wanted to hold her, calm her, but there was no time. They had to flee.

"What of this?" The boy kicked the body at his feet.

"Leave him," Davyd said. "His kin can bury him."

"May he rot first!" Tras spat and retrieved his bow. Swinging on his horse, he led the way down the trail while Bradon took rear guard.

Finding the mare was easy and she seemed to have regained strength during her brief rest. Keeping to a northerly path was harder since they tried to use streams to cover their tracks and those flowed to the east and sea.

They kept the horses moving until full dark then made a cold camp nearly a mile from any stream. There was little talk as they cared for their weary horses and shared the cold meats Alwyn's lady had packed for them.

Davyd knew his two companions had both lost kin to the raiders and were grieving, the boy most of all. Synda seemed in shock too and barely ate. Not content they were safe yet, he motioned for her to take her blankets and slide beneath some low-hanging bushes. She obeyed him without a word.

Bradon saw and approved. "I'm moving the horses away from us," he told Davyd. "If they come on them in the night, they might betray themselves before they find us."

"Agreed but split them up. If we can still reach two, that's better than nothing."

The older man nodded and led the horses away. With a word to Tras, he motioned for him to follow and learn the way.

Davyd blended into a tree's shadow and waited for them to return. No one could see Synda in this light and he knew she was safe until morning but it still worried him. He knew why the raiders wanted her and it enraged him to think any woman should have to choose between death and being used that way.

A hold is not a hold if no woman holds there. That's why there were hidden weapons in each hold. If raiders took it and the men died, the women had to fight, die, or accept new mates. Most women would give in and hope their kin rescued them but sometimes they fought or chose death—the only way they could sour a raider's victory. If they cursed them, sometimes they won.

The raiders could try to make a hold prosper under such a curse but it rarely worked. Crops withered in fields under Kala's displeasure and the animals bore dead young if Kal was invoked. Even quitting a cursed hold didn't work. The curse could follow the raiders.

There was only one way to lift such a curse and bring the hold back to a legal status—a woman with child.

Glancing at the bushes where his lady was hidden, he was glad she didn't know. She'd left Datyl for a manhunt and now she was being hunted. He flexed his hand on his sword hilt and vowed they would never take her from him.

"Davyd?"

"Come." Davyd moved his hand into the moonlight. The two guardsmen stepped out of the trees.

"I'll keep first watch," Davyd said. "Bradon, you take third. Tras, I want you to take mid-watch tonight."

"Yes sir." The boy's voice was flat and emotionless. "I'll kill them."

"Not tonight you won't. Mind the moonlight on your watch and stay in the shadows and wait. If you hear anything, wake us with a yell. Do *not* move from shelter until you have someone to kill."

"Yes sir."

"Get in your blankets. Roll under the bushes like the lady did. I want everyone to sleep under cover."

The boy obeyed and soon only he and Bradon were left. The older man was hiding the few signs they were there from the moonlight before he returned to stand beside him in the shadows. "I'll wake before the boy's watch is done. I don't think he'll sleep but…"

"Good. And thanks, Bradon, for being here."

"Let's just get her safe." He glanced at the bushes. "And get word to the Third Guard. This will be hard on Alwyn and Janas."

And on your lady. He almost said that out loud but stopped. The guardsman was trying not to think of his own son and he shouldn't remind him. No, he was concentrating on the here and now as guardsmen had to do. "Get some sleep."

The man obeyed but ignored blankets. Sliding under the bushes, he blended into the darkness.

Chapter 12 - Raiders

7 Tyras 850

DAVYD WOKE when it was barely dawn, blinking his eyes to clear them and resisting the urge to stretch. He had to be careful. Slowly he turned his head so he was looking at the clearing instead of the densely packed trunks of the bush that sheltered him.

Bradon was standing against the trunk of a tree, his head down and one knee cocked as he rested. Faintly surprised to see him so still, Davyd didn't immediately see the dark stain on his chest. When he did his heart quickened and his jaw tightened. He froze and wondered if the others were still asleep.

Where were their attackers? They'd gotten Bradon. There was no way he could stay so still without being dead. That stain had to be blood.

Knowing the light of day might betray their hiding place, he slowly flexed his muscles and laid hand on his sword. It was drawn and ready beside him but he didn't know if Tras was so prepared.

Remembering the boy was at his feet, he almost kicked him then thought better of it. He should wake Synda first. The boy was liable to move too slowly at first light.

Hoping Synda wouldn't make a rash move, he laid a hand on her ankle and squeezed, thinking hard of the need for stillness. Her foot moved but nothing else about her told him she was awake. He squeezed again and her foot twitched. She was clearly awake.

Blessing the gods that Sunborn could sometimes read strong emotions, he planned his next move.

Shifting his foot, he prodded Tras. When the boy responded by touching his booted ankle, he knew he was awake too.

He needed a rock but there weren't any close by. Hoping the Queen would forgive him, he carefully slipped his hand into the pouch around his waist and slid one of the crystals out. Moving awkwardly to keep from disturbing the bushes, he tossed it as far as he could.

The crystal caught the first sunlight and flashed as it arced through the clearing.

Someone shouted in surprise.

Another cursed as several men burst into the clearing.

Synda rolled out of her hiding place and ran. Davyd was only a split second slower but it was no use. Before he could get to his feet a sword point was at his throat and he was pinned.

"Don't kill him," a voice barked. "We want them alive."

The sword didn't waver. Davyd looked up into steel gray eyes and knew he would die if he made the slightest move. He let them take his sword.

Hearing Synda scream, he knew they'd caught her too. Of Tras there was no sound. He hoped the boy wasn't dead.

SYNDA BOILED as rough hands grabbed her and she was pushed around the bushes. Seeing the sword at Davyd's throat, her heart stopped.

"No," she screamed, then flinched as the blade moved closer, pricking his skin. Forcing herself to be calm, knowing they would kill Davyd, she abruptly quit fighting the grasping hands.

Think! She tried to use a Temple charm but her thoughts roiled. Outwardly calm, she felt her guards relax a little.

No, not yet. She had to get the sword away from his throat.

Glancing at Bradon, she saw he was dead, his throat cut and his body tied to the tree. She shuddered and looked for Tras.

Not seeing him until a filthy raider pulled his limp body around the bush, she thought he was dead. The boy groaned and she knew he was alive.

She had to save them. Davyd was helpless and Tras wounded.

"You give up easily when your man is threatened." A raider stepped closer and she could smell the foul stench of his unwashed body. Somehow she managed to look at him and not at Davyd's clenched jaw.

"He's my man," she said and knew she didn't mean just her guardsman. No, Davyd was her love. She didn't have time to examine that thought but knew it was true. "He's sworn to me."

"Sworn to you?" The raider laughed. "A high-sounding name for a mating. And are you sworn to him? Did you do it in the Temple or at your father's hold?"

She glanced at Davyd, suddenly guessing what this beast meant and blushing furiously. Around her the raiders jeered and laughed at her color.

"She's Sunborn," Davyd suddenly declared. The sword pricked his neck again.

"Sunborn my nuts," one man spat but the leader waved him quiet.

"Let him speak," he ordered, motioned to the man who held him down. "Let's see what kind of lies he tells."

"I swear by Galton she's Sunborn," Davyd insisted as the sword moved away. "Look at her hair, her eyes. I'm her guardsman."

Synda gasped as a rough hand pulled the scarf off her hair and her braids came free. Coarse hands unbraided them. Their leader grabbed her chin and looked into her eyes. She knew he could see. Gold flecks of power stood out in the green of her irises and any idiot could tell she was. Wishing Davyd hadn't revealed that, she wanted to strike the hands that wouldn't go away.

When one grabbed her between her thighs she cried out and struggled.

The leader growled at him then turned back to Davyd.

"Not Sunborn. No Sunborn would travel with only three men. No, you think we'll let her go because of that hair."

Hands were tangled in her hair and Synda boiled but couldn't fight them all. How could he not recognize power? She should—she stopped, appalled at the thought that crossed her mind. Use Starfire against them? No, she couldn't. It was against the law.

"It would be cruel to let her go, man," the leader said, his smile savage. "You killed eight of my friends—you and this one." He jabbed angrily at the groggy Tras. "If I kill you, she still needs protection. We'll keep her well at Hold Granol."

"Granol?" Tras managed to say. "Farkon. You killed my kin but Father will take back what's ours."

"Shut him up."

The boy was hit again with such a sickening thud that Synda feared his head was broken.

"What happed to the women? How did you lose them all?" Davy asked.

"There was a she-wolf. My sister joined them in Sefron and opened the gates to us. The she-wolf killed her."

Synda focused on that, thinking that might have been Rosa. She needed to know what to do. Would she have allies? What would they do to her? They spoke of keeping her safe but she doubted that would be without price.

"She killed the others too," someone snarled. "And Grady and Burt."

Davyd gave him a savage smile. "She made a good accounting then." The sword danced around his throat.

"Rosa?" Synda breathed the name and the leader gave her a sharp look.

"Aye, that was her name," the leader growled. "But you won't follow her. She's dead and buried and you'll get no chance to do the same. No, you'll live to be my lady."

"No," she refused, knowing what he planned now. "I'll not give myself to you."

"Let's see if she says that with rugur on her lips," a man cracked and laughed.

Looking helplessly at Davyd, Synda felt someone grab her breeches. She kicked as he tried to pull them down but another grabbed her foot. She started to panic and felt the power surge.

"Not here," the leader snarled and shoved his men away. "Put your pricks away. We do it right and at the hold."

Synda was set on her feet again but she held on to her anger and let it build until it blocked her fear. She would die first.

"I say we do it in front of him," a man snarled at Davyd. "He killed our brothers."

"No." The leader looked coldly at Davyd. "Wait until we're gone then kill them. Bring their bodies back to the hold. They'll be buried with their kin."

"NO!" Synda suddenly exploded, no longer scared for herself. Sending Starfire coursing along her arms, she tore free of her captors. They screamed, nursing seared hands and nerves burned by Starfire.

Sending another burst through the air at the raider who kept Davyd pinned, she heard him scream as if from a distance. Then she quit thinking under the force of her anger, shocking anyone who dared touch her or her man.

Davyd rolled as the warrior screamed, narrowly avoiding the sword than plunged down. Grabbing it, he felt a warning tingle of Starfire and dropped it. Chopping the neck of the nearest raider with a stiffened hand, he felt him drop. Moving on to another he used the disciplined moves of the Prime.

He kept away from Synda. One raider after another screamed and fled from her. Her hair stood on end in a true nimbus of power and he knew she was using too much.

She sent Starfire into anyone who touched her. Two dropped their weapons and fled and he guessed they'd dealt with Sunborn before. Others took the shock full force through their weapons. Their leader crawled away with a look of terror on his face.

Finally she threw one last burst at the bushes where they'd hid and they burst into flame. She fainted, her energy spent.

Killing the only raider left, Davyd raced to her side. Remembering his mother's warnings, he didn't touch her but held his hands a bare inch above her body. When no warning sparks flew, he checked her pulse. It was weak but she lived.

Desperate to save her, he grabbed her arms and willed some of his strength to flow to her. Feeling something give inside, he held on to her. There was a sensation of pushing but it was slow. Not knowing what else to do, he lay along her body and kissed her to increase the flow. It worked.

He felt weak when it was done but her pulse was stronger. Wishing he had more skill than that or even a bit more Sunborn blood, he dug in his belt pouch until he found the next best thing. Sylynum.

He'd found the toxic herb growing near the hold's fields and picked it. He should have told Synda he had it. Opening her lips, he crammed nearly a dozen small leaves into her pretty cheek.

He couldn't use it but he knew the Sunborn needed it. Somehow it was related to Starfire. Since he had no *Kural* to give her, the raw herb would have to do.

Satisfied he'd done all he could do, he looked around the clearing. The fire in the green bushes had gone out but they still sent a column of smoke into the heavens. They needed to move before the smoke betrayed them. The surviving raiders could also come back.

Doubting they would take Synda now, he figured they would kill them all rather than risk her waking again.

Gathering up weapons, he killed two more raiders who lay unconscious and burned from the Starfire. Checking Tras, he found the boy was still out cold but his pulse was strong.

His neck was sticky. Brushing it impatiently, he found he was bleeding. It hadn't killed him so it must not be bad. Grabbing a couple of leaves, he plastered them to his cuts and hoped that would do the trick.

He needed the horses. Not knowing exactly where they were, he had to guess. In the first place he checked he found his gelding and Bradon's horse dead and cursed the raiders for that. A second hunt turned up Synda's mare but Tras's stallion was nowhere to be seen.

Leading the mare back, he slung the girl across her saddle and moved her a good mile from the scene of their battle. Rolling her under a bush for protection, he fished out another earring and laid it in her hand to show he would be back. He must get Tras.

The meditation crystal. He'd forgotten that. He needed to find it. Once back at the camp site he checked Tras then looked for the crystal. He felt weak, even light-headed, but kept doggedly on. Finally getting down on his hands and knees he searched for the object in the leaves but it was nowhere to be found.

Despairing of ever finding it, he gave up. Tras needed to be safe and he couldn't leave the girl alone any longer. Who knew how long her sleep would last? All he knew was she would be ravenous when she woke and he'd better be there with food.

He couldn't believe how unearthly she looked when she used her Starfire. It seemed to come from everywhere around her and spark from anywhere they dared touch. He knew, having felt small shocks, that it was painful and could cause death, but he'd never seen more than a few controlled displays of it. What Synda did was *not* controlled. She'd raged and she'd made her power felt. It scared him to think the slender girl he lusted after could do so much damage.

Lifting Tras on to the patient mare, he was caught off guard by a savage kick. The mare snorted and shied as the boy flung himself off the other side and fell.

"Tras, stop!"

The boy stumbled to his feet, knife in hand.

"It's Davyd." He tripped him up and nearly disarmed him, sitting on him until the boy's vision cleared. "It's Davyd."

"You're Davyd?" Tras mumbled, his eyes blurry and dilated. "Where's Bradon?"

"Dead." Davyd didn't sweeten it. "The raiders are gone and I left Synda hidden. We've got to get to her."

"Where's Bradon?" the boy repeated again.

"Dead." Davyd wondered how hard he'd been hit. "We need to bury him."

Tras seemed to understand the third time he said it and he let him up. Cutting the big warrior down, he laid the body across the mare's back. The guardsman's throat was cut and one hand nearly severed across the fingers. He tucked that hand awkwardly beneath the body before making the boy get on the mare behind him. He was in no condition to walk.

Walking by the girl's hiding place once, he had to backtrack and check under several bushes before he found her.

Gods he was tired.

He forced himself to keep moving long enough to feed Tras and choke down some food himself. Then they cleared an area of leaves and began digging a grave.

The boy seemed to gain energy as they worked but Davyd found it hard to keep going. Somehow they managed to finish it. He let Tras go through the man's pouches and remove his weapons and other things of value, only stopping him when he started to remove a coil of hair and an amulet from a pouch around Bradon's neck.

"That's a bridal pledge. My father has one. You leave it so their marriage continues after death."

The boy's head was clearer now and he understood. Leaving it alone, he cut his mentor's tunic to show the pledge scar on his upper arm, then arranged him in the grave. Laying him on his right side with his face pointing north, he let the world know that Bradon had died with honor. He faced toward Primus, the ancient city of the colonists.

Bradon's weapons would go to his family so Davyd laid a raider's sword with him. Since he doubted the raiders had families or deserved to be buried with weapons, it would do.

Finally the work was done and the body covered properly. Leaves were scattered again on most of the grave but they stamped the earth down hard on and laid wood for a fire. Knowing the smoke could betray them, he didn't light it.

He had to rest. Not sure when Synda would wake, he finally gave in.

Ordering Tras to hide in the upper branches of a tree to sleep with his bow beside him, Davyd crept under the bushes beside Synda. His arms around her so he would know when she woke, he finally slept.

Chapter 13 – Hold

MONAR YORKSON eyed the prosperous hold they were approaching, wondering how they would receive so many armed men. It was still before noon and an unusual time for guests to arrive but he had no intention of staying unless Davyd was here. No, he just wanted news.

He kept the horses to a walk, stopping twice on the ride up to the hold to give them more time. Each time he halved his band so only four rode with him to the gates. Even so there was no sign of any women and only a trio of men greeted him. No, his force was not welcome.

"Pardon, holder, for riding across your lands." Monar bowed in his saddle, his hand carefully away from his sword. "We seek no shelter from you but only news of our kin. I'm Monar Yorkson."

There was an immediate easing of tension and he knew Davyd had been here. The old man he thought was the holder stepped forward with a grim smile. "Welcome son of York."

"Is my brother here?" Monar asked without ceremony. Hoping he was, he glanced at the gates but the holder dashed his hopes.

"No, I wish they were. They left here early yesterday with two of my people. They should be at Hold Farkon now."

"Where is that? How far?"

"I'll ride with them." One of the holder's men spoke up. "Uncle, give me leave."

"You have it."

The man slipped through the gates. The holder's wife also appeared and Monar slipped off his stallion to join them on foot.

"Yes, I've met you," the holder said. "Last year I traded you a dozen hides for a new plow blade. Your wife was with child."

"Yes." Monar abruptly remembered the transaction. "Alwyn, isn't it?" He hoped he had the name right. Only Mother Rayna seemed to remember every customer each time.

"Right." The man gave him a broad smile. "Janas, meet another of the York brothers. Monar owns the store in Sefron."

"And you look even more handsome than your brother," Janas said. "And what did your wife have?"

"A son." Monar saw the usual mix of emotions on her face. It was good luck to have a daughter first but he was happy with his son. "He's healthy and I'm pleased."

"Then she's doubly blessed." Janas smiled again. "Now I've met two of you. Is there another coming later?"

Monar started to say there were four more then caught her meaning. "No, I'm the only one chasing Davyd. The other four are at home."

"Does Davyd owe you for the men and supplies?" he asked Alwyn.

"No, he paid a good price for them. They were welcome to stay another day but I'm sure he didn't know you followed so close."

"No, he wouldn't." He looked up to see the holder's man standing by with his horse. "Come again to Sefron, Alwyn. I'll give you a good deal on those ax heads you wanted."

The holder laughed. "You've got a merchant's memory. Just get those two safe. The lady has friends here and we like your brother too."

Monar nodded. Turning to the new man, he offered his hand. "Welcome."

"Thanks. I'm Kran Alwynhold." He was a fine man in his twenties and obviously knew how to use the sword at his hip. "I'll go with you to the North Road."

"Good." Monar made no comment on the distance. He meant to find Davyd before then. Noting the man preferred naming his allegiance to the hold rather than his father, he would introduce him to his men the same way.

"We'll be off, Alwyn and Lady Janas." Monar made a courtly bow to the holder's lady and got a pleased smile. "Thank you for your hospitality to my kin."

"You're welcome. And come back with your lady sometime. You will be guested here."

"Agreed," Monar replied with a smile. "And may all your wine be sweet."

Mounting up again, he headed his men north. He would find Davyd today. He was sure of it.

SYNDA WOKE from a deep sleep with a gnawing hunger and recognized the sensation at once. There was something bitter in her mouth too and she found it irritating until she moved it between cheek and gum. Sylynum! Where had she got sylynum? She nearly gagged on the bitter herb.

Somehow she managed to crawl over Davyd and stumble a few steps before she spat it out. It came out as a green glob and she gagged.

"Steady." Davyd was suddenly there, his hands on her shoulders. "Take a deep breath. You can't afford to lose it."

She struggled for control, waiting until the nausea passed. Finally she could look at him and saw the leaves plastered to his neck and the paleness of his face. He was safe. Without thinking she went into his arms.

Davyd held her.

She didn't want to let him go. Raising her lips to his she felt dizzy.

"Stop that." He caught her. "Tras, get down here."

"How long was I out?" she asked as he helped her sit down. "And who gave me sylynum?"

"Four hours, nearly five. I had the sylynum."

"Thank you." She gave him a weak smile.

"What's sylynum?" Tras joined them, his face as worn as theirs.

"Eat." Davyd handed her dried kivak and turned to answer the boy. "Sylynum is a herb the Sunborn need after they expend a lot of Starfire or do a lot of healing. Usually they have pills or Kural but we had neither. I found the herb near your hold and kept it with me in case Synda needed it."

"You could have made a tea." Synda wrinkled her nose. "I don't think I'll ever get the taste out of my mouth."

"No time," Davyd said. "You went too far, Synda. If we'd been in Gardon, my mother would have sent for a ranked healer. I couldn't."

"What happened to the raiders?" Tras finally asked. "I don't remember anything after they hit me."

"I don't remember much either." Synda looked at Davyd. "Not after that pit bait gave the order to…" She couldn't say it.

"…to kill me?" Davyd finished for her with a grim smile.

Tras stared.

"The leader gave the order for them to kill us, Tras, and he meant to take Synda," he explained. "She didn't agree. She shot Starfire all over the place and not one of the raiders stayed. They're probably still running back to the hold."

Synda remembered how much she wanted to kill them. Now she felt like she had, every nerve ending weak and dulled.

Tras was grinning but it looked lopsided to her. Was he all right? She should check him. She tried to say that but lacked the will.

Davyd knelt beside her. "You need more food and rest. Tell me what you need and I'll find it."

"You can't find Kural," she managed to say. "Make me a tea if you have sylynum left. Put in kivak, sylynum, and kamomyl if you have it. And I need meat."

Tras pressed some dried meat into her hand and she tore into it almost savagely. She didn't even notice when the boy started the fire and dug out their only pot to fix tea. The boy emptied the last water out of the waterskins and went to fetch more.

Davyd watched her closely, guessing her reaction was normal but still worried. Standing behind her, he stroked her loose hair and moved her head back to rest against his legs then casually checked the pulse in her throat. She stiffened then relaxed against him in a gesture of trust he found touching.

Her pulse was strong but he mistrusted it. Fighting the urge to move on, he made the decision to stay where they were. She needed to rest.

He needed to rest. Tempted to drink some of the tea he brewed for her, he squelched the thought. Sylynum wouldn't kill him in small amounts but it could make him sick. He couldn't afford it.

Tras didn't look good either. Certain the boy was still suffering from his head wound, Davyd knew he should be checked more carefully. When Synda was ready, he'd ask her what to do. He knew only to watch out for blackouts and unequal eyes. Once when Wydon fell from his horse his father made him stay awake nearly half the night before he could sleep.

"Who's buried?" Synda abruptly asked. "There's someone buried here." She made to move but he stopped her.

"Bradon. We built the fire to keep the animals away."

"Bradon?" She looked lost then her eyes teared up. "He died. I saw him."

"I know. He fought but they got him. It happens."

"No," she moaned. "Davyd, no. I want to go home."

He held her, pillowing her head against his shoulder as she cried. "Hush, my lady. It's not all this bad. We'll get you to Gardon then home. Hush." He didn't know how many times he repeated that but it seemed like she would never stop crying. Finally he kissed the top of her head then his eyes met the boy's.

Tras was watching, stunned by what he'd done.

Knowing he could do nothing to defend himself, Davyd acted like it hadn't happened. Instead he noted the boy had brought more than just water. Behind him was the missing stallion, his bridle still hanging neatly on his saddle horn and his halter rope dangling. The horse seemed just as curious as his master.

"Synda, look." He made her straighten up and look at the horse. "The gods are being kind to us now. I thought for sure the raiders had taken that horse."

She looked just in time to see Tras turn and the surprise on his face made her go from tears to giggles all at once. Thinking the boy didn't know the horse was behind him, she found it hilarious.

Davyd almost laughed with her when the boy came on into the clearing and simply pointed to the tethered mare. The stallion ambled over and dropped his head to nibble at the scraps of grass the mare had left as if he'd been there all along.

"Does he always loose his ties?" Davyd asked while he dumped the last of the herbs into the boiling water.

"Not always," Tras told him. "Sometimes. Bradon knew it but he also knew he wouldn't go far. He put him with the mare. If I had whistled for him, he would have come."

"But not to me," Davyd guessed. "Smart horse."

"Too smart. He was following us."

Davyd knew what he was getting at. It was bad enough that the mare left tracks not once but twice. If the stallion had done it too, there were two trails for the raiders to follow. They should move camp.

"We'll move before nightfall," he said and heard a murmur of protest from the girl. "I don't think they'll try to take Synda again but we won't take chances. We'll go up the stream."

"Yes sir."

"But I want to take a look at that head of yours first. Sit down."

The boy sat without protest. Feeling his skull for any signs of a crack, he wasn't surprised when Synda brushed his hands away and felt.

"Concussion," she reported. "not a major one. No skull fractures. He should sleep though."

"Sleep?"

"Yes." Synda put a weary hand to her head. "He should sleep. Is that tea ready?"

"Yes." Davyd fished out the herbs and tested the temperature with one finger. Finding it too hot, he added a bit of cool water and swirled it to settle the herbs. Pouring it into one of their trail cups, he stopped to swirl it twice more and handed her the cup with only a trace of herbs in it.

She drank it down, making a face at the taste, but finishing it anyway.

"Let's move camp now," Davyd said to Tras. "And get away from this fire. Since we all need sleep, I want us secure."

The boy nodded and moved to bridle his horse. The mare was next. Davyd helped Synda on her and climbed up behind. Leaving the drowned fire behind them, they rode upstream then across a rocky bank to a cliff that promised caves.

This time they didn't take the horses all the way to the campsite he scouted but stopped them some distance away. Taking a chance the mare would stay with the loose stallion, they removed their harnesses and hung them in trees before the camping gear was taken up in the rocks.

Tras found a shallow cave on a rock shelf. They struggled up the slope. It wasn't an easy climb but Davyd was all in favor of that. Another trail led up and over into a dip then higher into the rocks. They could retreat but attackers would have a hard time finding an easy road to where they took shelter.

It would do.

Davyd settled Synda as comfortably as he could then told Tras to sleep. Holding his own weariness at bay, he sat by their path to the ground and waited, only moving when he needed to check one or the other.

Gods he was tired. He knew he wasn't hurt nearly as bad as the others but he felt like he hadn't slept in days. Even the hour or so of sleep he'd gotten with Synda was no relief. He felt like he could sleep for a week.

A bit of meat and some dried kivak helped him stay awake until nearly sunset then Synda was suddenly up and looking at him.

"You need sleep." She knelt beside him and placed cold hands on his temples. For a moment he thought she meant to kiss him but then she frowned.

"You're all out of balance. Did I hit you with Starfire?"

"No," Davyd said. "No, I think I pushed too hard."

"Pushed?" Her frown deepened and she bit her lip. "I don't know what you mean."

"Neither do I," Davyd admitted. "I tried to give you some energy. Something happened and I think I did but…"

She stared at him. "You can't do that! You're Kalryn. You shouldn't even know it can be done."

Putting her hands back on his temples, she read him again. Suddenly Davyd could feel her warm presence inside him. She soothed nerves and shifted something and the aching weariness lifted a little. She skirted around the edges of his mind, not touching his center, but she was there and he could feel her soothing touch.

Finally she broke the contact. "I don't know how you did it but you did. Do you have Sunborn blood somewhere?"

"Not in two generations. My mother has some though."

She studied him doubtfully.

"I thank you for your gift." She finally broke the silence with a grave little smile. "You're balanced now but I think I'd better take the next watch. You need sleep more than me now."

"Synda, no. You shouldn't have to."

"I want to. I need to watch this slope, right?" She pointed down the path they'd taken upwards. "And listen for any sounds I don't know — like scraping."

"Yes."

"Then I'll wake you if I hear something. And you'll go to sleep. If not, I'll make you sleep. You know I can do it."

"You can do a sleep set?" Davyd demanded.

"Yes."

"Don't do it to me. Not here."

"I won't if you sleep. We need to move on in the morning."

"Wake Tras when the moons rise," Davyd said. "And there's still food in the pack. We may have to hunt tomorrow."

"Yes sir. Now don't talk to the watcher."

Giving her a weak smile when she gave his words back to him, he moved to the blankets. Seeing her settling into a meditation pose, he tried to watch with her but he slept.

It was midnight when she woke him. Mostly asleep, he didn't react when she crept under his blankets and stretched out beside him. When she snuggled close, he just accepted it and went back to sleep as if it were a strange dream.

It was nearly dawn when he discovered he was holding her, her fine hair in his face and her legs curled against his. Were they back on the beach? He wondered if all the rest had been a dream but then he caught sight of Tras. The boy wasn't watching them. In fact he wasn't looking at anything. He was sound asleep and there was no one on guard!

He stiffened, his arms tightening around Synda. She quickly woke but stayed still. He only knew she was awake by the change in her breathing. Moving his mouth close to her ear, he whispered. "Why is there no one on guard?"

"Because no one can get up here without making a horrible racket." Synda shifted to look up at him and one of his hands fell on her breast. "There are animals down there—I think gaks—and they'll let us know if someone comes."

"And how do you know that?"

"I woke Tras and asked him then I told him to go back to sleep."

"And he did?"

"I helped him." Synda stuck up her chin. "He wanted to do guard duty and I told him no. I said I would wake you."

"You didn't."

"You woke up anyway. I didn't want him to know I was sleeping with you. And there was no point in waking you if I wanted this. You would have given me all the blankets and moved."

"Damn right." Davyd hastily moved his hand and rolled away and up in a fluid move. "Synda, you know better. We've been through this."

"We have." She followed him up and stood far too close to him. "But I don't want what you want."

His jaw dropped. "Don't want?" He felt a rush of anger. "You don't want this?"

Pulling her close, he tilted her head back to give her a deep kiss, his arms snaking around her back to press her hips against his as she hotly responded. His manhood hardened as she melted in his arms and he lifted her then felt her legs wrapping around his hips.

Gods, he wanted her! When that raider grabbed her and started to pull her breeches down, he had nearly died with the urge to kill him.

His tongue teased her mouth and she clung to him when he would have ended the kiss, her arms wrapped around his neck. Finally they had to breathe. Laying her fingers across his lips, she held him back.

With a groan he set her down, knowing he'd played the rutting stallion again but he couldn't help it. Even knowing she could kill him with a touch seemed like a good price to pay for her pleasure.

"Davyd, not here." She looked up at him, a sensuous smile dancing on her lips. "But I want you. If I hunt you, will you accept?"

"Yes!"

"Then wait until Gardon," she said, her eyes dark with desire and her hair seeming to crackle in the night air. "When your service to me is done and I have leave to hunt, I'll come to you. Remember your promise."

She backed away then, smoothly scooping up a blanket and taking it to another part of their shelter. Before he could fathom what he had done, she was wrapped up and fast asleep.

Released from her spell, Davyd groaned and buried his head in his hands.

Gods. What had he done?

Chapter 14 - Promise

8 Tyras 850

DAVYD BROODED over his morning tea and shot hot glances at the sleeping girl. It was nearly mid-morning and he wanted to leave but neither Tras nor the girl showed any signs of stirring. He could leave them there and do his errand alone but he wanted Tras awake before he left.

He hoped the girl wouldn't wake. She'd played him last night and he knew it, challenging him before extracting a promise he wished he'd never given. What would his father say? What would his mothers say if they knew he would be hunted?

He didn't want to even think about Mother Nan's reaction. *Her* grandfather had been a Sunborn and a real villain from what he'd heard. He'd taken a Kalryn favorite and used her till she bore him a son then stole her children away.

Pitfire! Synda would take *his* child just like old Platon took his grandmother.

She shouldn't hunt him. He was Kalryn and her guardsman besides. Even if she waited until his service was done, it wasn't proper. She should hunt—or marry—some Sunborn lord who could match her power and give her children with hair like hers and power besides.

He didn't want her in the hunt. Knowing she'd be there only for the child he could give her, he didn't want to do it. A father should be there for his children and he knew he couldn't let his firstborn be taken away and raised by others—especially not Synda. She was just a child herself.

He felt like a failure. Remembering the meditation crystal he lost, he knew he had to go back and find it. If it was lost, all his profit from the trees would be eaten up repaying the Queen. He doubted he'd ever get another royal commission.

It was in this black mood Tras found him. The boy looked well rested but his face got just as glum as his when he saw it. Forced to remember his dead kin, he sat down by the fire and took the cup Davyd offered him.

"What do we do next?" the boy asked. "The North Road?"

"Not yet. I have to go back to where they attacked us."

"Why?" Tras looked stunned. "Why go back now?"

"I lost something—something very precious that doesn't belong to me. I wasn't thinking straight yesterday and couldn't find it."

"As precious as the girl?" Tras glanced at her as she stirred. "I could swear you would die for…"

"I nearly did and Bradon did. No, she's precious to me and knows it but I have to leave you here for half a day. That should be time enough to go back and find it and return."

"We should all go. You need more eyes."

"No. If those raiders see her again, they'll kill her too. They've learned she can kill them."

"Did she?" Tras looked aghast.

"No, she didn't," Davyd admitted. "She hit enough of them with Starfire but none died. I killed four but they'll probably put the blame on her. I didn't use a sword and there's no mark of a blade on them."

"No mark?" Tras looked uneasy. "How could you?"

"The Prime. It's a Temple discipline to improve coordination and speed but you *can* kill with it. I did. Several times."

"And you know it? Why does a trader know something like that?"

"A lot of guardsmen know the Prime. Depending on who teaches you and what guard you join, you might learn it too. My parents both knew it and taught me."

"I wondered how you came to be so good at it." Synda spoke from her blankets, sitting up and brushing her hands through her hair. She looked wide awake and he guessed she'd been listening. "Tras, it's true that both Kalryn and Sunborn practice the Prime."

Davyd avoided looking at her, unwilling to be entranced by that hair again. Tras, though, had no qualms and watched her until Davyd cleared his throat.

"Synda, I want you and Tras to stay here. I've got to find that crystal. I couldn't find it yesterday."

"I thought that was what you threw." Synda paused in her braiding. "But you can't go alone. What if the raiders come here? We should stick together."

"No, I'll not risk you for it."

"Then let me replace it. I have a crystal of my own. Since you lost it defending me, I'm willing."

"No," Davyd exploded, then stopped when Tras looked shocked. "It was *my* loss and *I* will answer for it."

She looked exasperated. "Then we'll all go back. I will not stay here without you. We all go or you accept my gift."

She looked stubborn and Davyd knew she wouldn't give in but how could he take the gift she offered? Did she really think he could hide from the queen that it wasn't one of the crystals he purchased? Surely she knew Fara would ask. If she didn't, he would have to tell her.

He balked at the thought of taking her too but saw no other way. The boy was no match for her wiles and he didn't relish the thought of binding and gagging a Sunborn—if he could. Remembering the power she threw off, the wild beauty of her enraged, he didn't think he wanted to try.

"All right. We'll all go but you'll give your word to hide if we see any men."

"I won't." Synda calmly retorted.

His jaw dropped at her open rebellion but then his lips tightened and he glared at her. "Synda, you will or I *will* leave you here with Tras—bound, gagged, and Starfire be damned!"

"You can't handle Starfire!"

"Not if I'm wearing metal," he shot back at her. "But I can bind you with metal and you'll be as vulnerable as me."

"Why do you think I used the Prime instead of a sword? I know what Starfire can do. I know about warding wands too. I don't have one of those but I bet sitting you on top of a naked sword would have the same effect."

"It would," she confirmed then looked like she wanted to call the words back. "But you wouldn't."

"Don't count on it," he snarled. "Give me your word you'll obey me today."

She glared at him, then abruptly surrendered, giving him a nod.

"Say it."

"I'll obey you today," she slowly said, giving no more than he asked for. "Until sunset and no longer."

And stay away from my bed he wanted to shout but didn't dare. Tras didn't know and he meant to keep that secret. Wishing she would forget it, he knew it was a vain hope.

"Until sunset," Davyd answered. "And may we be at the North Road by then."

THE TRAIL back to the clearing was faster. It was barely noon when they left the creek they followed and went back into the woods. Once Davyd stopped them to rescue his packs off the gelding. Small scavengers had already torn into the carcass and he knew larger ones would come soon. Seeing the saddle was already shredded, he left it.

Tras watched the woods as he freed the saddle from Bradon's horse and hung it in a tree. Synda didn't look at the horses at all but kept her face averted and her nose covered to avoid the smell of rotting meat.

"Pit bait!" Tras said that one word and kept watch, his mouth clamped shut.

"Yes, pit bait," Davyd agreed. "And Kal will make then answer for it."

He abhorred the waste of the animals but knew why the raiders had done it. He might have had to do it himself if he were faced with the right situation. A man afoot was not nearly the threat as one mounted. No doubt the raiders hoped to find all the horses and leave them with no choice but to fight.

Scanning the ground in the clearing, he found no sign that other men had been there after his visit yesterday. Reassured by that, he rejoined the girl on the mare and rode toward the scene of their battle.

A mutter of men's voices put an end to his ease. His nerves tightened as he quickly backed the mare to one side of the trail.

Motioning for Tras to take the other side, he quickly dropped Synda off his horse but she had no time to hide.

A lone man appeared, looking surprised to see them. He immediately reined back but Davyd knew he was no raider.

"Wait!" he barked at Tras. The boy stopped, his sword in hand.

"Who are you?" Davyd demanded of the newcomer.

The stranger was clean-shaven and the horse good quality.

"Marl Batson, guardsman to York's." The man shouted his reply, warning his fellows.

The girl gasped and Davyd felt a huge sense of relief even as two more guardsmen burst into view.

Yelling his own name, the next thing he knew he was being pulled off his horse and into a rough hug.

"Gods!" His brother pounded his back, then pushed him away to look at him. "I thought for sure…"

"Not yet." Davyd grinned foolishly, overjoyed to see him. "You're late."

"Late!" Monar let out an exasperated bellow. "If you had stayed put one day—" He swung at him.

Davyd ducked, his reflexes still sharp, but he wasn't prepared for the fury that followed.

"Stop!" Synda was suddenly there, madder than a bee. "You leave him alone!"

"Synda, no!" Davyd flung himself on top of his brother. Fearing Starfire, he looked up at his vexed lady.

They were surrounded now by a loose ring of horsemen, some with swords drawn as they watched the reunion uncertainly. Afraid of what they might do, he got off his brother and tried to look like nothing was wrong.

"Synda, this is my brother. Monar's come to give us escort to Sefron."

She seemed not the least bit mollified. "Why did he hit you? That's no way for kin to act."

"He didn't touch me," Davyd hurriedly said. "And I've ducked his arm before. Simmer down."

Some of the men were grinning now and sheathing their swords even as Monar took the hand his brother offered and climbed to his feet. He eyed the lady.

"And this is the delicate Sunborn lady you were guarding?"

Davyd looked at Synda and saw her as his brother did. Clad in riding breeches and knee-length tunic from two days ago, she'd been under bushes and slept in them since. Her hair was neatly braided but there were dirt smudges on her sunburned face and hands. She was a far cry from the fragile lady of Datyl.

"This is Lady Synda of Datyl," Davyd confirmed. "And she's not delicate when she needs to be strong. If you've seen the raiders, you know."

There was a murmur of respect and the guardsmen bowed their heads to the lady.

Monar gave her a deep bow that looked out of place in the woods.

"Greetings, Lady Synda. I didn't mean to doubt you," he gracefully apologized. "It's just that the picture Lady Alva painted of you was quite different."

She looked surprised then smiled. "How is she? I know I've worried her but…" she gestured around her.

"You'll see her soon. We've got a few things to settle here and then we'll be off."

"What of the raiders?" Davyd asked. "Some still lived after yesterday."

"Dead. They tried to fight us at the hold. We sent word to Alwyn what happened."

That reminded him. Davyd looked around for Tras but the boy was nowhere to be seen. His stallion was there, his lead held by a guardsman, but there was no sign of him.

"Tras, come out. These are kin."

A rustle of movement spooked the horses as the holder came out of a bush, his sword in hand.

"Hold!" Monar snapped at the closest men. They froze, their swords half out of their scabbards.

"This is Tras Alwynson." Davyd motioned for him to sheath his sword. "He stood by me when we were attacked. He's an ally and a friend."

"Welcome, Tras, and join us." Monar offered his hand.

"You sent word to my father? He'll think we're all dead."

"No, I sent word when we reached the hold and we already had a prisoner screaming about a Sunborn witch and the fire of the gods. I didn't credit most of the tale but we knew some of you lived to put such terror into him."

Davyd glanced at his lady and saw her blushing a faint pink, her eyes suddenly intent on the ground. He smiled and wished she could know what terror she'd put into his heart and her anger hadn't even been directed at him.

"They gave you no trouble?" Davyd asked and heard a chuckle. Several of his brother's men smiled and he recognized some. They had served his family before.

"Not a lot," Monar drily reported. "We were reaching the hold when they burst out of the woods as if the pit demons were swarming after them. Three never even saw us until they were at the hold and we weren't hiding."

"Those died quickly. We already knew they were raiders. The others fought but we took one prisoner. He babbled like a babe, screaming about a lady with fiery hair. He called her Kala and begged for mercy."

"He deserved no mercy."

"He got none." Monar hesitated. "I sent him to Hold Alwyn with our guide. He'll get short justice there. All the hold folk died and three were Alwyn's children."

"I know." Davyd looked at the youth who stood silently grieving and made a quick decision. "Tras, if Synda agrees, you're free to return to your hold. Your family needs you more than we do now."

Synda looked grave. "I give you leave, Tras, but ask a small favor."

"Anything."

"Don't tell Bradon's family how he…"

"Don't tell them everything. Tell them he was caught by a sneak-thief and nearly sacrificed his hand fighting them off before he died of a slashed throat. What happened after they don't need to know."

Tras nodded, his face grim. "I didn't see. I thought he fell asleep."

"Him?" Davyd let his disbelief show. "No, he was standing by the wrong tree. It can happen to anyone. Remember to keep a tree at your back too wide for a man to get his arms around."

"Yes sir." Tras looked relieved. "If I may?" He looked to Monar for permission and Davyd's brother nodded. Without another word he took his stallion and left.

"Why did you come back here?" Monar asked. "Once we knew you weren't dead we thought you'd keep moving."

"I lost a crystal," Davyd quietly said. "I had to use it to save her life."

His brother gave him a stern look but none of the grief he expected. "A tough choice to make but I would have chosen lives too." He touched his belt pouch.

Davyd's eyes widened at the gesture. Seeing a round shape there, he felt chagrined and relieved at the same time. "It took no hurt?"

"Later." Monar turned to his men. "Let's finish the burials and get away from this place. I want to be at the North Road by this time tomorrow."

His men answered with a chorus of ayes and backed their horses away, leaving only two Davyd knew. With a start he saw one held his own horse and shot a grin of thanks to his brother. Finally things would be better and Synda safe.

"Wydon took charge of your cargo," Monar reported as the second warrior brought the lady's horse to her. "If we hurry, we'll meet him at the North Road."

"And the trees?" Davyd asked, recalling his investment for the first time in days. "Still alive?"

"They were when I saw them. Mount up."

Brushing by a guardsman, Davyd lifted Synda on to her mare. Their hands touched and he felt the tremor in hers. Remembering his promise, his joy at being found faded. If only Monar had caught up with them a day earlier.

Regretting the promise even as he longed for her, he turned back to his brother as if nothing was amiss.

Chapter 15 - Gardon

10 Hoth 850

THE CITY OF GARDON wasn't as big or as old as Datyl but it hummed with youthful life. Here there were horses on the streets and it wasn't uncommon for a man to wear a sword. Lawlessness was kept in check by the city guards and the brown uniformed guards who protected Gardon's outlying holds.

Having discharged his duty to Synda and delivered the meditation crystals to Gardon's queen, Davyd slipped quickly back into the routine of his family. After the three-day rest they all took at the end of a journey, he started seeing to the trees Wydon had delivered. The wine belonged to his family—an agreement made before he even left for Datyl—but the trees and other purchases were his to trade.

With Monar headed back to Sefron, he thought he would go with him but his father asked Wydon to take the caravan already prepared. That left him with time to sell the trees. Wishing he could go sooner, he put his efforts into selling the four-year-old trees at a good profit and made himself scarce in the public areas of the store. He dreaded the appearance of a woman in hunter's red.

His father had accepted the report he made of his adventures and he dutifully wrote it down for his brothers but omitted the promise Synda got from him and the reason she came to Gardon. Hoping she would reconsider and hunt someone closer to her station, he didn't tell a soul what she intended. With luck he'd be away from Gardon before she hunted and he meant to stay away if he could.

He wasn't needed here. With four sisters and three brothers still at home, he was just an extra pair of hands. No, he was better used on the road—just like Wydon. Someday Donal would join them and he supposed his sisters would wed men who were capable traders.

Glynda had. Her Nathan was gone now—killed in an accident less than a year after their marriage—but he had been promising. Glynda still mourned him but her two-year-old daughter and her status as second in the store helped ease her pain. Davyd hoped she'd find another to take Nathan's place but didn't push. Less than six months older than her, Davyd was closest to his widowed sister.

Returning to the store just before the sunset song, he smiled at Glynda as she waited on a customer then joined seventeen-year-old Adlar behind the counter. Straightening a display of teas, he kept himself busy until the first bells of the sunset song rang out and it was time to hang the shutters and close the store.

Helping with the heavy wooden shutters was a task he enjoyed since it meant the work day was done. As he manhandled a shutter into place, his sister showed her customer out and joined them.

"Davyd." She smiled at him as he hung another on an iron bracket and fastened it into place. "Mother Nan was wondering if you'd be back for supper."

"I try to be." He gave her an answering smile. "I sold all but two of the trees."

"Good. What price?"

"I'll tell at supper." He turned to watch as Adlar hung the last shutter. York's was a large business and covered nearly three lots with the store and had living areas and storage on another. There were cellars and storage rooms below too and two more floors of quarters above. It was easily the largest store in Gardon.

It still seemed crowded to him with most of the family home. The babble of his sisters and even the good-natured rivalry among his brothers bothered him after weeks away. He couldn't wait to get back on the trail and have the quiet solitude of trees around him.

Soon. His trees were nearly gone and his other responsibilities done. Once he came up with a cargo for Sefron he was sure his father would let him go. Maybe he could return to Hold Alwyn with suitable goods. The hold tanned good leather and the little flute he brought back from there got Glynda's attention. Claiming it had perfect tone, she wanted more to sell. He hoped the maker hadn't been one of those who died at Hold Farkon.

He still had the brown mare. Thinking she'd be good enough to breed, he sent her out to pasture with the other horses the family owned and tried to forget the girl who rode her last.

Lingering in the store after Glynda and Adlar left, he soaked up the quiet. It was nearly dark with the shutters in place and the merchandise lay hidden in pools of dark shadow.

"Davyd?" A slender figure appeared in the doorway. "Glynda said you were back."

"Yes, Mother. I was just enjoying the quiet."

His birth-mother was almost as tall as he was and still slender after bearing four sons. She was past fifty, being just three years younger than his father, but she didn't look it. The few gray hairs Nan had seemed only to enhance her light brown hair and her blue eyes were as clear as ever. She looked like a full-blood Sunborn but had only a quarter of that blood—her sole inheritance from her grandfather.

"I know what you mean. Your father needed quiet every time he returned. It must be worse after days in the forest."

"No," Davyd denied. "I would have given anything to have Wydon or even Donal for company."

"Donal is growing up," Nan said. "It won't be long before he leaves home too."

"Surely Adlar will leave first. He's seventeen."

"No, I think Donal will be next. He's had something on his mind ever since he returned from his fostering—and he asked to come back before the harvest."

Davyd knew that was odd. The holder who fostered them was a retired guardsman and one of the few his father acknowledged was better than him with a sword. Since part of the fostering price was helping at harvest, it was strange to find Donal already back. He had assumed his father recalled him when word came he was missing.

"Let's go into dinner. We'll talk later."

"Yes Mother." He offered her his arm and tried not to think about his real problem. He knew his mother wasn't a telepath but she was quick to sense moods. He thought about the trees and knew his family would be pleased at their disposal. He had only two trees left and he had a plan for them.

The dining hall was easily the largest room outside of the store itself. Over forty feet long and twenty wide, it was used for many purposes when the family wasn't eating. When a new shipment arrived, it was the sorting room and the family ate in the smaller rooms upstairs. Tonight, though, it was clear of all but family and their household servants and guards.

With most of the children able to do their own chores, they had few servants now. A cook and two assistants oversaw the kitchen and served the meals and three laundresses doubled as maids. Hop, his tree tender, was still there too. The rest of the staff consisted of ten guards. Some went home to their families at night but there were always two in the small guard room and two more sleeping half the night. York's had never been robbed but his father took no chances. Since the household guards were the first to be chosen for a caravan, they never lacked for good men in those positions.

Davyd took the seat next to his mother. With Monar and Wydon on the road, that was his place. She sat next to his father and Rayna, his second mother, was on his father's other side. The rest of the children were scattered in whatever order they picked. He found little Aldo sitting next to him and smiled. His youngest brother would tag after him any chance he could.

He eyed Donal during the meal, trying to decide if he really would fly the nest, but couldn't see it. Donal was serious but no more than normal. Thinking his mother was imagining things, he joined the light banter that went with the meal. His news must wait until dessert.

Finally his father asked for a report on the day's activities. Glynda dutifully reported sales, naming the most prominent folk who bought from her. Then it was Adlar's turn and even six-year-old Byka reported her own best sale of the day. Rayna reported the acquisition of some new cloth and a shipment of kamomyl tea then his mother reported her own progress in the tea room. When they were done, his father looked at him.

"Lord Robar will be here tomorrow to buy ten trees at fifteen solaris each," David reported and saw the smiles. "That's a profit of nine solaris per tree. He's also agreed to buy Hop's contract for eight solaris which Hop gets." He smiled at the tree tender as the nearest guardsman thumped him on the back in congratulations. The man looked dazed at the amount. Davyd had only asked him whether he would go with the trees earlier and assured him Robar was a good man to work for.

"That leaves you with two," his father said. "Wouldn't Robar take them as well?"

"No, he wanted only the ten best. I gave him choice. I suggest the last two trees be given to the Temple for the garden court." Davyd said that in a rush, keeping his eyes on Mother Rayna. "They'll be harder to keep alive without Hop and the Temple will appreciate them."

"So you'll settle for a profit of ninety solaris?" Rayna asked. "You could have more."

"Or those trees could be lost all together," York commented.

The other members of the family waited for the decision. Mother Rayna was the merchant but if York overruled her…

"That's it," Davyd said. "I meant to learn more about their care but…" he shrugged. "And I expected to lose two on the journey. Hop was better than I hoped." He smiled at the tender.

"Giving to the Temple would be good." Mother Nan broke her silence. "Not only will the Temple remember it but it might create a new market. Tyran apple trees can't be grown from seeds so they'll want more of the grafted trees."

Rayna looked thoughtful. Davyd hoped she would agree. Even though the trees were his, he wanted her approval. She had built the business and taught him the trade.

"Sometimes it's better to give thanks for good fortune," Rayna finally said. "And we have had a *very* good year."

Davyd tried not to look embarrassed when his family looked at him. A thanks offering—he hadn't intended the trees to be that.

"Yes, we've had a good year," York gruffly agreed. "Let the Temple have the two Robar doesn't pick."

"Agreed," Rayna promptly said and was echoed by Nan. They turned to him.

"You have the final vote," his father reminded him. "You own the trees."

"Yes sir. Agreed."

"You should take them to the Temple," York said. "If you want company, I have business there tomorrow."

"Yes sir." Davyd hoped he wouldn't see her but the Temple was large and it was unlikely he'd leave the garden court. "Lord Robar will be here before the noon song."

Rayna perked up. "York, Robar is fond of Datyl's honey wine. Can we have a case brought up from the cellars?"

"Of course." York looked at his fourth son. "Let's make it two, Adlar. It's his sister marrying Prince Valdyn."

"Yes sir."

"When is the wedding?" Davyd asked.

"At Harvest Court," his mother answered. "Valdyn is away until then. Oh, the Queen came up with another wedding gift for him. Lady Synda is painting a portrait of Lyda. She's staying at the Citadel now."

Davyd couldn't hide his relief. "Not at the Temple."

As soon as he saw his father's frown, he knew he'd given him suspicions. Trying to recover, he continued. "Her business was with the Temple when I agreed to escort her."

"You're not in her service now," York gruffly reminded him.

"No sir." He sounded so relieved that his brothers laughed. "She's a talented artist but I've no wish to escort her again."

His father seemed satisfied with that but now Mother Nan was looking at him. Would it never stop? He concentrated on his dessert and was glad when Glynda asked a question about rearranging the cookware they stocked.

Adlar unexpectedly took exception to her plan and there was a heated debate about whether some smaller pots would sell better in a display of their own. Even his father seemed interested as Adlar insisted the pots were housewares and Glynda argued they were only good for men on the trail and should be in the camping wares. Donal came in on Glynda's side and it looked like he was forgotten.

He hoped he was. He didn't want to talk about Synda and that blasted promise. Maybe she'd given up on asking him and was looking for a better man. The thought of another holding her was disquieting though and he shoved it from his mind.

SYNDA HADN'T forgotten him. Waking late that night from a dream in which he held her, she wished it was real and longed to see him again but she'd given her word at the Temple that she would look at others.

Alva had been scandalized that she wanted to hunt her guardsman but the head of the Temple had been more lenient even when she told him of the promise she'd shamefully extracted from

Davyd. That was skirting very close to compulsion and she knew it but the priest hadn't condemned her. Instead Justus made her promise to give it a month's time before she hunted and she was required to stay at court where she might meet men of her station.

She hadn't changed her mind. Lord Jon was nice but she wasn't surprised to find out he had an understanding with a lady and would wed her when her fertility began. Another that she liked was Lord Robar but he was wed and devoted to his lady. Although she could cross marriage lines with a hunt, she didn't want to put a strain on their young marriage.

None of the others even attracted her although some seemed to know why she was here and paid her undue amounts of attention. She'd put them off.

Finding she couldn't sleep, she left her bed. Going to the easel she kept covered and away from Alva's prying eyes, she lit a lamp and carefully uncovered the unfinished painting of her love.

He was smiling, his arms crossed and his stance relaxed as he looked at her. His brown eyes twinkled in one of her best effects and his lips were slightly parted as if he were thinking about hers. She shivered, remembering his kisses and aching for more. Only eight days had passed but she missed him. Wishing they were back in the tree, she hugged herself and imagined the feel of his whiskers on her neck and his arms around her.

It was so unfair. Because he was Kalryn everyone was telling her to wait. She could still hunt him—that choice was hers alone—but they disapproved. Even when she told them of other children, even couples, in Datyl who were of mixed blood, they said wait. She didn't want to wait.

Covering the portrait again, she sighed. Tomorrow she would spend the day with Lyda and let Alva go her own way. Glad she'd found at least one new friend in Gardon's Citadel, she used her painting of Valdyn's bride to keep her companion at bay. She was tired of arguing with Alva.

Hoping she could go back to sleep, Synda climbed back into bed and tried to blank her mind. When that didn't work, she deliberately thought of the night in the cliff camp and the kiss she'd provoked from him. This time, though, she didn't ask to be let go. With her fantasies wandering through her mind, she fell asleep and dreamed of him.

Chapter 16 - Trees

11 Hoth 850

IN THE SMALL yard behind York's Davyd followed his customer as Lord Robar looked over the trees he was buying. He was an extra. With the price already set, he was just there to give proper attention to the man who might someday be prime minister. The real players in this scene were Lord Robar's forester and the tree tender as they looked over each tree and pointed out reasons it should or shouldn't be selected to Lord Robar.

Davyd followed along, listening to the conversation and learning what he should look for on future purchases. The grower on Midway had been good to him and the forester could find only minor faults with the trees he rejected. Finally two were set aside and Robar motioned for the others to be loaded in his wagon.

"A fine lot." The Sunlord turned to him. "I hate to leave even the two but..."

"But the price is high."

"No, the price was fair," Robar corrected him. "I've tried to get apple trees before. These are the first I've seen worth the price and I've paid more for ones that died in one season. Your man has the touch with them."

"Hop does," Davyd admitted. He could have asked for a higher price? He filed that away for the future and other customers. "If York's tries for another shipment, we may wait until he's free again."

"You may not have to wait," Robar said. "If these trees winter well, I'll send him back with you. I'll want first offer on the new shipment."

"When the time comes. I've no plans to deal for them again this year. It's too late in the season."

Robar nodded. "I'm glad I heard of these. Tell Mistress Rayna thanks for the wine as well."

"I will." Davyd glanced at the cases in the wagon. His mother had proved right again and the Sunlord had bought both.

"I heard of your adventure," Robar said. "Lady Synda paints a lurid tale of it. Is it true that a boar pitched you twenty feet up a tree?"

Davyd grinned, surprised she was using his version of the tale. "Not quite but his breath inspired me to jump that high."

"I'll bet. I've hunted wild boars before. If our ancestors had known how dangerous they were, I doubt we'd have any pigs on Syra today."

"True," Davyd agreed. "But their meat is tasty."

"Yes, there is that. Well, I'm glad you made it back safe. Synda is firm friends with my sister and a good addition to the court. I also know it would have grieved the queen if you'd been lost. She's fond of your family."

"That's what she said," Davyd remarked, still surprised by her admission. "But I was more worried about the crystals. I didn't like losing one for even a short time."

"I didn't know you had but I doubt she would have been pleased about the crystals without you delivering them. She values good men more than that. So do I."

Davyd didn't doubt him. Robar was well known for his fairness. Raised as one of the prince's companions, he was one of four men who could become king if something happened to Prince Valdyn and he was favored by most. Certainly he'd be prime minister!

"I'm glad one of York's sons has asked to be in the Guard. I wish I could have lured you away too." "No, I'll not go," Davyd replied. Inwardly he was stunned by the revelation. Donal? It had to be Donal. Wondering what had got into his younger brother, he wanted to find him and ask. "Besides, I recall you want more trees."

"There is that but I would give those up to have you in the Guard. We need more good men."

"Yes sir." Davyd didn't know what else to say.

"I must be going." Robar clasped his hand and put his writ into it. "One hundred fifty solaris plus twelve for the wine. Let me know when you go for more trees."

"Yes, my lord." Davyd accepted the writ with a bob of his head and watched as Robar mounted the wagon. Hop was already settled, his small trunk of personal possessions jammed between two pots. Davyd waved to him and waited until the wagon pulled through the yard gates and into the street.

Thinking he had time to talk to Donal, he turned to see his father watching from a doorway.

"Well done," his father said and strode toward the remaining trees. "Why didn't he choose these?"

"One has a broken branch and the other wasn't as tall as the others. Father, has Donal applied for the Guard?"

His father hesitated. "Yes. I asked him to wait until Rayna agreed but the deadline for this year's applications was too short. We're waiting to hear whether he'll be accepted or not."

"Surely he will be. He's a York."

"That means nothing to the Guard. If it *did* count, I wouldn't want Donal to be one of them."

"That wasn't what I meant," Davyd denied. "He's as good as any of us with a sword and a good leader. I've seen how his friends follow him."

"There is that. Your mothers don't know his plans yet and I don't want them to until he's accepted. I know Rayna will fight it. She's hoping he'll go on the road too."

"And what do you want, Father?" Davyd knew Rayna's plans for him. She'd made no secret of what it would mean to have four traders out there buying for York's.

"I want him to follow his own path. You chose yours. Donal has his own right to choose."

"But you would like him in the Guard?" Davyd pressed, remembering his father's devotion to the queen.

"I would like one of you boys in the Guard. I'm too old to serve Fara now and most of you have made your choices. If Donal wants the Guard, I'll back him in it."

"So will I," Donal decided. "There's enough of us in trade."

"More than enough. I don't regret becoming a merchant but I think it would be unwise for us to concentrate solely on it. Having Donal in the Guard will let the others know they have choices too. Not everyone is suited to this life."

"I know. I enjoy traveling and have a knack for buying, but the selling part is...." Davyd shrugged.

"You're getting better at it," his father said. "I think Robar is pleased with the price and I know Rayna was. She plans to send you to Datyl again."

"When?" Davyd asked, his mouth suddenly dry. "Soon?"

"No. I'm calling for a family meeting after the harvest and there will be no journeys till after that. If Donal goes into the Guard, we'll announce it then too."

"Yes sir." Davyd remembered seeing troops of 15-year-old boys being paraded in their new uniforms at the harvest games. "I can take the next caravan to Sefron?"

His father studied him. "When we have one. I thought you would want more time at home."

"Father, the rains are coming. I'd like to get one more caravan in before winter." Davyd tried to justify it. "And you don't need extra help in the store right now."

"That's true enough," York answered and rubbed his gray beard. "With Glynda and Adlar arguing over displays, I could use less."

He looked thoughtful. "We've already decided to send Adlar to Sefron to help your brother. It's time he went to his own store and that will free Monar to do more trading. Monar knows but we've not told Adlar yet."

"And Glynda?"

"She says she wants to stay in Gardon and I know she wouldn't do well with Dylla. Here, at least, she is second to Rayna. It's better to send Adlar off."

"Yes sir."

"If you or Wydon were to get married and settle somewhere, it would be different," York suddenly said.

Davyd couldn't hide his reaction.

"I thought there was something to this girl. You've been moping around here ever since you returned and trying to get away from Gardon."

"I didn't know it showed," Davyd said, his jaw set.

"It does to me. How the hell did you fall for her?"

"I don't know," Davyd confessed. "I knew she was beautiful when I took the post but I kept my distance. It's just that, well, it's hard to keep your distance when you have to keep warm."

"You didn't touch her?"

"A kiss." He made no excuses. "And a promise. We couldn't violate the law and I thought she would leave it be, but she got a promise from me."

"What promise?"

"She came to Gardon for a manhunt. I said I wouldn't reject the scroll if it came to me."

His father groaned and he knew he'd done the wrong thing.

"If I'm gone, it can't come to me."

"You won't be gone," his father snapped. "You can't duck a promise like that."

"But she tricked me," Davyd protested. "And I don't want her. I can't want her."

"Because she's Sunborn?" His father folded his arms and glared at him. "Davyd, you promised and you'll honor it. You'll regret it all your life if you don't."

"Father, could you honor a promise like that?" He knew as soon as the words were out that his father would. No matter what it cost him, he wouldn't break his word. *But he never would have made it.*

"Davyd, *if* she comes to you, you *will* honor it," York said, his sympathy gone. "Then you'll go get a wife and get her out of your system. There's many a woman who would be proud to have you."

"Yes sir." Davyd glumly accepted the order. "But I would rather leave Gardon."

"I would like to send you," his father said. "But Justus wants to see you and I've no doubt it's about this. I wish I'd known sooner."

"I'm sorry." Davyd had a wild thought about running but one look at his father's face told him he'd get no chance. Justus wanted to see him? The Black Priest? Recalling his father's comment about having business at the Temple, he knew he'd made it easier.

"Well, it won't be the manhunt today," his father said. "If she's at court, she hasn't donned the robes. That much I know about the ritual."

With that last bit of comfort, Davyd loaded the trees into a handcart. As they prepared to leave his father went to the guardroom and chose two of the household guards. Flanked by them, father and son pulled the handcart down the streets to the Temple.

Chapter 17 – Temple

11 Hoth 850

THE TEMPLE of the Flame was a series of buildings off the Great Square. Its first domed building was tucked in next to the arena and flanking the Citadel of Gardon. Across from it was its counterpart, the Tax Hall, where much of the city's administration took place.

Davyd remembered what his tutor had told him about the Great Square. The Temple on its west side saw to the welfare of the people, the Citadel on the north kept them safe, and the Tax Hall on the east paid for it all. It was the core of Gardon but the city had long since opened up smaller versions of the buildings to provide for the needs of the growing city.

The Grand Temple remained unparalleled in splendor, its three-story golden dome shining brightly in the sunlight. Most days Davyd would enter the Temple through there but not today. Because of the cart, his father guided them down a side street to the Garden Court.

This gate was rarely used by armed men but there was a warden there. Once his father dismissed the guards and they surrendered their weapons, it was an easy matter to get entry and even easier to find the priest in charge of trees. The priest was delighted with the gift and speedily recorded their offering before they left them in his charge.

The Garden Court was as unique as the Grand Temple. Sandwiched between two stone buildings, it had a roof made of glass panels and a waterfall fed by the city aqueduct. At this season some of the panels were gone to let the heat of summer escape and a few were replaced with plain wood to cut down on sunlight burning the leaves of the plants below.

It was an engineering marvel but Davyd had seen it before. Only pausing once to admire a bank of rare flowers, he followed his father through to the innermost courts of the Temple.

A guide soon joined them. Dressed in the flowing robes of a senior priestess, she greeted his father by name and seemed to know why he was there. She smiled once at him but directed her few words to his father. Davyd felt like a child being led to classes as they entered another building flanking the court and climbed to the top floor.

"Master Justus? York and his son are here. They were sent for."

"I know."

The Black Priest turned to smile at York then eyed Davyd, his violet eyes seeming so out of place against his dark skin. His hair was cropped closer than a guardsman's and he wore his rank beads on a horsehair braid looped at his belt. Davyd resisted the urge to count them. There were too many and the braid was doubled and redoubled to keep it from hanging low. Justus was legendary and his word was law in the Temple.

"Greetings, York. It's good to see you again."

"Thank you, my lord." York bowed his head. "You asked to see my son."

"I did. This one is Davyd?"

"Yes sir. He's my third son and not yet twenty-two."

"I see." Justus smiled at him and Davyd was surprised to feel the warmth of the man. "And you're a son of Nan. You have the look of her."

"Yes sir."

"Come sit with me. I think your father had other business to tend to today." He looked at York. "Davyd won't be long."

"Thank you." York accepted his dismissal. Giving him a warning look, he bowed and left them alone.

Davyd couldn't believe that anyone outside of the queen could dismiss his father so casually. Suddenly irritated by this man's power he was even more irritated because he knew Synda was the reason for this meeting.

"I've spoken with Synda of Datyl," the priest said as he offered Davyd a seat. He quit smiling when Davyd made no move to sit down. "Sit."

Davyd automatically reacted to the command in his voice and sat, then flushed as he realized the priest made him do it. Standing again, he tried not to lose his temper.

"So you recognize a subtle command." Justus gave a satisfied smile. "One point in your favor. I thought Synda might have ordered you against your will."

"Not with that," Davyd said, realizing he was being tested. "As far as I know I was under no compulsion."

"Then she won't be punished," Justus said. "She said you weren't but it sounded like you were. In any case, the promise she made you give is voided here and now. You are free to decide for yourself whether or not to accept her hunt."

"She still means to hunt me? I hoped...."

"I've forbidden her to hunt until she's met the men of the court, but she will hunt. What did you hope?"

"I hoped she would find someone of her own station." Davyd didn't stop to think. "I'm only Kalryn."

"You are not *only* Kalryn." Justus stopped him. "There are few Kalryn like you and fewer still like your father. York has proved his worth many times."

"I'm too old to stand all day," he suddenly announced and chose a chair for himself. "You have the choice now."

Davyd hesitated then sat down again. He wanted to leave but he also wanted to hear what this legendary man had to say.

"I understand you brought meditation crystals with you from Datyl and two hundred cases of wine *and* apple trees. A shipment of goods most men wouldn't leave but you did. Why did you follow Synda off the ship?"

"I was sworn to her," Davyd instantly replied. "I couldn't let her drown."

"And that's all?" Justus quirked an eyebrow. "You did it just because you were sworn to her?"

"Yes sir. At the time that was the only reason."

"At the time," Justus repeated. "Well, it's a good reason but many men wouldn't do it. You're commended for that."

Davyd said nothing, not sure he wanted to be commended. Remembering the unhealthy feelings he had for the girl, he couldn't meet the priest's eyes.

"I know it's hard for a man alone to keep his distance from a beautiful woman," Justus continued. "Especially when you must keep her safe and warm. I assume you slept close?"

"Yes sir," Davyd mumbled. "We had to the first night. After that I tried to keep her warm in other ways."

"So she told me," Justus drily commented. "She must have been a trial for you."

"Yes sir. Not that she meant to be, but—"

"I think she tried to be more than either of you realize. From what I know of her family, you're the first man she's been alone with for any length of time. Her father was hunted and Synda never knew him. Even her mother set her adrift when she became an adult. It's no wonder she's formed an attachment for you."

"She can find another," Davyd grimly replied. He remembered her lonely tale though. She seemed to accept it as normal when she told him about her parents but he knew it wasn't.

"That might not be best for her," the priest said. "Synda, whether she knows it or not, is looking for a family to belong to but she's scared too. The only person who raised her was her mother and she was rejected by her. She's afraid to open her heart to anyone for fear she'll be rejected again. A child won't reject her though and that's why she is set on doing a manhunt."

"I wish I could forbid her to hunt and make her marry," Justus continued. "The manhunt was not intended for all women everywhere but just for the few who could find no mates unrelated to them."

"I can't change the law and I can't forbid her hunt. I can only insist she look at the choices available and see if there is someone she'll marry instead. You understand I can't stop her if she chooses to give you the scroll?"

"Yes sir. What if I left?"

The priest studied him. "That's something for you and your family to decide. Most of all, you need to look in your heart and ask yourself if you wish to avoid the choice or make it and be done with it."

"Davyd, you assume you're unworthy and that's foolish. I've not seen you before but all that I've heard has been good. Synda could do far worse than choosing you either for the hunt or marriage."

"But I'm Kalryn."

"Are you?" the priest asked with a faint smile. "Your great-grandfather wasn't. It's only because the women of your family have always loved Kalryn men that you are what you are. That was their right and they took it. Now Synda wants to exercise her choice and do the same. Is it any different?"

"Yes!" Davyd exploded then hastily lowered his voice. "She's a full blood and she should marry someone with power."

"I see." The priest looked disappointed.

"Davyd, do you know why they say I am so old?" Justus abruptly asked. "No, I see you don't. I *am* old. I remember the founding of Sefron two hundred years ago and another hundred years before that. The records say I am three hundred and forty-six years old. I was born in the year 505."

Davyd stared. The man didn't look more than forty.

"I am what happens when too many Sunborn marry Sunborn," Justus sadly explained. "Most children born like me die within days. I was lucky, but I can't age without help. Unless I meet with an accident or choose to end my life, I'll just continue and never look any older."

Davyd waited for him to go on, thinking the man was blessed but his tone suggested not.

"The price you don't see is something few know," Justus said. "And I must have your word that you'll tell no one about it."

"I—you have my word."

"I am denied children."

Davyd stared at him.

"Long life I have but no woman will ever bear me a child. I've tried many times and I know it for truth. I would like a child but it will never happen."

Davyd was shocked and sorry all at once. He tried to think which he would like but couldn't. Would he want to live long at that price? He didn't know.

"Do you remember your history? Our ancestors freed the Kalryn from certain death on another world for two reasons. First, they abhorred the waste of a promising race. Secondly, they did it because they were dying. Few women could bear children and the great ship was near empty. There were just a few thousand Sunborn when the Kalryn were saved."

"Our ancestors thought mating with the Kalryn was the answer and it was. We left the ship so the Kalryn could have the skies and forests they needed. We left the stars so we could renew our race."

Davyd knew the story from his childhood but his mother had told it from the Kalryn point of view. He thought the Sunborn needed the planet and simply decided to bring the Kalryn with them.

"Our ancestors mated and there are very few who can say they have pure blood now. Like you, there's Sunborn blood in nearly every Kalryn you meet and almost every Sunborn family has some Kalryn blood. It may be in small amounts but every Sunborn woman gives thanks when she becomes fertile that it's there — even Synda."

"She can't be Kalryn," Davyd protested. "I've seen her throw Starfire."

"Yes, she has power," Justus frowned at him, "but that is simply her birthright from her parents — just like you've inherited your father's height. Right now I think she'd gladly give it away."

"She can't."

"No, she can't. It can be taken from her but there must be proof of a crime first. That brings me to another question I must ask you. Did she kill with Starfire?"

Davyd blinked. "No, no, she didn't."

"She thought she might have and *that* was a more serious matter than her choice to hunt."

"She sent them running and shocked two badly," Davyd explained. "They were still alive when I killed them." He had no regrets about that.

"I see." Justus didn't judge him. "If the gods are merciful, they'll have a chance to atone."

"Yes sir." He knew the legend about rebirth but hoped those raiders wouldn't get it.

"We must end this." The priest rose to his feet and Davyd followed. "Keep in mind that Synda *can* bear children but her children may not if she chooses unwisely. The law allows her to choose Kalryn. It is no different than a Sunborn lord choosing a Kalryn lady and she will *not* be censured for it."

"Yes sir. But I will still pray to Kala that she chooses another when she hunts."

"That is your right," the priest said. "Just remember the promise you made is not valid. You must decide when you get the scroll."

"Yes sir." Davyd got the words out but couldn't agree. A promise made was binding and he knew it would stay in his heart until he knew she'd chosen another.

Let her choose another. He didn't think he could bear to part with her again.

Chapter 18 - Lyda

12 Hoth 850

SYNDA EYED HER subject critically, trying to decide if her smile was the same as yesterday or not. Her green eyes went from the half-done painting to the young woman she was supposed to capture with an exasperated air.

"Now what's wrong?" Lyda asked, her hands going up to her golden hair then down to smooth her dress. She was beautiful, her features nearly perfect and her body slender and lovely in the deep blue gown she'd chosen.

"You smile differently today," Synda promptly said.

Lyda laughed, surprised at her answer.

"That's better," Synda said, satisfied her smile was back. Before it could fade, she checked her work and added a few more strokes to the face.

"Synda, you are a piece of work," Lyda said, her brilliant blue eyes shining. "Did you give Davyd Yorkson so much grief when you were with him?"

Synda paused, her hand suspended in midair as she shot a guilty look at the covered easel.

Lyda saw and her smile faded. "Synda, I was joking."

She eyed the easel, her curiosity showing, but didn't leave the small stone pillar where her clasped hands rested. "Did you sketch him?"

"Of course." Synda tried to sound matter-of-fact. "I sketch everyone I find interesting. Half *The Seawind's* crew posed for me."

"Somehow I can't see Davyd posing like this." Lyda froze for nearly a minute then laughed at her face. "I doubt he can stand still."

"Oh, he can." Synda made a few more strokes. "I've seen him stay quiet for *hours* at a time." In spite of herself, she sounded aggravated and Lyda laughed again.

"That sounds like Valdyn," she declared and moved her hands then hastily put them back when Synda motioned to them. "Sorry."

"I've tagged along on hunts, you see. The first time I got caught and Robar was so mad he talked Valdyn into leaving me."

Synda paused, shocked.

"Oh, they didn't really leave. No, they just hid out of sight. You see, they had planned the hunt for days and even ducked their guards—Valdyn didn't do that often—and then I was there to spoil it."

She wasn't smiling any more. "I thought it was a game then but they really scared me. I *did* panic until I finally spotted Valdyn high in a tree. He was watching me."

"So what did you do?" Synda had to ask, remembering her fear when she thought Davyd had left her.

"I sat down and played until they came out," Lyda said. "I even made like I was taking a nap." She smiled at her expression. "Valdyn still swears I really did take a nap but I didn't."

"You took a nap? How old were you?"

"Eight. Valdyn and Robar were thirteen."

Synda stared at her, then set her brush down as she tried to imagine a girl of eight tagging along on a hunt. She thought *she* was daring for having left Datyl but...

"Oh, I wasn't in any *danger*." Lyda mistook her reaction. "We were in the Protectrate on lands my father owned. It's just that we'd gone quite a way from the hold before they caught me."

"And you were just eight?" Synda was amazed. "I rarely left my house at that age!"

Lyda sighed. "Well, you didn't have brothers to tag after. I had two and it was a lot more fun following them than staying home and learning the proper way to bake bread."

"Two?" Synda picked up her brush again and made a few more strokes in the gown. "I didn't know you had another. Will I meet him?"

"Probably not." Lyda frowned. "Mowyt doesn't like the court and he rarely comes home. He's half-Kalryn and chose to follow that path instead of being Sunborn." She said that without a trace of censure. "He's more comfortable with a sword than in a Council chamber."

"I see." Synda's answer was automatic. She was surprised anyone would choose to be Kalryn over Sunborn. "Do you miss him?"

"Oh, he's around. He's a captain in the guard. My new villa is in *his* quad so I'll get to see more of him. Valdyn wouldn't let me have a villa unless it was there."

"You aren't going to live in the Citadel?"

"Goddess, no!" Lyda made a face. "I love the queen but can you imagine being with her day after day? And Valdyn would look to her for everything. That's all right when it's business," she hastily added, "but I want to order my own household. I can't do that here."

"I guess you can't." Synda remembered her mother's rules and how many she'd broken or discarded in her own household. She really couldn't live like her mother did. "But what does your mother think about you not living here?"

"She's gone." Lyda was frank, her eyes on her hands as she nervously adjusted them.

"I'm so sorry," Synda quickly apologized. "I didn't know."

"Don't be sorry. She's with my father. I was only nine when he died but Mother took it hard. I think she only stayed to raise me. Anyway, she was never the same afterward and now she's with him again. She's happy."

"I never knew my father. Mother did a manhunt to get me. I'm not even sure who he is."

"And now you want to hunt?" Lyda was astonished. "Didn't they tell you so you wouldn't hunt kin?"

"I didn't want to know. I just asked if he had close kin in Gardon and was told he didn't. And I'm sure he's not related to the man I want anyway."

"The man you want?" Lyda cocked her head. "You know which one? I didn't think you'd had enough time."

"Oh, I know," Synda said with a little smile. "But I don't know what his family will say. He's Kalryn, you see."

"Kalryn?" Lyda's eyes widened. "You want a half-blood child?"

"From the right man I'll take one." Synda bent her head to her work, hiding her flushed cheeks. "But only from him."

"Tell me." Lyda abruptly quit the podium.

"Please." Synda gestured to her spot but her friend looked immovable.

"You've only met a few and I only know of one you talk about…" Lyda gave a mischievous smile then laughed. "Oh, this is wonderful."

Synda blushed deeper, wishing for the first time she hadn't spent so much time with her.

"You like Davyd Yorkson!" Lyda smiled. "And you mean to hunt him?"

"Yes," Synda answered, her face hot from embarrassment. "I want him."

"Goddess," Lyda declared and grabbed her hand. "There's nothing to be embarrassed about. He's a fine man. If I didn't have Valdyn as my beloved, I might even be tempted by the sons of York."

"You wouldn't! Not Davyd."

"No, not Davyd," she responded with a wicked look. "No, I took a long look at Monar and another at Wydon. Davyd is really the plainest of the three."

"He's *not.*" Synda hotly defended him then realized she'd been baited. "I can't believe you ever looked at any of them."

"You're right," Lyda calmly answered. "No, I knew Valdyn was mine. Mother said I would even quit crying when he picked me up from my cradle."

She moved back to her place, rearranging herself in her pose. "Mother said he nearly died of embarrassment the first time I told him I would marry him. I remember it too. He was only nine and I was three."

Synda was envious of her friend's tenacity in getting the man she wanted. She listened to tale after tale about how she aggravated the man she was soon to marry and then got his love but couldn't imagine doing the same to Davyd. No, Davyd would simply walk away and she would never see him again. The very thought of losing him hurt.

Laying down her brush, she flexed her hand to relieve the stiffness there. It was time to quit. Looking at her model, she stopped her in mid-story. "We're done for the day."

"Good." Lyda let her hands drop and stretched her arms before sitting down in a chair. "I wondered if you were going to work all afternoon."

"I'm sorry. You should have asked for a break."

"No problem and I do enjoy talking to you. There are few people who can stand my running mouth for so long."

"Oh, but you tell stories so well," Synda promptly responded. "I didn't know girls could go on hunts or how to get a man to look at you like a woman." Lyda had definitely given her pointers.

"What worked with Valdyn may not work on Davyd," Lyda told her. "Can I see the painting you're doing of him?"

Synda hesitated, but she wanted to show off her best work. Before she could think twice, she flipped the cover off the easel and let her friend look.

She was further along now. The tunic wasn't done because she was still unsure of the front but his face and arms were done in loving detail. On one hand she had started a ring.

Lyda stared at the painting, careful not to touch it, but her expression showed what she thought. Synda watched her, happy with the awe she saw there. It really was her best work.

"It's wonderful." Lyda finally said then motioned to his hands. "But what are you doing there?"

"A ring," Synda said. "He showed me the symbol of his house and I thought I'd include it. Wait a moment."

She went to her sketching table and found the earring he'd given her. "He had to use the ear wires for fish hooks, but he left me this." She held out the medallion. "It's the symbol of his house."

"No, it's not," Lyda said. "There aren't enough stones."

"Not enough stones? But I…"

"Oh, it's close," Lyda assured her. "But there's a stone on each side of the Y. The one in the arms is a ryl stone and not garnet. The garnet is to the right and there's a safyr on the left. I've seen it often enough."

"The trio of stones stands for the three owners of the store," Lyda explained. "That's Nan, Rayna, and York. Nan is Davyd's mother — she spends a lot of time at court. Rayna stays at the store and manages it."

"I didn't know." Synda looked at her medallion and tried to remember what Davyd had said about it. She would have to change that detail in the painting. "Why do they have a triangle? It makes it look busy."

"That's the three cities. Gardon at the bottom and Sefron and Datyl at the top. Since they trade with all three, they put them on their arms. Someday they might even have a store in Datyl. They put one in Sefron when Monar got married."

"I wish they would. I mean Datyl needs more trade."

Her friend laughed, seeing through her little lie. "Tell me about Datyl. I've not been there and I would really like to go."

Synda obeyed, relieved Lyda was content to talk of other things. She still found Gardon strange and longed for the clean, quiet streets of home.

DAVYD ROLLED another case of wine up the steps of the cellar, pushing the cart that held it up the tracks to either side of the stairs. Stacking it with the other six he'd already brought up, he rolled the cart back down the steps and went to get another.

Not having to think much to do this task, he'd taken it on and let Adlar tend to something else so he could be alone. He needed to think and the children weren't likely to bother him down here. Except for Aldo and Adlar, no one knew he was working down here. He had told his tagalong brother to help someone else today.

He didn't want to think about Aldo or even Donal. As he pushed another case up the stairs, he tried to banish his brothers and sisters from his mind and think only of his decision. Should he stay or go?

Davyd wanted to run but he knew that would displease his father. He could take almost anything but not that. Worse, it would set his mothers against him. Anything that upset his father hit them worse and they weren't quiet when one of them failed the family.

Actually, it was Rayna that wasn't quiet, he corrected with a grim smile. Nan would say little but Rayna was verbal enough for both. When he was a child, he hated having Rayna find out his misdeeds because she would haul him out to the store and make him sit in a corner until one of his other parents rescued him.

She never told anyone outside the family exactly what he'd done but every customer who came into the store knew the child in the corner was being punished. It was the one thing all the children in the family dreaded.

His mother was better. She would ask them to explain where Rayna didn't and make them set their own punishment. She knew if they set one too light. If she caught them at that, it was his father who passed judgment. That could take hours or even weeks if he was on the road.

Davyd paused in the dim cellar to read the labeling on a sack he'd passed before. Noting the sack held seed from last year, he frowned and looked around for others. Seeing there was only the one, he hauled it closer to the stairs. It should have been sold in the spring. He doubted anyone would buy it now.

Looking around the first cellar, he couldn't see any other tag ends of merchandise but vowed to check the other cellars. It wasn't like Rayna to overlook even one sack of seed. It was kona too.

Carrying the lantern into another cellar, he looked around there. Cloth, wine, plow blades, tools, and a few swords accepted in trade were objects he noticed. There was also a solitary gitar on a shelf. Looking only for lone items that might have been overlooked, he took the gitar and swords. He might be able to trade those in Garwys. It was only a few hours away.

He didn't want to risk his father's displeasure. Admitting that, he decided he would have to stay and wait for the hunt. When the time came, he would either refuse her or accept, but he wouldn't run.

Maybe his father was right and he should seek a wife.

Chapter 19 - Edan

13 Hoth 850

SYNDA SIGHED, ready for yet another public dinner in the feast hall. She wondered who would sit next to her today. It wouldn't be Robar or Jon or that tiresome Jaffry—she was glad he only sat beside her once. No, every day the seating arrangement was changed so she had two new partners to meet.

Lyda would be across the table from her. If she didn't like the men, she would talk to her friend.

Wishing she could just eat in her rooms and forget this business, she walked into the feast hall alone. Lady Alva was already there and looking irritated by her late arrival but Synda didn't care. The queen wasn't here and she was not that late.

"Lady Synda," Alva greeted her with a tight smile. "You look lovely today."

"Thank you." Synda smiled back, knowing she was just polite. She'd deliberately worn russet and gold instead of her favorite green and they did little for her eyes.

"Let me present Lord Edan." Alva smiled at the Sunlord she'd been talking to. "Edan is one of Valdyn's Companions and a member of the Seven."

"I'm honored." Synda gave him a curtsey and obediently smiled. Another Companion? How many were there? She'd already met two.

Edan was pleasant looking and almost handsome in his own way. His hair was brown but not dark enough to suit her and his eyes were a grayish color with a few flecks of gold in their depths. His surcoat was a dark shade of green with a row of neatly tied points down the front. The sleeves were slashed to show flashes of yellow beneath.

He had a ready smile as he studied her, looking her over from head to foot like some animal he might buy. He must have liked what he saw because his smile was deeper as he bowed.

She hated this. Knowing Alva was behind the fluctuating dinner seating, she was beginning to hate her too. She didn't want to know every eligible man in Gardon. Still she'd given her word and must wait ten more days before she could begin the hunt.

She smiled politely and asked the first question that popped into her mind. "How many Companions are there?"

Edan looked surprised but took it in stride. "Four now, my lady. Once there were six but two have left Gardon," he explained, his smile a little warmer. "Which ones have you met?"

"You, Robar, and Jon," she told him, relieved there weren't more. "I heard Lord Tarus was one too."

"He is but he's dedicated to the Temple. I doubt he'll come to court unless he's lured here by tales of your beauty."

"That would have to be stretched to move anyone from the Temple," Synda retorted but her sting was gone. She liked the compliment and was warming to the man.

The dinner bell sounded and those waiting moved to their assigned seats to wait for the queen. Synda was relieved to see an older man and his wife standing on her right. She needn't worry about him. She smiled across at her friend, then straightened as Gardon's queen swept into the room.

Queen Fara was a stately woman with honey brown hair and a figure that belied the age of her son. She was also a powerful woman with a personality which warmed people to her even as she demanded their loyalty and service. Synda had been surprised to meet her but the queen had welcomed her within two days of her arrival then asked her to come to the Citadel and paint her future daughter-in-law. Even now she smiled at her before turning to others.

"Lords and ladies," Fara said. "Let us be grateful for the bounty of this table and the good fortune the gods grant us." The ritual blessing done, she took her seat.

Synda smiled at her friend. The servants were collecting the first course from the long tables down the center of the hall. It was almost a dance, each servant shifting about the table to dish up soup from the big tureens and leaving room for the next as they moved on to the stacks of rolls and cheeses. Not a drop was spilled or a roll dropped by the staff but neither did there seem to be any order in the way they took turns. Synda wondered how they did it without bumping into each other. She accepted the plate a servant set in front of her and allowed another to pour chilled wine into her cup.

"You come from Datyl?" Lord Edan claimed her attention just when she wanted to eat. "Do you attend public dinners there?"

"Never." She was more honest than she meant to be and saw his surprise. "I mean I've only been presented at court and never dined. I don't think anyone does."

"I see." Edan grinned. "I can assure you they do though. When the Companions visited King Regan showed up how elaborate a feast could be."

"Better than this?"

"The food wasn't any better," Edan said, "but you had to wait hours to get it. They even had jugglers before the first course."

She stared at him, appalled, then had to giggle.

"After the first night we ate before the feast so we wouldn't starve to death," Edan finished and she had to use her napkin to smother her laugh.

"Edan tells the most outrageous tales," Lyda said, "and he stretches them too. My brother said it took three days before they learned."

"Oh, stop." Synda could see Alva's disapproving face. "I can see it. King Regan just loves a spectacle."

"He's a good king," she hastily went on, "but Datyl's court is so big and stuffy with all the ceremony. Mother hated it."

"We'll keep that in mind. Won't we, Lord Mark?"

Her other neighbor was smiling too. "Indeed." He inclined his head to her. "And it's nice to know Gardon's court isn't stuffy yet. Please let me know if it gets there." He sounded like he meant it and Synda wondered exactly who he was.

"I will," she said then paid attention to her soup, her face flushed as she tried to remember who was who here.

"You weren't introduced," Edan said so low she barely heard it over the chatter in the hall. "Mark is one of the Three. If there's an excess of stuffiness, he can stop it."

"I didn't know."

"He knows," Edan assured her. "And I'm sure he enjoyed your comments."

Synda wondered and suffered until the first course was removed. Relieved when Mark turned to her again with a warm smile and introduced his wife, she relaxed and started to enjoy the company again.

She liked Edan but thought guiltily of Davyd. She tried to compare the two and thought they were much the same. Edan had the same confidence but his talk was all of the court and council. She found it interesting tonight but knew she would tire of it.

Thinking back, she realized Davyd never mentioned politics. He admired Gardon's queen and was firmly loyal to her but his talk was mostly of his trade and his family. She had enjoyed listening to him.

"Would you mind if I sketched you?" She stopped Edan in the middle of a tale about some lord or other. "I don't mean now but later."

Lyda looked surprised. She hadn't asked to sketch anyone else. Alva looked far too smug as she took another bite of roast gak. Synda hoped she'd eat too much then hastily amended the thought. If she did, she would be up all night and moaning about it.

"I would be honored," Edan warmly replied. "I heard you were painting Lyda but I thought she was the only one."

"That's a commission," Synda said. "And I rarely paint a full portrait without one because it takes weeks to get it right. No, I'd just like to sketch you. I work very quickly at that."

"Then I'll be honored to have a sketch by such a lovely lady," Edan told her.

Synda suggested after dinner and surprised him with the lateness of the hour but he was agreeable. With that promise given, Synda paid attention to her meal. Even Alva's disapproval didn't dampen her spirits as she thought of sketching later.

STRETCHING out his long legs by the fireplace, Davyd listened to the patter of rain outside with a frown. Of all the days to go to Garwys, he'd picked a wet one. It hadn't started raining until evening but still he dreaded doing the last of his business out in the wet and late summer storms often went on for days.

The conversation in the inn was subdued too. His guardsmen, the two his father had insisted he take, sat at another table with a promising young woman to keep them interested. He simply shook his head at another, even prettier than the first, when she tried to join him. He was in no mood for harlots.

She was good at her trade and took the warning, joining another likely prospect instead. Davyd wished he'd paid extra for a private suite but he was unlikely to make enough to cover the cost on the few trade items he'd brought with him.

He didn't have the seed. Once Rayna realized what bag he was talking about, she appropriated it, saying it wasn't forgotten at all. He tried to ask her why but none of his parents seemed the least bit curious about the seed.

Seeing that was no use, he'd proposed selling the swords, gitar, and a few other items he'd found and asked permission to do it in Garwys. His father agreed readily enough, only asking him to take Donal with him. Aldo had asked to go but his father had promised him another trip instead. He was glad of that. The ten-year-old was too eager and would have wasted the time he and Donal had together.

He hadn't told Donal he knew he was going into the Guard. Unwilling to break the confidence his father had given him where others might hear, he'd waited until now.

Looking up as his brother rejoined him, he thought Donal was well grown for his age. His curly hair was almost black but there were strands of brown in it—even reds. A legacy from their mother, it was even lighter when he was a babe. That, combined with their father's good looks, made him catch the women's eyes in spite of his age.

He was too serious though. Davyd knew that was a recent development and guessed he was still searching for ways to tell their family what he meant to do. Having the same problem with Synda, he understood his reserve.

"Have you heard from the Guard yet?" he asked his brother and saw the shock on his face then his relief. "Father told me."

"No, not yet," Donal replied, his glance going to their guards and back again. "I didn't think you knew."

"I've known for nearly a week but I think Mother suspects. She said you'd be the next to leave home."

"She did?" Donal looked chagrined. "I thought Adlar would be."

"Oh, Adlar will." Davyd smiled, realizing his brother didn't know what his father planned for him. "But it won't be before the harvest. If you're going to join the Guard, you'll parade then."

"True." Donal returned his smile but it was shaky. "They may not take me this year."

"Maybe, but they might. You'll be old enough."

"By less than a month. I asked to come back early because of that but—well, maybe I should wait a year," he said in a rush.

"And maybe you shouldn't. Actually, I think it's too late for you to wait. Lord Robar saw your application."

His brother's jaw dropped.

Davyd gave him a smug smile. "He mentioned it to me before Father did."

"What did he say?" Donal leaned closer, nearly toppling the pitcher in his eagerness. "Am I in?"

"He didn't say." Davyd quit teasing and straightened in his chair. "He did say he was happy one of us applied. He didn't even say who but I knew it wasn't Monar or Wydon and I can't see Adlar doing it."

"It was me," Donal confirmed, his face showing his disappointment. "I thought I would hear by now."

"I know but Robar was really pleased to see the application. I don't think he would be if he intended to reject it."

"He doesn't have final say. The Captain's Council does."

"Really? I thought his word carried more weight than that."

"No, I checked. There's a meeting of the captains and they discuss each application. If someone can speak for the applicant, they might call them for an interview but that hasn't happened yet." He looked almost panicky.

"Relax," David said. "How many of those captains shop at York's?"

His brother hesitated.

"And how many have you waited on this summer? I know you work in the store."

His brother looked thoughtful.

"It may be enough have met you and judged you that you won't *need* an interview," Davyd finished. "It's possible."

"Yes, but I can't see them doing it and two of my friends have been called for interviews already."

"Did they make it?"

"Baron thinks he did but Wes is sure he blew it. He hasn't heard for sure but at least he got an interview."

"Don't worry so much," Davyd admonished. "If you don't get at least an interview, I'm sure Mother Rayna will raise prices on them."

Donal looked surprised then grinned. "Yeah, she would."

Davyd turned the subject to other members of the family then to the swords they had to trade. Content that Donal knew he approved of his decision to join the Guard, he hoped he *would* get accepted. He could tell his brother wanted it badly and he didn't want to see him disappointed. Hopefully there will be enough openings in the ranks this year for his brother to qualify.

Later he wondered what he could do to ease the blow if Donal wasn't chosen. Maybe a year as his trading partner would help until he could apply for the Guard again. With that thought, he went to sleep.

SYNDA crept out of her bed and back to the covered painting with anticipation. She had it. She knew she had it.

Lighting the lamps, she looked over the sketch of Lord Edan with a critical eye then at the portrait of Davyd. Yes, she had it.

Slowly she corrected the front of Davyd's surcoat, twice consulting the finer detail in a corner of the sketch she'd done. Having only seen Davyd in that surcoat twice, she'd mistakenly given him buttons instead of points.

Tomorrow she'd give Edan his completed sketch but tonight she was using it. He was such a nice man. She'd agreed to have him for tea tomorrow. Wondering how it would feel to be held by him, her thoughts quickly returned to Davyd. Where was he now? What was he doing?

IT HAPPENED. Davyd looked down at the red scroll in his hand and knew it was Synda's. He tried to throw it away but his family was watching. Wydon wasn't smiling. Monar and his wife were and he thought that was strange. Would they close the store in Sefron for this?

His father had a stern expression and shook his head when he tried to throw it away. He couldn't do it.

Turning to face the woman in red, he handed the scroll back to her and then Synda was in his arms and his family was gone. She kissed him and he held her close, tasting her sweet delight. He moaned when he moved over her bare breasts and filled her with his seed.

Suddenly it was over. He was alone and she was gone. Knowing he would never see her again, he cried her name.

"Davyd, wake up!" Donal shook him and just like that he was awake and back in the room they shared. His brother stared at him, his concerned face half-lit by the night candle. "You were having a nightmare."

Davyd blinked then sat up in bed to scrub his face with his hands. It was a dream, nothing more than a dream. He tried to tell himself that but it was no use. He knew the rules of the manhunt.

"You were calling *her* name. Were you back on the ship?"

"No." He tried to ignore the warmth in his loins. "No, it wasn't there."

"I didn't know you had nightmares," Donal said, seeming more mature than his fourteen years. "You should talk to Mother about them."

"No!" Davyd exploded and saw his brother's shock. "Donal, I can't. She's not to know about this."

"Why? It could be a foreseeing."

"It's *not* a foreseeing," Davyd ground out. "I just made a stupid promise and she's making me suffer for it." Even when he said the words he knew it wasn't true. No, he'd been trying to tell himself for days that he could have her in the hunt and that would be it but he couldn't do it. If he ever shared her bed, he'd want to stay there.

"What promise? Did you break it?"

"No, not yet." Davyd rubbed his hands through his hair. "But I can't tell you about it—not until Synda leaves Gardon."

Donal looked ready to argue but stopped. "Well, I don't think you should escort her back. Maybe Father will."

Gods, he hadn't thought of that. It would be natural for her to ask for him and he couldn't do it. Whether or not she hunted him, he knew he didn't dare escort her. She would tempt him. And if she hunted someone else—he couldn't bear to think of her with another man.

"Davyd? Do you love her?"

"Yes," he snarled and it felt like a release to finally admit it. "I was stupid and fell in love with her." He looked at his little brother. "Don't *ever* fall in love with someone you can't have!"

"I won't," Donal promised, his face grim. "But what are you doing to do?"

"Not a damned thing," Davyd answered. "I won't see her again if I can help it."

He felt defeated and anguished at the idea. "And Father suggested I get a wife." He heard his brother gasp. "I pity any woman who would take me now."

Rolling over in his bed, he turned his face to the wall and hoped his brother would leave him alone.

He wanted her. Galton help him, he wanted her.

Chapter 20 - Choice

14 Hoth 850

SYNDA listened to the pouring rain outside and tried to concentrate on her painting. They'd lit every lamp in her quarters and even asked for more to dispel the day's gloom so she could get the proper light on Lyda.

Lyda seemed out of sorts too. She dutifully maintained her pose but she wasn't talkative today. Synda was glad she was nearly done with her face because she wouldn't smile. Instead she seemed tight as a bow and just as depressed by the rain as she was.

"Is Valdyn due back soon?" Synda asked as she put another stroke of blue paint on her dress. "It's not very long until the Harvest Court."

"Yes," Lyda said and shot a glance toward the window, "but it might not be for a week or so. In any case, he'd find shelter in this storm."

"It must be hard to wait for a man to come home," Synda commented. "I'm glad I won't have to."

"You should be glad to have one coming home," Lyda snapped. "I don't see why you want to hunt at all."

Synda stared at her in shock, stunned by her sudden criticism.

"Or maybe you think you can use Edan instead of Davyd. You should leave *him* alone."

"Why?" Synda asked. "He seems nice enough."

"Because you don't love him. And he's looking for a wife who will stay here. His career is here."

"I don't want him for a husband." Synda's hand trembled and she hurriedly put down the brush. "I only want a child."

"And I thought you loved Davyd." Lyda threw up her hands before striding over to whip the cover off the portrait. She even turned the easel toward her. "I thought that was why you painted him. It looked like you loved him."

Synda stared at the painting and her heart pounded as she saw him looking back at her, that smile on his lips. "I do." Miserably she turned back to her paints but Lyda wasn't done.

"Then why encourage Edan?" Lyda demanded. "If Davyd is the one you want, you should be after him. You should marry him."

"I can't. Justus made me promise. I have to look at others."

"Justus has no business denying a choice," Lyda snapped. "And he can't make you delay. Who knows how long you'll be fertile? When were your cycles?"

"Ten days ago," Synda answered, her heart sinking as she realized she'd have to wait another month if she waited at all. "I have another week before…"

"Before you're on the wrong side of your cycle? No, you don't. You have six days."

"Before I can go back to the Temple. I'll hunt next month."

"*If* you're fertile next month." Lyda was implacable.

"Stop it!" Synda clapped her hands over her ears. "I will be. Mother was fertile eight years. I can…" She started to cry.

Lyda abruptly stopped taunting her and tried to hold her but Synda brushed her away.

"Synda, please don't cry." Lyda begged then stopped as Lady Alva burst into the room. Behind her was Edan.

"What's this?" Alva demanded and Synda cried even harder. "Synda, what?"

"I," She gasped for air. "Auntie, I—I'm fertile now. I want to… hunt."

"Hush, child." Alva gathered her into her arms.

Edan was staring at the painting then at her. Before she could gather her wits, the Sunlord abruptly left.

"Edan, wait!" Lyda caught up with him. "I'm sorry. You shouldn't have seen that."

"Seen what?" Edan turned on her. "That she likes Davyd Yorkson enough to *paint* him? Oh, I recognized him," he spoke quickly, his words bitter. "And I should have known she was a hunter."

"You didn't? She didn't mean to deceive you. I know she didn't."

"It's no matter." Edan's jaw was set and his eyes cold. "I knew last night she'd go back to Datyl. She'll take no child of mine with her."

Roughly opening the door, he left her standing there. Lyda didn't know what to do. She'd only thought to provoke Synda into admitting she loved Davyd. Thinking she might be liking Edan too, she didn't want her to hunt him. No, Synda should follow her heart like she did. She should *marry* Davyd and forget this hunt.

She could still hear her crying. Wishing she hadn't started it, Lyda went back into the bedroom and looked miserably at the portrait of Davyd. It was so well done. It made her own portrait look second rate but she didn't mind. Synda loved him. She couldn't have put so much into the painting if there wasn't anything to give.

"You." Alva looked accusingly at her. "Did you know she was worried about her cycles?"

"Not until today," Lyda said. "I'm sorry. I provoked this."

"Sorry isn't enough," Alva snapped. "Here I was trying to get her to choose someone else and..." She stared at the painting, her jaw set. "If I'd known that guardsman was in her heart—"

"Davyd is not *just* a guardsman." Lyda rose to his defense. "He's from one of the finest families in Gardon! His father backed the queen *first* when she took power and he has the King's Star. And his mother—Lady Nan *is* Sunborn. If you opened your eyes wider, you would see that Davyd is as noble as any man at this court!"

Seeing she'd stunned her into silence, Lyda turned and walked out, her anger still boiling as she thought of how that *woman* had summarily dismissed Davyd as being *just* a guardsman and not suitable for her little girl.

They were both fools. She wished Valdyn were here.

FOUR riders and their pack horses waded through the rising wet to the gates of Gardon, only stopping once to identify themselves to the soaked guardsmen at the west gate. They walked their horses through wet streets with heads bowed to keep the worst of the rain off their faces and trusted the soaked horses not to run into the few pedestrians still out in the weather.

Davyd held his stallion down to a walk and tried to ignore the smell of wet horsehide. It was miserable riding in the rain. If their trading hadn't been done and Donal anxious to get back, he would have sat out the storm in Garwys.

He needn't travel again. The Harvest Festival was just a week away and he knew he had no time to go elsewhere to trade. No, he would have to stay now until the family meeting was done. Maybe he could go to Sefron with Adlar and Monar and put together a caravan there.

He hated rain.

Glad to see his father's store, he rode past the open front and yelled inside for someone to open the gates. His youngest brother yelled back.

Turning his horse back to the yard, he got there just as the gates were unbolted by Aldo but his twin was there too. Mala grinned up at him as he rode his horse in, rain dripping off the end of her nose.

"Get inside, younglings," Davyd gruffly ordered. "Nan will warm your hides if she finds you out here without cloaks." He gave Mala a warm hug, realizing he'd barely talked to his third sister this trip. She smiled unrepentantly before he shoved her toward the kitchen door. Her brother was less reluctant but he knew he'd be put to work tending the horses if he stayed.

"Let's get them under shelter," Davyd told his men. Putting geldings and his stallion in two stalls and the two mares together, they managed to make four stalls do for all six.

Donal pitched hay and grained them while Davyd helped a guard strip harness off and dry the horses. The other guard dried the harness as quickly as it came off and stacked it on racks for cleaning. They were done in record time and left the horses comfortably settled.

Hauling one of the heavy packs in through the kitchen, Davyd got the expected yell from the cook as she saw him tracking in water. Davyd grinned and tried to hug her but Vita ducked away with a shriek and a laugh from his wet arms. Listening to her scold, he grinned and took his pack into the dining room. The others were already waiting on the roughest of the tables.

"What did you bring?" Mother Rayna asked, her brown eyes assessing the packs. "Tools?"

"Yes." Davyd shed his wet cloak, handing it to Mala. "I traded four of the swords for eight ax-heads, five spear heads, and two dozen arrowheads."

"And the rest? No, wait a moment. Donal." She turned to his brother with a frown. "There was a messenger for you. You're to see York about it."

His brother froze, hope lighting his face. "Where is he?"

"He went to the Tax Hall. You might be able to catch him there."

"Great!" Donal grabbed his sodden cloak back from Mala and went rushing through the store.

"Don't run through the store," Rayna shouted then turned back to Davyd with a puzzled frown. "What did you do to him?"

"Me?" Davyd struggled not to grin. "He just likes rain."

Rayna noticed her daughter. "Mala, get that cloak hung up. There's no sense in making work for someone with those drips."

"Yes Mother."

"And get upstairs and get yourself dry. You should be in the store."

"Yes Mother," Mala responded, but the grin she gave Davyd wasn't the least bit repentant.

He knew it was close to the Sunset Song. If she dallied even a little bit, she'd miss the closing of the store.

"Mother, are there many customers? These can wait and I'll help."

"On a day like this?" Rayna looked at him like he was daft. "We'll be lucky to make one more sale before sunset. I didn't even expect you back until tomorrow."

"We were done and we got good prices for dealing in the rain."

"And you'll probably catch cold," Rayna scolded. "I wish Nan could see you. Go upstairs and get changed. You can make your report later. I want to hear how Donal did too."

Davyd obeyed, thankful she hadn't been more curious as to why Donal ran. Hoping it was the interview, he climbed up to the second floor and changed in the room he shared with Wydon. Since they were rarely both here sharing a room was as practical for them as Adlar sharing a room with Monar. Only Donal and Aldo seemed cramped for space.

If Donal and Adlar both left, it would leave the rooms pretty empty. Thinking of that, he looked around the room he shared. It was big enough. There were two beds, a desk, a table, a warming stove for cold nights, and enough shelves to stash the things they owned. They tended to share clothes as most brothers did so the ones hanging on the hooks and filling the trunks were mostly his mixed in with a few of Wydon's.

He tried to imagine what it would be like to have a room of his own and couldn't. Having grown up in this room with his brother, he was loath to mess with the few belongings Wydon kept here. It just wasn't done.

Thinking how Glynda might take over one of their rooms, he wondered if it might be better. Surely he and Monar and Wydon could share. Maybe even Donal would do that. If he were accepted into the Guard, he'd be in their barracks for at least three years.

Glynda might like being on the second floor instead of the third where the girls had their rooms. He could bring it up at the family meeting. He used that to banish his worries about Synda and what she would do.

JUSTUS QUIETLY closed the door of Synda's room and joined the others who waited by the fireplace. Stretching his hands out to the warm flames, he regarded Lady Alva and the two who waited with her.

"Well, Justus, are you going to keep her in suspense?" the third lady demanded and he raised an eyebrow to his queen.

"She knows the answer," Justus said. "Lady Synda will come to the Temple tomorrow and prepare."

Alva looked away. Of course she knew Synda's heart was set.

"Is her fertility likely to end?" Fara asked. "I understood from Lyda that she fears that."

"No. No, I did a deep scan and there's no sign it will happen so soon. She's been fertile for less than half a year. There is just simply no point in waiting for her to change her mind."

"I don't think my son will agree to a manhunt," the queen's companion said. "He's not York and I doubt he'll give a child he can't raise. This would be his first born too."

"That's my opinion too," Justus said. "And I would prefer that they marry. I know he cares for her and she is definitely bound to him. I doubt she'll willingly have a child by another man."

"That isn't something I care to think about." The queen motioned to the two portraits which were now on display. The one of Lyda was far better than she hoped but even her untrained eyes could see that Davyd's, while still incomplete, surpassed it. "She has too much talent not to pass it on to her children."

"That's what her mother was told." Alva spoke up. "And she agreed and bore her when she didn't want a child at all. I know she was glad to leave her raising to tutors and teachers. When I met her, Synda was a very lonely girl."

"All the more reason she shouldn't hunt," Justus said. "She needs someone to provide the home she never had—a home with family."

He turned to the queen. "I've no wish to see her mother's mistakes repeated by her. A flower must have roots to grow."

"Then we need to sow the seeds deep but not too deep." Fara smiled at the analogy then turned to her companion. "Nan, tell us what you think Davyd will do. I know what York would say but I don't know your son. How can we get these two together?"

Nan thought, a tiny frown line appearing between her eyes, then gradually told them about her son.

YORK STARED out into the black night, seeing the water on the streets had risen in the last hour and the gutters were no longer so quick in taking it away. The bricks of the pavement shone black in the street lights and the few people who walked the streets were mostly in the uniforms of the guard.

He leaned against the door jamb and waited, worried for his wife. Even though a guardsman had brought word she would be late, he worried about her and the queen she served. It was unlike Fara to hold her so late and he wondered what had happened.

The supper hour was long past and he'd sent his younger children upstairs. Glynda was waiting too, having sent her daughter up with Mala.

"Is she coming?"

Davyd was at his elbow and he shifted so his son could join him in the doorway.

"What could be keeping her?"

"Crown business," York gruffly answered. "She won't be long."

His son looked skeptical but so was he.

"Well, I wish she'd get here. It's too wet tonight."

"The queen may keep her overnight. She's done it before when the weather was like this."

"But they sent a guardsman. At least she won't come home without an escort."

"No, she won't," York confirmed. "They take good care of her."

They waited in companionable silence and watched the rain. It still fell in a steady stream and pocked the puddles they could see by street light.

"Father? Was the news what Donal wanted?"

"The interview?" York looked over his shoulder to see if anyone was near. "Yes. He goes tomorrow morning. I was going to ask them to delay it a day but you got back. Now there's no need."

"Good. I know he wants it."

"Yes, he does," York replied. "And I'm sure he'll get it. Except for his age, they can find no fault with him."

"He'll be fifteen though. That's what the law requires."

"Barely fifteen," York grumbled. "But that can't be helped. Your mother would bear an autumn child."

Davyd grinned, remembering that. It was true that Donal and Byka were the only children born in the fall. The rest of them were born between spring and midsummer which was the best time for children to be born. Privately he thought Byka was a surprise but the six-year-old was still much loved by the family. Until Glynda's girl came she was the undisputed pet.

"Is that why Bryndal is only three months older?" He thought of his second sister, the quiet one. He rarely thought about their birthdays. He knew his mothers had traded children when Donal was a couple of weeks old but the babies had undone that when they started walking. It was a joke in the family that Donal always knew his own mother, Bryndal knew hers, but Aldo got confused and insisted on following his father instead.

"Yes. They were both pregnant for half a year. I'm surprised you don't remember all the complaining that went on. You were six when Donal was born."

"Complaining? Like Glynda did?"

"Worse. Two of them complaining and three boys and a girl who would hide to get away from it."

"Sorry, Father," Davyd belatedly apologized. "I really don't remember it."

"Well, they never did it again. One breeding woman is hard to handle, son, but two makes you want to hit the road. Remember that."

"Yes sir." Davyd thought his chances of doing that with Synda were small. Depressed by the idea, he started to tell his father what he had decided but York straightened and looked down the street.

"There's your mother." Reaching behind him, he brought out the lantern and went to meet the guardsmen escorting his wife home.

Nan was warmly wrapped in her cloak and had clogs on her shoes to keep them above the puddles. The four guardsmen weren't so well garbed. They wore boots and short cloaks they could doff in a hurry to defend their charge. York was glad to see her so well protected as he bade the guardsmen good night at his door.

"It's late," York told his wife as he helped her up the two short steps. "I thought she might keep you all night."

"No, I wanted to come home," Nan replied and let him unfasten her cloak and lift it from her shoulders, only briefing touching his warm hands with her colder ones. "I don't like staying when I know you worry."

He gave her a fond smile. "Davyd and Donal are back." He hung up her cloak to dry then secured the door for the night.

"Good!" She turned to their son. "Good trading?"

"A small profit. No loss at least," Davyd said.

"He did well and Rayna is pleased," York said. "I'm sure she'll tell you about it."

"Yes, she will," Nan said. "And she's still up?"

"Yes."

Soon they were settled in the dining hall with mugs of mulled wine. Rayna had Davyd repeat his report and show off some of the tools. It was only when that was done that York asked his wife why she was delayed.

"It was just some foolishness between Lady Lyda and the artist. Since Lyda was upset, Fara had to get involved and…" She gave a small shrug. "It's over now. Synda went back to the Temple tonight."

"Is she all right?" Davyd asked.

"Synda? Of course, Justus is tending her."

"Why would Justus tend a minor scrap?" York frowned.

"Oh, it wasn't *that* minor. Lyda took exception to Synda sketching Lord Edan. It seems she thought Synda was flirting with him. Since Lyda was her friend, it was upsetting for Synda. She hasn't had many friends in her life."

York glanced at his son and saw he was grimly listening to her tale. Thinking his son cared too much, he wished he could spare him this.

"I think Lord Edan would be a good match for her," Rayna said. "I mean, didn't she come to Gardon to look for a husband? Edan is single and a companion to Prince Valdyn. She could hardly do worse."

"No, she came for a manhunt," Nan corrected. "That's why she was at court. Justus wanted her to meet the best men so she could make her choice."

Both Rayna and Glynda looked shocked but it was his son York wanted to keep from hearing more. One look at his grim features told him he must get him away.

"Davyd, take those tools to the cellars," he spoke quietly but it was a command. "There's no need to leave them on the table all night."

"Yes sir." Davyd promptly answered him and gathered half the tools up. When he was gone, York turned to his wives.

"I think a manhunt is a poor topic this time of night. Let's finish our wine and go to bed."

"Yes York." Nan took his suggestion with a meekness he mistrusted.

Thinking the subject closed, he relaxed when Glynda announced she was done. Giving him a peck on the cheek, his oldest daughter headed off to bed.

Sorting the tools Davyd had left, he paid little attention to his son's return until Nan left off speaking to Rayna about household matters and raised her voice.

"I did see some of Synda's work today," she said just as Davyd passed her. "The portrait of Lyda is wonderful. It looks so alive even though it isn't quite done. And she painted another of Davyd which is truly a masterpiece."

Both York and Rayna turned to their son.

"She sketched me a lot aboard ship," Davyd explained, not looking at them. "I let her because it kept her from bothering the crew."

"Sensible," York said but his wife wasn't done.

"She has a good memory," Nan said. "She hasn't seen you at all since you left her at the Temple but she has had Lyda sitting for her every day for weeks."

"Nan, it's bedtime." York broke in, irritated by her insensible gossip. "If you would rather stay down here and talk about a painting, you're welcome to it, but Davyd and I have work in the morning."

She tried to catch his eye but he deliberately ignored the message there. For the first time in years he left his wives sitting at the table.

She couldn't know about the promise. She wasn't that cruel.

Chapter 21 - Edan

15 Hoth 850

MIDMORNING at the Inn of the Flowing Cup was a good time. Barely four blocks from the Citadel and two blocks from York's, the Inn was always busy. At mealtimes there were guardsmen and families here but at midmorning it was mostly visited by traders looking for a deal and people willing to sell.

York preferred to do his trading here where the food was good and the drink plentiful. When he wasn't at home, his children knew to check here first. Today Davyd had come with him to listen for his own opportunities. He needed to put together another caravan and this was the place to find product.

Hearing someone mention his father's name, Davyd lowered his mug and rose just as one of his father's friends reached their table.

"York," the holder said, pumping his father's hand with a glad smile. "It's been long."

"That it has, Jylad," his father answered with a smile of his own. "I thought you'd gone back to Sefron."

"No, not there." The holder's smile slipped. "I took up a hold in the Protectrate. I was just bringing my stock for the auction."

"Stock? I can't see you farming."

"Not cattle," the holder replied. "No, I breed horses. I've got five prime two-year-olds to sell for the track and a few more besides. Which son is this?" he abruptly asked. "Not Monar."

"No, this is Davyd. My third son by Nan," York answered. "Davyd, Jylad was a top trainer at Sefron's track. He moved his family here—was it four years ago?"

"Six, but I didn't find you for a couple of years."

"Yes, that was it. Join us." York motioned to one of the chairs.

The Flowing Cup was larger than most inns with nearly forty tables set up between three rooms and a half dozen apprentices helping the innkeeper and his three daughters. As usual one spotted the new arrival at their table and brought a fresh mug which the holder paid for with a couple of coppers.

"Are you interested in horses this year?" the holder asked as he helped himself to the teapot. "I've got a yearling stallion I'm sure you'd like. He comes from the line of Galewind too."

"He sounds good, but no. I rarely have time for yearlings anymore."

"I bet." The holder eyed Davyd. "And you've got the look of a man who has a good horse."

"I do," Davyd said. "And I have a couple of good mares to breed him to."

"Ah, then business is done." The holder didn't seem disappointed. "How's the family, York? Added more girls?"

"One," his father said. "A granddaughter. She's Glynda's girl."

"Congratulations! How old?"

"She's two and Monar's boy is four months old."

The holder hesitated then grinned. "It never stops does it? Just when the wife — *wives* — quit, the kids start. I bet this one even has plans along that line." He motioned to Davyd.

"Not yet," Davyd said. "I'll wait for a wedding."

"Good! Too many men have the child first and then the wedding. Bad deal all the way around."

"And how is your family?" York interjected. "All well?"

"Most of them," the holder reported, his smile fading. "I lost my youngest girl but she's at peace. My two oldest boys are wed now — the third is who I've come to see."

"Which one is that?"

"Jydar," the holder supplied. "He's starting his third year in the Bowmen. We usually spend the harvest together."

"Good custom. My family is also gathering for it. Monar has a store in Sefron now and I'm sending one of Rayna's boys to help him out." He paused, then bent a little closer. "And Donal is applying for the guard."

"Donal?" The holder hesitated, then smiled. "Gods, is he that old already?"

"Barely. He turns fifteen in two days."

Davyd heard that with dismay. "I haven't found a gift."

"Well, you'd best start looking," York told him. "But make it something useful. There's not much room in the barracks."

"No horses," the holder said. "He'll rarely get to ride in the guard. That's why Jydar wanted the Bowmen. He hates to walk."

"I wish I'd known he was there. Tell him to come by York's and I'll have him to dinner."

"I'll do that," the holder said. "If he stays in the city long enough. They're sending them out to the Protectrate to train."

"I heard. It sounds like they'll be more ready to take the field. It's a good move."

"That's what I thought," Jylad said. "Well, I must be off. Good trading, York." With that he took his cup and rose, moving to another table not far away where he knew someone else.

"He breeds good horses," York commented. "But I think we'd do better to buy ones already old enough to work."

"I think so." Davyd watched the man work the room and thought of the brown mare. He was sorely tempted to sell her and rid himself of the last reminder of Synda. He didn't need to breed her to his stallion.

"Don't go buying the yearling," his father cautioned. "Any colt of Galewind's line that hasn't been cut must go for at least a hundred solaris. It's not a good deal unless you mean to race him."

"I wasn't thinking of that. I was thinking of selling that brown mare. She's a sweet-moving horse and well-trained but I really don't need her."

"True," his father agreed, "but let me look at her first. She may do for one of your sisters."

"Yes sir." Davyd wanted to just sell her and be done with it but she was a good horse.

"Let's get back. It's nearly the noon hour and they'll need the tables."

Davyd finished his tea and started to follow his father then froze.

Lord Edan! Staring at the Sunlord just inside the door, he remembered his mother's comments then moved stiffly after his father. If he didn't see him, it would be best. He doubted he could be civil to the man who might win Synda.

The Sunlord didn't notice him. Busy talking to a guard captain Davyd faintly recognized, Edan didn't even glance his way. It was only when he was halfway down the block that Davyd was relaxed enough to place the face of the captain.

"*Captain* Mowyt? When did *he* make captain?"

"Robar's brother?" York paused. "I don't know—maybe at Midsummer. He's not been one long. He is on the Captains' Council though. If he's here, your brother must be done with his interview."

With those words they hurried home and walked straight into a battlefield.

"STOP FOOLING with my displays" Glynda shouted at Adlar.

Davyd looked at the mess on the floor in disbelief as his sister angrily toppled a pan display next to her own.

"And that's for yours," she screamed and grabbed a pan, flourishing it at her brother.

"*What's this?*" York snapped, eyes blazing, as he wrenched the pan out of her upraised hand and spun her around. "Glynda, get out of this store."

She moved so fast Davyd barely saw her go. He couldn't blame her as his father turned on the stunned Adlar.

"You too. Get to your room and stay there." The words were barely out of his mouth before Adlar disappeared.

"I'll take care of it," Davyd promptly volunteered as his father glared at the mess on the floor. "Father, let me."

Without waiting for an answer, he set the cabinet upright and started to reload the shelves.

From somewhere Byka appeared then Bryndal and Mala were there. Ten-year-old Mala smoothly took over waiting on the lone customer as her brother and sisters straightened the displays.

York hesitated then walked on into the house, his face promising more punishment for the children who broke one of Rayna's rules. There would be no fighting in the store.

"What happened," Bryndal asked as she sorted the pans by size and shape. "How did these get on the floor?"

"You didn't hear?" Davyd was gruff. "Glynda didn't like Adlar's display."

"*His* display?" Bryndal nearly dropped a pan. "This wasn't *his* display. Mother Rayna set it up." She stopped and her eyes got wide. "Oh, when she hears..."

"Leave it be," Davyd advised her. "If she's lucky, Father will settle it instead of Rayna. Glynda is going to get it though."

"She should," six-year-old Byka declared. "Adlar didn't do anything. She just dumped it on the floor when she saw Father coming."

"Don't be silly, Byka," Bryndal snapped. "Adlar had to do something. You just missed it."

"Did not. He didn't do nothing."

Davyd just shrugged it off, knowing how Byka would defend Adlar. Just as Aldo tended to tag after him and Father, Byka was always around her brother. There had to be a reason Glynda flew into a rage. She just didn't do that. Not Glynda.

YORK STALKED down into the cellars, not daring to follow his children upstairs yet. Knowing he needed to get his temper under control, he started stacking and restacking crates. It worked. Slowly he quit cursing and started noting what the goods were and how much of each.

Gods, what had gotten into Glynda? She knew the rules and even enforced them with the younger children. Remembering his decision to send Adlar away instead of her, he cursed again. Did she want to go?

Thinking she might feel overlooked, he could feel some empathy for her. She was past twenty and ready for a store of her own.

It still didn't excuse what he saw. Remembering the customer, he knew word of the fight would be spreading on the streets already. The best he could hope for was a flock of suitors for his suddenly wayward daughter—suitors drawn by her dowry and name.

He shuddered, remembering what it was like when Rayna's dowry became known. She'd been his ward then and he had no thought of marrying her even when he was constantly tripping over the suitors who filled the store.

He'd finally told her to make her choice after a month of chaos, not dreaming she'd choose him. Then Nan had talked him into it, joining forces with Rayna. It was the first time the two ever teamed against him and he'd been defenseless—not that he regretted it now. No, once he began treating Rayna as a wife and quit thinking of her as a daughter, it had turned out all right. He had six children, including all his daughters, to show for that marriage.

He sat on a barrel of pickles and thought about his wives. They were so different. Nan was tall, slender, and looked like a full-blood Sunborn even though she was just a quarter blood. She also carried herself like one and he'd rarely seen her upset or crying. It was no wonder everyone instinctively said "Lady Nan" instead of the more appropriate "Mistress Nan." She was the cornerstone of their marriage and the one who made most of the household decisions.

Rayna was the other side. He'd known her since she was twelve and never ceased to be amazed by her skill at selling and her knack for remembering people's names and what they last bought. She kept written records too, but it hardly seemed necessary with her around. She rarely forgot.

She was different from Nan in other ways. Where Nan was tall and slender, Rayna was short and soft, barely coming up to his shoulder. Purely of Kalryn stock, she had inherited her build from her parents—both merchants—and passed it on to the children she bore. Glynda was the tallest of her children followed by Bryndal. He feared Aldo would never grow tall or get the reach he needed to be a decent swordsman and he knew what would upset his youngest son terribly.

If he sent Adlar away, Aldo would be the only boy living in the house. Thinking of that, he wondered if he *should* send him for fostering elsewhere. Adlar hadn't gone for more than a season. The boy knew he was a merchant and had no interest in swords. Would the same thing happen with Aldo? He would be better off.

Another thing for the family meeting. He sighed and rubbed the bridge of his nose. It seemed everything was happening at once. He had to think what to do with Glynda then there was Davyd. And Donal. He still hadn't told Rayna he was going into the Guard.

Wishing he could just leave, he steeled himself to face the family. First, he wanted to talk to Donal. Glynda could wait. She would wait. Maybe he would let Rayna deal with her. Glynda broke her rule in her store. Yes, let Rayna deal with her daughter.

With that resolved, he went back up the stairs to find Donal hovering around the door. One of the household guards was also waiting and he knew his son had kept him from being interrupted in his rage—just like his mother did.

"Thank you," he said to the guardsman and the man nodded, then left without a word. He hadn't really been needed but York knew Nan often asked one to keep her company in case the children needed her. No doubt Donal had simply followed her example.

"You kept your head," he said to his son. "Thanks."

"It was nothing," his son said, looking embarrassed. "I just knew you wanted to be alone."

"I'm glad anyway. Get us two cups of wine and come downstairs." With that, he headed back down.

When had his sons started taking care of him? He tried to think but it was a jumble. He wasn't that old—only fifty-eight—but Donal's thoughtfulness only served to emphasize what he'd known for a couple of years. His sons were doing what he could no longer do.

Davyd had wrestled the potted trees into the hand cart. He'd made an abortive move to help, but his son hadn't seen it. Thinking back he could see that Monar and Wydon—even Adlar—were doing the same. Only Aldo seemed unconcerned for him. He should have noticed it before.

"Father?"

"In here," he called back and his son came into the second cellar. His eyes went to the crates which were now neatly stacked against the walls. "I didn't drop any."

"No sir." Donal grinned and offered him one of the cups.

York took it then saw he'd left no place for Donal to sit. "Pull down a couple of crates and have a seat."

"Yes sir."

"How did the interview go?" York asked his son and knew the answer even before he spoke.

"Great! I think I gave good answers anyway. There weren't any I didn't know."

"Good. Then it just depends on how many slots they have this year."

"Yes sir. But Captain Mowyt said they were opening a new guardhouse in the thirty-second quad. They've got openings for forty boys because of it."

"Well, that's good news," York said. "It doesn't mean you'll be assigned over there though. No, they'll put veterans in the new quad and scatter the boys around in the units like they've done before."

"Yes sir, but we'll get on the streets faster."

"Don't count on it. The Guard puts you through three months of training before you join a unit. Even then you'll probably run errands for a while."

"I know."

"When will they send word?"

"They said all the boys will know this week," Donal quietly told him. "On my birthday."

York looked at him then decided to make light of it. "Well, you'll either have the best birthday of your life or the worst one. Let's hope Monar and Wydon are here by then."

"Yes sir." Donal sipped his wine.

"York?"

Surprised to hear his wife call him, York debated whether to answer but his son's expectant expression made it hard to refuse. He should get it over with.

"Down here, Nan. Is Rayna with you?" he asked as Nan brought another lantern into the room.

"Yes, we were shopping. No, she didn't come down with me. She's in the store. What are you doing down here?"

"Donal, ask Rayna to join us and give her another glass of wine. You tend the store."

"Yes sir." Handing his nearly full cup to his mother, he sped up the stairs.

"What is this about?" Nan looked at him.

"Just sit down and be quiet for a moment." Getting up, York took down two crates for his other wife. Determined to break the news on Donal, he saw no reason not to do it down here.

Rayna appeared looking a little surprised at the summons but took the seat he motioned her to without a word. He waited for her to drink some of her wine before he spoke.

"Donal interviewed for the Guard today and it looks like he might get in." As he expected Rayna looked stunned. Nan seemed less surprised but things rarely got past her.

"*If* he gets accepted this year, he has my blessing and will go. I'll take his place on the road if you think we need another trader."

"York, no," Nan protested. "Three is enough. We need you here."

"But..." Rayna sputtered and shot a glance at Nan. "York, we planned for him to take his turn. What if—what if Wydon gets married? That would take us to two."

"Then we back him up with Glynda just like we're giving Adlar to Monar. After today I wish Wydon would open his own store!" Neither of his wives looked surprised. "Is Wydon thinking about marriage? He hasn't said anything to me."

"Not that I know of," Rayna quickly replied. "He's just the next oldest."

"Well, I may ask him to open a store in Datyl anyway and send Glynda there. And when Bryndal starts throwing things in the store, we can send her too."

"Maybe she needs a husband," Nan quietly said. "Someone from Datyl might do nicely."

"I *know* she needs a husband," York retorted. "And after that little fit in the store, she might have them flocking here in droves. A customer saw the whole thing and I'm sure word will be around by nightfall that Glynda Nathan is ready to marry again."

"No." Rayna looked shocked, even guilty. "Goddess, I don't think she can hold them at bay."

"She won't have to." York brushed that away. "I'm not putting out the sign again. I had enough of that foolishness when you were ripe. And she will *not* work in the store until this blows over. Bryndal can work it. Better yet, I want Davyd out there. He doesn't have enough to occupy his mind right now."

"Can Adlar work too?" Nan asked. "Until he leaves that is."

"*If* he didn't start that argument I walked in on. If he did, I want him busy elsewhere too. And it's about time the younger children were given more work."

"Yes, my lord," Nan answered.

He looked at Rayna. "Rayna, I'll not debate Donal's choice. I *want* him in the Guard."

"Yes, my lord." She said it quietly and York knew she hadn't given in but neither had he. This was one time he must make her see that it wasn't just the business that counted. No, Donal was *his* son and he would see him follow his own path. He would serve the queen.

"I'm done," York said. "Rayna, you deal with your children. I don't even want to know how that argument started."

"Yes sir." She rose with her cup still in hand. "May they come to dinner?"

"Not tonight. I might say something I regret tonight."

"I'll see they eat in their rooms." Nan rose from her seat. "Are you coming up?"

"No, not yet. Send Aldo down with a writing pad. I'm going to finish the inventory of this cellar."

"And more lamps," Nan said. "You can barely read the boxes you stacked so neatly."

"And more lamps. I might as well get some work done."

He watched his wives depart then turned to his self-appointed task. If he worked hard enough, he might forget the problems that crowded in.

Chapter 22 - Preparation

15 Hoth 850

LIGHT SHONE through tall amber windows, casting bars of warm golden light on a stone staircase which led to only one place. Climbing three stories against the side of the Grand Temple, the staircase was straight and the walls barren of all but the gentle light. Those traveling this way left their cares down below in the unfiltered light of day so they could concentrate on what lay above.

Justus paused at the second level and eyed a door that was bolted today—a door that was the only concession to those too weak to make the full three floor climb to the true Temple. It was rarely used and since the Temple was reserved for Synda's preparation, it wouldn't be used today. No one would interrupt the soul searching the girl must do.

As he continued up the stairs, he mentally rehearsed the ritual questions he must ask and the others he meant to ask. Knowing the girl was making a mistake made it harder for him because he couldn't forbid her hunt. The law needed to be changed. Too many times the daughters of a manhunt chose to follow their mothers and thought a child could provide the love they needed from a husband and father.

He knew the roots of the manhunt. It was designed so a woman of Sunborn blood could find a father for her child who wasn't close kin. In those days she often married or was married to a man who was kin. Since she was unable to bear her husband's children, the manhunt was an acceptable solution.

It was also used by women who gave over their marriage right to the Temple. They were more discreet about the hunt, usually choosing young men studying in the Temple to father their children. They couldn't marry or even ask the fathers to acknowledge their children but they could pass on their genes to a new generation. The Temple, in response to the lack of fathers, assumed the role to raise them in a loving environment.

Wishing he could change the girl's mind, Justus ascended the last steps and stopped before the warning doors of the Temple.

"Here bring no metal for it is death." He read that warning aloud and obeyed, shedding his belt, his sandals, and even his outer robes to lay them neatly on the preparation table to one side of the door. Finally he stood in just an ankle-length white robe. It was straight cut and hung loosely on his shoulders, its stark whiteness in wonderful contrast to his ebony skin. Removing his smoothly polished signet last, he touched it to his lips before tucking it into his robe.

May Galton protect me. He invoked the Kalryn god without a qualm. Whether he was real or an invention of his ancestors didn't concern him. He needed his protection when he walked through the Temple's doors.

The doors were constructed of wood, even the hinges being of leather and wood so no metal was used. There were no door handles save for knotted ropes and he pulled one until the door was wide enough for him to enter. Touching the cool ceramic surface of the inside door, he pulled it shut then felt the ebb and flow of power that was the Temple of the Flame.

He glanced at the starry dome up above and the simple flame on the bare altar with dispassionate interest, knowing those to be just trappings like the pillows on the bare floor and the candelabras standing against the walls. If the Temple were an ordinary room, it would still hold the power he could feel on the edge of his consciousness — the power of the Flame.

As his eyes adjusted he could make out three figures in the dim light. The one lying prostrate before the altar was the girl who hunted and the other two were her guardians. Waiting until he could see which was Dava and which Karyn, he moved.

Not approaching the altar directly, Justus set his feet on a white pattern on the stone floor and followed it around the room in a complex pattern which cleared his mind and prepared him for the role he assumed. He could feel the residual power of other rituals in the room and tapped it as he passed the candelabras, sending Starfire from his fingers to the pure candles waiting there. When he was done the room dimly shone with the center candle of each set adding to the light of the stars. The warning tingle he'd felt was subdued now and the Temple was ready.

Standing before the altar, he looked at the waiting form of the girl with regret.

He must begin.

"Woman, why do you come to the Temple of the Flame?" he asked the ritual question and saw the girl stir.

"To seek a child." Her voice quavered but it was clear.

"To seek you must be fertile," he said. "Do you swear you are fertile and able to bear?"

"I swear I am fertile and able to bear," Synda replied.

He turned to the others. "Do the guardians confirm?"

"We do, master." The two answered in unison.

"Then rise Synda Verasdatter."

She was not made to rise on her own. Her guardians helped her to her knees before they sat on cushions behind her. Her eyes were like dark pools in her pale face and her hair was unbound. She looked frightened but determined to continue.

"You have been given this day to learn what a manhunt entails," Justus said. "And to think about the price of what you do. Have you thought?"

"Yes, master," Synda replied, her face as white as her robe in the dim light.

"And you still seek a child?"

"I do."

"Then I must repeat the warnings," Justus said. "You must go to the man you choose as a willing mate. There may be no maidenly resistance, no drawing back, once you take the scroll from his hands. You are his mate for a full three days and nights and he *will* plant his seed in you. Do you understand?"

"I do."

"You may not, under penalty of death, use Starfire against your mate." Justus began the second warning. "If he is rough, you may ask him to be gentle. If he hurts you, you may ask him to stop but you may not defend yourself with Starfire. There is no reprieve from this law. Do you understand?"

"I do." Synda's voice trembled.

Justus knew she would have to be prevented. She'd used Starfire before against men and, although that was justified, she might panic when the moment came and use it again. A suggestion planted deep in her mind and a dose of the right potions would keep her from using it at least in the initial mating.

"When the hunt is done, you must *walk away* from the man you hunted and never see him again except in public. You may never speak to him again without witnesses. You may never ask him to acknowledge the child you bear. If you do any of these things, you dishonor the hunt and may be banished to some place your mate does not go. Is that clear?"

"Yes." Her answer was so low he could barely hear it.

"Do you understand?" he asked again.

"Yes!"

He could hear her anguish.

Pitying her, he went on. "The Temple gives you this advice. Do not hunt a man you love but rather the man you admire. Don't pick the young for they think first of their own needs and don't pick the old because they may find their strength failing." He wondered with an irreverent thought if that included him. "Pick one of middle years who has learned patience and wisdom. Pick one who knows how to pleasure women."

He knew that advice fell on deaf ears. She would pick the man she loved and she would suffer for it. He could only hope Nan knew her son better than Synda did.

Finished with the formal ritual, he relaxed. "Synda, the first ritual is done. You can sit on the cushions." He sat cross-legged in front of her. Used to sitting on the cold stone floor of the Temple, he didn't use the cushions himself.

"Synda, you would be foolish to hunt a man you can marry," Justus said and saw her eyes widen. "The Temple has no objection to a union between you and Davyd Yorkson. Unless *you* have a reason you can't, you would be foolish to proceed with this."

"I can't," Synda weakly protested. "His life is here and I can't."

Justus knew what she couldn't say. Gardon wasn't her home. Torn adrift of the safety of Datyl, she was too insecure, too unprotected, to face life in the younger, more vibrant city. He frowned, knowing there was another choice, but he couldn't show it to her. No, he'd given his word to Lady Nan.

"I think you'll regret this hunt." Justus spoke softly and saw the dejection in her face. "You'll have a child by the man you want but you won't have the man and can never have him again. Is that really the price you want to pay to have this child?"

She didn't answer and he knew she loved him.

"You have two more days to stop this but after tonight you'll no longer be virgin. Do you understand why Dava must take your maiden blood?" He spoke frankly to ease her embarrassment. "It's done to spare you the pain of a first mating."

"I know." She was flushed. "I know it's done to brides too."

"Yes, but then your mother and his would witness. Tonight only the Temple will be there."

"My mother wouldn't care," Synda blurted out, the first admission she'd made of her mother's callousness to her.

"She should still be there." Wishing he could tell her mother what her hunt had cost her daughter, he went on. "And there's something I must ask you. Will you love this child if you get it? Or will you leave its raising to servants as your mother did to you?"

"I'll love it," she whispered. "I'll love it more dearly than my life."

His heart softened. Knowing the girl was seeking what she never had, he wondered again how a mother could let her daughter be so love-starved that she must have a child to find peace. At the same time she was so afraid of rejection that she couldn't accept the man she loved.

"I will not bar this hunt or force you to go to Sefron," Justus finally said. "But know this is the only hunt you may do in Gardon and the only time you may hunt a member of the house of York. If a child doesn't come of this, you may not do it again." He put the only stipulation he could on the hunt. "If you choose to hunt Davyd Yorkson, know it is the only time you may have him in this life."

He could see that upset her and it was good. Maybe, just maybe, she'd spare herself grief and Davyd too. He'd know tomorrow. Today he'd done all he could.

YORK LOOKED up from the dinner table, surprised to hear the door chime at this late hour. Looking to his sons, he waited to hear what word the night guard would bring.

"Are we missing anyone?" Donal asked. "Wydon?"

"Not at this hour," Davyd grimly told him. "Not unless it's bad."

York realized it could be the manhunt. He thought it might be when he saw a messenger from the Temple.

"Lord York?" The messenger came directly to him. "Lady Nan is needed at the Temple. I was sent to fetch her."

He hesitated then motioned to Donal to tell her. Both his wives had gone upstairs with the girls. They wouldn't be in bed at this hour though.

"Why mother?" Davyd asked the question he wanted to. "Surely someone in the Temple…"

"I don't know, my lord." The messenger was little more than a boy himself, his brow furrowed as he tried to answer. "Justus asked for her and I am here."

"Is the queen in the Temple?" York asked, his mouth dry. He could only think of one reason Nan would be summoned at such an hour and he didn't like it. Not Fara. Fara was far dearer to him than anyone save his wives ever guessed.

"I don't know." The messenger's eyes widened at the possibility. "There's been no word."

"Father, let me go to the Citadel," Davyd promptly offered. "If the queen is in the Temple, they'd know."

"Not if she took the Queen's Way. And they wouldn't let you past the gates at this hour. I've got Council right. I'll go." York quit speaking at his wife came down the stairs, still braiding her hair as she hurried.

"Let me." Intercepting her, he finished the braid and pinned it properly while his wife shot worried questions at the messenger.

"I'm going to the Citadel to check on Fara," York said. "If it's her…"

"It surely can't be her," Nan protested and saw the grave faces of her sons. "York, wait. I'll send word from the Temple when I know what this is about. They probably just need some herb only I know how to handle."

"Did they mention any herbs to you?" She shot at the messenger and the boy looked blank.

"Oh, pitfire," Nan declared. "Bryndal?" She called up the stairs.

"Yes Mother?"

"Stay up for two hours," Nan ordered. "If I must send for an herb, you know which is which."

"Yes Mother," Bryndal acknowledged, looking more mature than her fifteen years.

"York, don't worry. If it is the queen, I'll send for you. I know she would want me to." With those cryptic words, she followed the messenger to the door.

York followed, lifting his wife on to the extra horse the messenger brought with him. The horses were grey and painted with the sign of the Temple. They had no guards but anyone who stopped those horses on Temple business faced a curse and knew it. They were the only horses allowed to run on the streets of Gardon.

"Wait for word, love."

York nodded and watched until the horses turned a corner, then returned to his sons. His mind still on his wife and her errand, he barely noticed Rayna had come down stairs.

Setting a cup of wine in front of him, Rayna took the chair beside him. He clasped her hand, entwining her fingers in his to share his concern. She didn't smile but waited with him.

Davyd finished telling him some details he'd noticed that day but their minds weren't really on it. Even when Adlar repeated a joke he'd heard from a customer, the laughs were half-hearted. They sat and waited for news. Even Aldo waited at the table, half-forgotten and drowsy.

York waited. His hand was still holding Rayna's but he wasn't really comforted by the reassuring pressure of her fingers. He thought he should send Aldo to bed but he made no move to.

When the door chimed again, it came as a shock and a relief. Aldo started from his sleep and Davyd was on his feet before the echo died away, passing the slower guardsman.

It was the same messenger. The boy quickly strode into the room and went straight to him with a reassuring smile. "Lady Nan says to tell you it is *not* the queen but one of the ladies from Datyl. She'll remain at the Temple tonight."

York relaxed. Finally letting Rayna's hand go, he smiled at the messenger. "I thank you for the news. Adlar, get him a package of Starry Night."

He glanced at Davyd and knew what he wanted to ask. "Did Nan say which of the ladies from Datyl?"

"The young one," the messenger said. "She also said she would need no herbs and to tell Bryland, no, Bryndal she can go to bed."

"It mustn't be that serious then," York remarked, wondering why Nan was summoned to deal with this. "But I know my wife enjoys a night at the Temple now and then." He made light of it as Adlar returned.

"Thank you for returning so quickly," York said and handed the messenger the package. "Enjoy this small gift."

"Thank you sir." The messenger bowed, his smile wide. Starry Night was the most popular and pricey tea in Gardon. Sold exclusively at York's, it was a better gift than coin.

"Donal?" He motioned for him to show the messenger out but wasn't surprised when Davyd followed them.

"I'm off to bed," York announced. "Remember you work the store tomorrow and let your sisters sleep." It was close to the Harvest Festival and tomorrow was the Women's Day. Throughout the city men would be doing women's work and tending children so their wives and daughters might have a holiday.

"Yes Father," his sons replied and he motioned for Aldo to come with him. His youngest son made no protest and they parted company at the top of the stairs.

Rayna wouldn't be long. With Nan out of the house, she would want his company as much as he wanted hers. Nan had told him once that when he was away, his two wives slept together in his bed. It was on nights like these that he understood. Worried because Nan wasn't safely at home, he would hold the wife that was.

Why had the Temple summoned her?

Chapter 23 - Women's Day

16 Hoth 850

IT WAS STILL early when York began lifting the shutters down from the store windows. It was too early but he was impatient to see Nan and unable to dally over breakfast. His sons were cleaning the kitchen and he had opted to open the store.

Breakfast had been a simple affair. He'd made flatcakes spread with honey butter and added warmed up meat from the night before. Fruit they'd picked up at the market completed the meal. Without the women to help, he'd kept it simple.

Only Mala, Byka, and his little granddaughter had come downstairs to eat, the others having exercised their right to ignore the bells and sleep late on their holiday. He suspected Glynda was the most thankful of the lot because Donal had removed her daughter before she woke. Little Natra had a pair of lungs and tended to be very vocal in the mornings. Thankfully she rarely woke up fussy.

Taking down the last of the shutters and stowing them in the cabinets beneath the windows, he peered out into the street. Deserted. Well, it would fill soon enough.

Lastly he set about counting the coins in the cash box. There were only two solaris there. The rest were copper, sols, half-sols, and double sols. Rayna had taken out the writs last night and would deposit them later at the Tax Hall. They had accounts in banks too but she was paying off the tax on their business this month. So far it had been a good month and she was understandably proud of paying the taxes without going into the substantial savings of the store.

York was sometimes embarrassed when he thought of the money they'd accumulated. Having less than thirty solaris when he came to Gardon in Fara's employ, it wasn't uncommon for the store to make three times that in a week. He knew Davyd had cleared more than two hundred solaris from his one trip to Datyl. His son hadn't been paid for conveying the wine back but neither had York asked him to pay a quarter share into the business from all his ventures. No, the wine was why he was sent to Datyl. The rest of the commissions were his own. Since it had worked out well for his son, he didn't regret making that agreement before he left.

Taking the solaris out of the box, he stashed them in their usual hiding place and set the box in its place. He was ready for business.

"The kitchen is done and Cook checked it. She's satisfied." Davyd reported as he walked into the store.

"Good." York knew how possessive Vita was of her kitchen. Even a holiday wouldn't keep her away from it.

"Any sign of Mother?" Davyd took his own look down the street.

"Not one, but it's early yet."

"Not that early," Davyd replied. Right on the heels of his words the city bells started to ring the hour. Grinning at the timing, he opened the store's door. Across the street the baker opened his and gave him a cursory wave.

The city gates would be opening now and the first holders would stream into the city. Their women were more likely to ask for a holiday here than to rest in a bed at home. Since it was their day, those who lived close to Gardon got it.

"Let's finish the preparations," York said. "I want the bolts on that table. Those tools need to go over there." He pointed to a smaller table. "Let's pile the cloth up deep."

"Yes sir." Davyd knew the drill.

Every Women's Day they sold out of cloth. It was a good thing Monar was bringing more from Sefron. Other items they would see the last of were the ribbons, threads, and fine metal needles from Datyl. There were two spinning wheels set out too but those were priced high enough they may not sell.

When he was young, York never thought he'd be a trader, much less selling cloth and ribbons to women but now he simply regarded it as one of the facets of the trade. Since Rayna insisted they offer things for all members of a family, it drew business to them. Many holders came to York's first to get their major buying done then went on to other stores for things York's didn't carry. His prices tended to be higher in some cases but his goods were also the best quality. That and the convenience of finding tools and tea and cloth in one place brought people in.

The first customer arrived but Davyd was closer and waited on her with such attention the portly matron tittered and bought a whole bolt of cloth and spools of ribbons. York watched and noted Davyd had not forgotten how to sell. Even though she bought the whole bolt, he steered her to a color she wouldn't regret buying later.

Adlar joined them and took the next customer then Aldo appeared. Guessing Donal was watching his granddaughter, York set Aldo to watching for Nan and waited on a customer himself.

She arrived nearly an hour later and York almost cursed. The store was too busy for him to leave for long. He finished with his customer and asked Adlar to help her settle accounts then hurried after Nan. She was already on the stairs.

"Nan, is everything all right? Why did they keep you so long?"

"I'm sorry, love. I overslept this morning. Everything is fine now."

"And the lady from Datyl?"

"She's fine," Nan said. "It was nothing really. You'd better get back to the store."

Frustrated and unhappy with her answers, he knew she was right. This was one of their busiest days of the year.

"Later, husband." She stifled a yawn. "I'm still not slept out." She gave him a mischievous smile and headed up the stairs.

"Later, wife," York called after her, wondering about that self-satisfied smile and wishing he knew why. Better yet, he'd like to give her something to smile about. Not able to do that either, he turned back to the store.

Business was brisk until the Noon Song, then it dropped off and allowed them a breather. York sent Davyd to fix food and was pleased when Donal came back with a full plate.

"Everyone is up," Donal reported with a grin. "And Cook couldn't stay away from the kitchen when she saw Davyd in there. He dropped one of her pots."

"So she…?" York looked over the grilled steak, freshly cooked noodles and succulent vegetables with appreciation.

"Yes. She said she wasn't going to eat *his* cooking on her day off."

York gave thanks for Vita's stubbornness and enjoyed the meal. He wasn't even surprised when Aldo brought him a tart still warm from the oven. When Vita was defending her territory she often overdid it.

He sent the dishes back with Aldo and prepared to wait on a new customer but the few women he could see weren't crossing the street to York's. They were watching something.

York listened, hearing a rhythmic metallic beating and shouts of welcome. Stepping out of his store, he looked down the Es Way.

"It's Prince Valdyn!" Aldo shot back into the store and York knew he must have gone down the street to see.

York smiled, then waved to Donal to shut the half-doors and bar customers from the store. He didn't even stop Aldo from grabbing one of the few drums in the store's supply.

It was the prince. Fara's heir was riding slowly up the Es Way, his chestnut horse prancing and straining against his bit as the people banged pots and clapped around him. Valdyn looked embarrassed by the racket but kept a smile on his clean-shaven face as he led his men. He'd shed the close leather cap he usually wore and his honey-brown curls nearly matched the horse he rode.

Aldo picked up the rhythm on his drum when Valdyn came close to the store. Hearing a true drum, the prince's head turned sharply toward the sound and he waved at Aldo. His eyes met York's and the heir nodded before moving on.

York approved. If Valdyn had stopped at his store, it would have been wrong. With both his queen and his bride waiting, he should tend to duty first.

He'd known Valdyn since hours after his birth and had been an unofficial mentor to the prince both before and after his father died. Since he had no rank at court but was often there, the prince had sometimes come to him to discuss things he didn't want to share with his companions. It was an arrangement that pleased his parents and he'd been happy to do it.

He was pleased that Valdyn had turned out so well. The boy had to make a tough decision when his father died and he'd made it, giving his support to Fara in her bid to become queen in her own right. Too young to rule, the fifteen-year-old boy accepted the role of heir to his mother and not once since expressed any regret about not sitting on the throne.

He was twenty-six now and York wondered how old he would be when Fara did retire. She was nearly seventy. Yes, she was just past thirty-five when he first came into her employ. She was still fit though and Valdyn was needed in the field.

The prince would get a peaceful winter. Knowing the heir would be married soon, York sent a silent wish that his marriage to Lyda would be long and fruitful.

"Leave off," he told Aldo as the last of Valdyn's escort passed. Tousling his son's hair, he turned back to the store.

Busy with his customers he didn't see his other visitors arrive and his first clue that his older sons were there came when he looked up at the end of his deal and saw Monar waiting on a customer across the store. Making change for his client, he tried not to be irritated at missing their arrival. No doubt they'd gone straight into the yard with their goods and not passed the store.

Another customer claimed his attention. The next time he looked up Monar had a new one. With the number of customers today the girls had taken pity and returned to work. There were more than six men could handle and Aldo was still a boy.

"Husband," Rayna was suddenly at his side. "Let me finish this. I know Mistress Balda." She smiled at the matron who was looking over a bolt of cloth the wrong color for her. Since there were few bolts left, she was understandably dissatisfied.

With an excuse to her and a smile for his wife, York left the store. Gods he was tired. He paused at the dining hall and saw bolts and bolts of new cloth spilled onto two tables.

"Bryndal." He spied his short-haired daughter and pulled a bolt from the stack. "Take this one to Rayna. She has a customer."

"Yes Father." His fifteen-year-old daughter obeyed, leaving his granddaughter behind.

Natra crowed at seeing him and came running. Sweeping her up in his arms, York sat down at the table to give his granddaughter some attention.

"Here's tea, husband," Nan said, shifting some bolts so she could set it down. She gazed at him fondly. "I think you're going to be very glad when the Sunset Song rings out."

"Yes." York smiled then let his granddaughter go so he could drink his tea. "I'm not as young as I used to be."

"I know." Nan's voice was soft. She stepped behind him and started massaging his shoulders with her magic touch.

They were alone in the hall. Somehow his granddaughter had disappeared but York wasn't inclined to look for her. Feeling Nan's expert hands on his neck and shoulders, he relaxed. Closing his eyes, he relished the feel of her hands kneading his knotted muscles and felt them move over his shoulders to his neck. Her light fingers rested gently on his pulse then moved on. York knew that touch but didn't care. He was tired. If his healer-wife wanted to reassure herself, he would ignore it.

He wasn't as tired now and he was beginning to wish that he didn't have to go back to the store. Wishing he could disappear up the stairs and make like a man half his age, he caught his wife's erring hand and brought it to his lips.

Turning it over he nibbled the sensitive skin of her palm then quickly let it go as he realized they had company.

Dylla, Monar's wife, just smiled and set down a tray of light snacks beside his tea but York was embarrassed nonetheless. It was as bad as having one of his children see that little bit of love play and he couldn't wait for her to leave.

"I wish we could go upstairs," Nan whispered in his ear, a hint of laughter in her voice.

"You aren't the only one," York replied in a fierce whisper. "I missed you."

"I know." Nan kept her voice low. "I'm sorry I stayed at the Temple but it would have been really late coming home."

York wondered exactly what his wife did there but was reluctant to ask. Sometimes she would tell him but other times she kept quiet about her duties. When that was the case no amount of pressing would get her to tell what she did. He'd learned to wait until his wife offered details.

"Rayna kept me warm," York absently told his wife. He twisted to look at her with a twinkle in his eye. "But tonight I want *both* sides warm."

"You're an old stallion." Nan blushed as badly as one of his daughters. "But I'll be there."

They had no more time since several of the children seemed to converge on the dining hall at once. With a start York heard the last of the Sunset Song and knew the store was closing. He'd worked later than he thought.

"Let me help close." York patted her hand and left her with a smile on his lips. Life was good.

HOURS LATER he contentedly nursed a cup of tea and looked around the table at his six sons, the girls having retired upstairs after dinner to catch up on Dylla's news and admire her new son. Finally they had time to do more than share reports of how business was going.

Not that it went badly. The receipts for day totaled well over fifty solaris in writs and coin. Since the average day in the store brought in less than twenty, he was happy. All but two bolts of cloth from the previous stock were sold and Rayna planned to mark those down because of their pattern. If they still didn't sell, his daughters would make them into storage bags for other goods. Such things rarely went to waste.

"It's good to have everyone together this year," he finally commented with an eye on Donal and his three traveling sons. "I think it may be a while before we can do it again."

"Surely not, Father," Wydon said. "So long as Dylla's kin live in Sefron and…"

"We'll be further scattered next year," York abruptly told him. "And it isn't a good time to be away from the stores—not when the Women's Day comes around."

"That's true," Monar agreed, "but I can get away by promising the receipts of this one day to my journeyman and Dylla's brothers—once the cost of the goods comes out of course. They'll tend the whole store for a full month just for this one day."

"It would still be better to have our gathering day at another time," York said. "If the roads and seas were passable in winter, I'd prefer to do it then but high summer seems to be the best time. Planting is done then and the crops are still growing so money is short."

"But it's also the best time for trading," Wydon said. "I would hate to lose the best weather."

"I know," York replied. "In any case, I think it will get harder as the years go by to gather at all."

He glanced at Adlar and wished he could keep him at home but the decision was made. He only needed to tell Adlar. "Today I was glad to have all of you here to help out," he began, his eyes on each of them in turn. "But most days we don't need so many hands. I think it's time Monar chooses his second for the Sefron store."

"Now?" Monar looked dismayed. "How can I? The girls aren't here."

The three younger boys looked confused but Davyd and Wydon just grinned. Aldo was the first to take him seriously and rose from his chair.

"Father, I—" He took a step toward the stairs, then waited.

"There's no need to fetch them down. Although I'm sure Glynda will be glad to go if Adlar refuses to go to Sefron."

"Me?" Adlar caught that last part. "I'm going?" His voice cracked and he looked stunned.

"Yes, brother, if you're willing," Monar said. "Dylla is looking forward to having you there and I need another man in the store who can deal as well as Mother.

"I thought Glynda would go. She's older."

"I've got other plans for Glynda," York told him. "And she and Dylla would not get along. No, it's better that you go and leave Monar a little more freedom to trade."

"You have a home, brother," Monar said. "And I plan to leave the day after the Harvest Court."

"I'll be ready." Adlar still looked stunned.

York braced himself for the next task, knowing it wouldn't please one of his sons. Before he could begin, the girls boiled down the stairs to give Adlar their congratulations. They were marshalled up again by Nan when things calmed down but Rayna dallied in the kitchen.

"What plans for Glynda, Father?" Monar was puzzled. "I don't recall…"

"It's time she had a store of her own too." York was grim as he thought of the fight in the store. "Nan says she's done with grieving and it's time she moved on. The only problem is who will back her."

He looked at Davyd before turning to his second son. "Wydon, what do you think of opening a store in Datyl?"

"Datyl?" His second son glanced at Davyd. "I think it would prosper and we could use a permanent base there. Especially if they could line up cargo quicker. I've had to leave one ship and wait for another while I was buying and I don't care to do that."

"Would you help Glynda set up a store? It could be your base."

Wydon lost his smile and didn't answer.

"I could go to Datyl, Father," Monar quickly inserted. "I've set up one store and I'm sure I could start another."

York shook his head. "I thought Wydon could use the experience and the base."

"York, why not Davyd?" Rayna sweetly suggested as she set a fresh pot of tea on the table. "He's been to Datyl."

"Not Davyd. If Wydon isn't interested, it will have to wait."

His sons looked puzzled and Davyd embarrassed but York didn't care. He would not force Davyd into a situation where he must see the lady he loved and not be able to speak to her. He knew the price of the manhunt.

Wydon studied Davyd then gave in. "Father, if it has to be me, I'll do it. Once it's established though and Glynda has good people around her, I'd like to return to the road."

"Agreed." York knew Wydon was a wanderer. He enjoyed trading and caravanning and was the best at it. He was restless too. If he'd been on his own, he might have followed Valdyn south as the prince tried to locate a city-state they knew was there somewhere.

"So Monar and Adlar are based in Sefron, Wydon and Glynda in Datyl, and Davyd here." York went over the assignments for his adult children. "Davyd will travel of course."

"Yes sir." His son looked relieved.

"And I've a mind to go to Datyl soon myself," York said. "It's been a long time and I know Rayna's never been."

"I never wanted to go," Rayna said as she gathered up cups. "It can't be as pretty as they say anyway."

"It is though," Davyd said. "Wide streets and everyone looks prosperous. In just the short time I was there I had three good offers for work."

"Offers?" York frowned. "How much?"

"Twenty to thirty solaris per year," Davyd said. "But I couldn't
see why anyone would need a guardsman. There are darn few
people who wear swords there."

"I got similar offers," Wydon drawled, "but not that much.
Most wanted me to escort them like you did Lady Synda. They
thought hiring a guardsman would save them money over what
Jarol charges."

"Jarol? I didn't hear about him."

"His cadre offers escort to Sunborn traveling to Sefron and
sometimes here. It's a lucrative trade and he usually gets a high
price. He was in Sefron though when *The Seawind* reached port. I
saw him before I left."

"I didn't know about him," Davyd said. "And I wish he had
taken that job."

Remembering the ordeal Davyd went through, his brothers
looked sympathetic.

"At least you got a good profit from it," Wydon said. "And
Monar didn't kill you for losing a crystal."

"I wouldn't have killed him," Monar protested. "But I was sure
we'd have to make good on the ones I didn't find. And I would
have missed you too."

"I'm sure." Davyd shot back.

"Pitfire, Davyd!" Monar exploded. "When I *did* find the one
you lost, I nearly threw it at a tree. By then I was so mad at not
finding *you* that I didn't give a copper for it!"

Turning to his father, he added. "And then when I did find
him, I thought that Sunborn lady was going to kill me for pulling
him off his horse and throwing a punch at him."

The words were out before anyone knew it. York heard them
in stunned silence and saw Davyd turn white as linen. The others
laughed but it faded away when he didn't join them.

Rayna appeared again in the awkward silence. Gathering up
more cups for the sink, she looked at Monar. "Did she tell you she's
come to Gardon for a manhunt?"

Monar's gaze went to Davyd. "No, I didn't know."

"It wasn't common knowledge," York snapped. "At least not
until my wives took an interest in it. Half the city might know by
now."

"York, I—" Rayna looked shocked by his anger.

"That's enough. Rayna, the hour is late."

"Yes, my lord." His wife gave in with a promptness that stunned her sons and left the last dishes on the table. "Tonight?"

"No," York said. "I sleep alone."

She looked ready to protest that but he was in no mood to share her bed. Suddenly he didn't want either of his wives. For the last two days he'd felt them conspiring and he'd had enough. His sons looked embarrassed by his public rejection but he didn't care. Rayna should not interfere with Davyd. Neither should Nan. And who shared *his* bed was *his* choice.

"In the morning, my lord." Rayna made light of it and kissed him on the cheek before climbing the stairs. An uncomfortable silence fell in her wake.

"Father, why would she hunt here?" Aldo innocently asked, his eyes wide at what he'd just seen. "Don't they have deer on Datyl?"

York looked at his youngest then had to grin. "Yes, Aldo. It's just that some think the deer are better in woods they've never seen."

The tension eased as Aldo accepted his answer.

"I think we're done." He looked at Donal and decided to keep the news of his son's application quiet until tomorrow. They would know then whether he was in. "Tomorrow is Donal's birthday. Let's make it a memorable one."

His sons, even Davyd, grinned at Donal's flushed face. Fifteen years was always memorable since it marked the boundary between childhood and adulthood. He wouldn't be counted full grown until he turned twenty but he was no longer a child and would be assuming the duties of a man.

Monar and Wydon both teased their brother and watched his blush darken as they suggested he get experience in new areas. Adlar, being the next youngest, was more sympathetic to Donal. Aldo looked envious but the effect was lost when he yawned.

"Aldo, off to bed with you. The rest of you don't stay up late. We've got sorting to do tomorrow."

"Yes sir," his sons answered and he climbed the stairs. When Davyd didn't follow, he knew Monar had detained him. Wishing the hunt was over and done with, he ached for his son.

Chapter 24 - Waiting

17 Hoth 850

IN A CORNER of the Garden Court sealed off from the rest, Synda of Datyl tried to calm herself with her meditation crystal. She rolled it from palm to palm and across the backs of her hands in more difficult moves but she couldn't seem to quiet her nerves.

Four more hours. Goddess, she hated to wait. These last three days of preparation were all waiting. She knew what she wanted and finally tonight she would face Davyd and give him the scroll. Her hands trembled as she thought of him and what he would do. The warmth in her middle grew at the thought of him taking her…

The crystal slipped and left her hands. She stammered an excuse at Alva's startled reaction. She hadn't dropped the crystal in years. Moving gracefully in her red robes, she bent to pick it up.

"Are you still sore?" Alva asked. "If so…"

"Not at all, aunt," Synda quickly replied. "I'm ready today."

"I know that," Alva said. "And I've told you I'll say no more about it. Dava just warned me that you could be sore and she will heal it if you want her to."

"I don't need it." Synda flashed the ball in her hands to show she was calm but she was far from it. What if he refused her? He couldn't. He'd given her his promise. Holding that close to her heart gave her courage. More than that she recalled his kiss and his touch and knew he wanted her too.

She would have his child. Davyd wouldn't join her in Datyl while his family was here but she would have his child. She tried to imagine a little boy just like him but it was hard. She wasn't ready to think about the child. She wanted his father too much.

"Synda?"

Turning toward the gate of the garden, Synda hesitated.

"It is you, isn't it?" Lyda looked at her uncertainly. "Please say something. I don't want you to be mad at me."

"I'm not mad," Synda quickly reassured her. "But should you be here?"

"Not normally but I came to be prepared for my wedding and Dava said I could see you. Valdyn is back," she declared, looking radiant. "We'll be married tomorrow then Fara will present me to the Council during Harvest Court."

"I could have my child before you do." Lyda gave her a wicked grin and ignored the gasp from Alva. "And I just know it'll be a boy. I've even got a name picked out."

"I haven't thought about names," Synda said with a stab of envy. "What name?"

"Dykon, Dykon Valdynson. It's a good name for a king."

"Dykon?" Synda tried the name out. "Yes, I like it. I haven't thought about names."

"You should." Lyda suddenly looked somber. "If *you* don't name the child, it won't have one and the Temple says it's best to start calling the child by name before it's born. Of course, you want to wait until you know what sex it is."

Synda had to smile. "Lyda, I wish you well." She touched her friend's hand. "And I think you'll have a son too."

Her friend smiled back. "When you finish your hunt, you'll have to meet Valdyn. He is just the most perfect man—did I tell you he's found our enemy?"

"No, where?"

"Almost on the Amron," Lyda told her. "Not quite on the river which is why our searchers missed it. They call it Lykos and they fly the Banner of the Wolf. He'll have to go back next year and try to make contact, but we'll have the winter together. He's found it. The queen was so pleased."

"Lady Lyda?" Dava was at the gate. "We're ready for you and the queen is here. Come along."

"Yes, priestess." Lyda looked a little scared as she gave Synda a hug. "Kala's blessing, Synda."

"You too." Synda let her go. *We'll have the winter together.* Suddenly that seemed like a long time and she wished she could keep Davyd that long. Remembering her home in Datyl, she shoved the thought from her mind. She couldn't stay here and he wouldn't go there. Hadn't he said he'd stay where his family was? And he'd called Datyl weak.

Remembering his acid comments about her home, she knew it was no use. She couldn't contemplate staying in Gardon either.

Everywhere there were swords and rough men ready to use them. She couldn't raise a child here. She couldn't even go shopping without a guard.

"She shouldn't have talked about the Wolf," Karyn said as she joined her, her hand clasping the hand of a little girl. "That doesn't concern you—not now."

"I know." Synda covered up her true thoughts. "But who is this?" She smiled at the little girl.

"Well, you know I've hunted and this is my daughter from that hunt," Karyn said with understandable pride. "Narys, say hello to Lady Synda."

"Hello," Narys politely said. "Are you hunting a man?"

"Yes," Synda answered, embarrassed to have that question come from such a young girl. "I'm wanting a child just like you."

"Well, I'm half Kalryn," Narys announced in a grown-up voice. "My father serves the queen."

"He does?" Synda wondered how much she knew about him and was envious. "I never knew what my father did."

"Narys, go play with your friends now," her mother told her with an affectionate smile. "And stay away from the public courts today."

"Yes Mother," the child responded and skipped away.

Synda watched her go, wishing she could have talked to her longer. She hadn't met many children that young.

"My daughter is still at the age where she'll say what she thinks," Karyn said. "And I've no wish for her to tell the world who her father is."

"She knows?"

"I've not kept it from her. Since *he* doesn't object and neither do his wives, she can know."

"Wives?" Synda felt like she'd missed something. "You hunted a man with more than one wife?"

"Yes." Karyn seemed amused by her reaction. "I am still friends with them. I can't speak to *him* or even see him without it being public but I can and do stay friends with his family. That's the advantage of choosing a man of middle years who is happily married. I couldn't have done that with an unmarried man."

Settling herself on a bench, she motioned for Synda to join her. "Let me tell you how I chose my man and how my hunt was done."

Synda knew this was another step in her preparation but she was curious. She wouldn't change her mind about Davyd but she was curious about these wives who consented to let their husband be hunted. She didn't even know anyone who had more than one wife.

"The father of my child was a guardsman for the queen. He even came to Gardon in her service before she wed King Alden. He was the captain of her guard and then, when Alden needed a man for special missions, he picked him," Karyn explained. "He holds a Council right for his service to the king and was one of the first in Gardon to be awarded a King's Star. He's a good man."

"When I met him some seven years ago, this guardsman was already married to two women and had nine children. I thought him a perfect tyrant when I found out he was wed to two and kept them in the same house but he wasn't. No, he was the nicest man I'd ever met." Her eyes shone. "And he never forgot his family. Every time I saw him he had a son in tow. His children are devoted to him."

"You could tell the man put family first. I wanted that in a man."

"Davyd loves his family," Synda told her. "He was forever talking about his brothers and sisters and his brother came searching for us."

"I know," Karyn replied. "And I would expect that of a York. They're a tight family. The problem is Davyd is young and untried *and* unmarried. What if he followed you to Datyl? Could you keep from talking to him?"

"If I had to, but he doesn't like Datyl. All he ever talked about was Gardon."

"That's natural enough. He grew up here. A man should be loyal to his home city. In any case, we weren't really talking about him."

"Synda, if I could do it again, I would still choose this father for my child but I would prefer to be a member of his family and not have the restrictions of the hunt on me. He couldn't be there when Narys was born and I had to ask Justus to stand in for her father. He caught her and named her, but still…"

"Synda, I would have given anything to be able to show her off to him. She was perfect and her hair was black when she was born. I thought for sure she'd grow up looking like him."

She gave her a wistful smile. "I'm better off than most. Although I can't speak to him, I can speak to his wives and they're willing to count Narys as part of their family. If something should happen to me, I know they would take her in and that's rare when you hunt a man."

Synda was envious and wished she could say the same for Davyd but she didn't know him that well and she'd only met one of his brothers. She'd heard some about the family from Lyda but that only made her more aware of what she didn't have. Her mother hadn't cared.

"My story is really rare," Karyn repeated. "I have friends here in the Temple who hunted priests and they seem the happiest. Their children know they have a father here and many find out before their teens who it is. It's hard to keep such a secret here."

"But those who hunt outside the Temple have the hardest time. Some go on to marry another and have more children but their firstborn is theirs alone. Others never marry but dream about the man they hunted. Some had no wish to have children at all and did it out of duty."

"Then there was one who crossed the lines and had to be banished. She followed the man she hunted and demanded that he marry her. He refused and she tried to kill herself and the child. The Temple had to restrain her. They sent her to Kala's Island and she may never return."

"I won't be such a fool," Synda said. "And I won't kill my child."

"Good, but choose wisely, Synda. If you love Davyd, you might want to keep the door open so you can marry him. If you hunt him, the door is closed."

"He'll never marry me. He won't."

"How can you know if you don't ask?" Karyn demanded. "His father married one with Sunborn blood — why wouldn't his son?"

Synda looked at her in surprise. Before she could say anything the bells of the fifth hour rang and Justus appeared, motioning to her. Three more hours.

THE HOUR was almost here. The tables of the dining hall were overflowing with good food and wine as the household prepared to celebrate Donal's birthday.

Davyd looked over the fare with a practiced eye and decided Cook had outdone herself. There would be three kinds of meat tonight—chickens, beef, and roast pig—and three kinds of bread. Everything was in threes and he knew she was trying to bring luck to the household. There were even three tables. The family table was set crosswise in the room. The other tables had been added at each end to make a U-shape. Tonight some of Donal's friends and family friends would be joining them for this feast.

At one end of the dining hall was a portable altar to Galton, the God of Protection. The other gods sat in their niches in the family shrine but tonight was Galton's night. With Donal choosing to join the Guard, Galton would be his patron and take precedence for him.

When Glynda and Bryndal came of age, he knew Kala had been invoked. He'd been here for Glynda's choosing but had missed Bryndal's. He'd been on a ship bound for Datyl when she turned fifteen and offered her long hair to Kala.

He'd chosen Galton. Davyd touched the figure of the god reverently, then checked the offering plate before him. It was clean and burnished to a high shine. Beside it stood a small bowl of alka and the knife used for first blood.

His older brothers were doing the same thing and he had to grin. Of the six boys in his family only Donal hadn't come into the hall. Busy entertaining his guests in the store, he had only his father for support until their mothers rang the dinner gong.

Remembering how he'd felt, his anticipation and dread that he'd do something wrong, Davyd sympathized with his brother.

"Is everything ready?" Nan came out of the kitchen and looked over the tables and altar one last time. "Yes, I see it is."

She turned to her boys. "I hope you remembered there would be none of *those* gifts tonight."

"In front of our sisters?" Wydon grinned. "No, Mother. We'll give those in private."

"Good." She pinned Davyd next. "And I want no one disappearing after dinner."

Davyd stammered an answer, not sure why she thought he would do that. It was Wydon. He glanced at his older brother and decided she must have mixed them up. She must really be nervous tonight.

"Now where's Rayna?" Nan looked around. "Aldo, go fetch her."

Aldo went dashing up the stairs and brought the breathless Rayna down. She fussed with her hair then her dress before Nan hugged her and spoke a few words to calm her.

They looked a pair. Dressed alike in the house colors of russet and gold, they still looked very different. Nan was tall and noble looking but Rayna was plump and short. She was still a good height for a woman but beside Nan she looked too short and too plump. If it wasn't for her sharp mind and the respect others had for her, she could easily have been mistaken for a crafter's wife.

No, she couldn't. Davyd corrected that thought almost as quickly as it crossed his mind. Mother Rayna had the same confidence and bearing his mother did. She was used to commanding them and, moreover, she had their father's backing. She might not look as noble as Mother Nan but Davyd knew she was just as strong.

"Now." Nan put her hand on the gong chord and waited for Rayna to join her. Tonight they rang the gong together and showed the unity of the house. Donal was *their* son.

After that there was the greeting of guests and a sorting out of places before everyone was gathered in a semicircle around the altar. Davyd joined his siblings and knelt in the first line and just to one side behind their brother, his sword at his side and his gift at his feet. His mothers stood to the right of the altar to watch as York prepared his son.

"Today Donal, my son, is fifteen and he has made his first life choice—to follow Galton and be a protector of those who need it. Not just those who may have the coin, but those who need it. I'm proud of him."

York finished his speech and looked at Nan. "And what does the mother who bore him say?"

"Husband, I grant his choice and wish him happiness with all my heart," Nan promptly responded. "And let there be no one to keep him from what he knows is right."

"And what does the mother who suckled him say?" York turned to Rayna with a smile.

"Husband, we must each follow our heart and go where it says. As I once chose you over all others, let Donal choose his own life. If his heart tells him he must serve the queen above family, then let it be so. And let him be the best guardsman in the queen's service!"

Davyd felt Glynda stir beside him and guessed she hadn't known. Now the entire family knew.

"Then I let my son choose his own way in the world and let him know that in three days' time he *will* join the Second Guard of Gardon." York made the announcement smoothly as he smiled at his son. "Word came today."

Davyd grinned for just an instant but sobered again. This wasn't the time for congratulations.

"Today I offer my son to Galton," York continued. "Let the god protect him in his chosen path and watch over him and his charges. I will no longer treat him as a son to be ordered but as a man to be dealt with. I see him now as the man he'll become and the man he is—equal with any man under the law. He's no longer my child."

Davyd remembered when his father said those words to him. He knew it was just now hitting Donal that he would be called on to make his own decisions and couldn't ask his father to make them for him. Likewise, if he broke the law, he would be held accountable and could no longer hide behind his youth.

"Donal, do you take the responsibility of managing your own life from me? Will you stand as a man?" York asked the first questions.

"I will." Donal's face was pale when he looked up at his father.

"And you choose Galton to guide your steps and guard your path from this day forward?"

"I do." Donal made his choice and Davyd knew it was good. Only Adlar had chosen Kal over the Protector.

"Then know you will be called on to shed blood for him and someday, when the time is right, give your life. Let it not be without honor." York gave the ritual warning.

Davyd shivered, remembering the clearing and the raiders who pinned him down. That could have been his time.

"Do you accept the price?"

"I do," Donal answered.

His father studied him then turned to the altar. Picking up the bowl of alka and the short knife, he turned back to his son. "Show you have the courage of your convictions. Take the knife and shed first blood and swear you will follow Galton from his day forward."

Donal licked his lips then took the knife from his palm. Dipping it into the alka, he covered the blade with the healing liquid. No one said a word or even breathed while he drew the knife firmly across his upper arm. A thin red line followed the knife's path and blood oozed from his wound.

He'd chosen his sword arm too. Most chose their shield arm because it was safer but not his brother.

"Well done and deep enough." His father approved the wound and handed him the ritual paper. The words of his oath were already on it since he'd penned it earlier that day.

Donal rubbed his wound with the paper and brought it away covered with blood. "I offer my first blood to Galton the Protector and ask him to take me into his service. I swear I will follow him faithfully through this life and, if he wishes it, into the next. Let this blood shed by my hand be my witness." He crumpled up the paper and put it in the offering bowl his father held.

York picked up the altar candle and held it over the bowl. "Let all here witness Donal Yorkson is sworn to Galton." With that he touched the flame to the paper and it flared up in a bright flash and was gone. Only a trace of ash remained in the offering bowl. It was done.

"Mothers." York looked to his wives and they stepped forward to clean their son's wound and bind it. There would be no special healing for this one and Donal would wear the mark of it the rest of his life. The wound wasn't deep but Davyd remembered how his had stung when they poured alka on it. It hurt for more than a day afterward. Fortunately, this was the only blood sacrifice Galton required—only the one for courage.

York smiled at the assembled guests and family then turned back to Donal. "Your brothers have outdone themselves and each of them has come to me with a sword. I don't know what you'd do with five swords." There was a chuckle and Donal grinned with them. "So I let them choose which one was the best. All of them were fine swords and would have served you well but Davyd's..." He motioned to him.

Davyd rose, smoothly drawing the sword from its scabbard and held it across his outstretched palms.

"This sword was forged by Edryk of Datyl." Davyd smiled at the recognition in his brother's eyes. "It was given to me by a widow who had no sons and sought an honorable man to wield it. Its last owner, Rykar Salson, put no blemish on it and died in Galton's favor. I swore to his wife that his sword would never be dishonored."

He laid the well-used sword in his brother's hands. "I give the sword and the oath to you." Smiling at his brother's amazement, he pointed to the maker's mark at the base of the guard.

He hadn't known for certain that the sword was by Edryk of Datyl when he got it but a visit to an armorer had confirmed it. He'd been offered not three solaris, but twenty for it. More than a hundred years old, the sword was made by a true master and had stood the test of time. It was a fitting gift for his little brother.

"Thank you," Donal stammered. "I never thought I'd see one of these."

"I know. When it came to my hands, I didn't believe it. Take care of it." Handing the scabbard to his brother, he stepped back in his place.

"The rest of the gifts will wait," York told the assembly. "Let's eat."

With those words he broke the tableau. Monar and Adlar had to look at the sword again then Donal's friends crowded around. Baron and Wes had both made the Guard and were here to share his joy.

"I didn't know he was applying for the Guard." Glynda spoke softly as she sat next to Davyd. "The mothers never mentioned it. I thought he would be here to work the store."

"Don't worry about it." Davyd frowned at her. "I'll be here when I can and the twins need the experience."

It was only during the second course that he remembered Glyda hadn't been told she was leaving. She was upstairs when Father told them. Shooting a glance at his sister, he debated how much she knew.

"When do you want to leave for Datyl?" he finally asked.

"Anytime you…" Glynda looked at him in shock then her eyes turned to Wydon. "I mean Wydon. It's Wydon going with me, isn't it? I knew it had to be one of you."

"So that fight in the store?" Davyd sat back in his chair, then saw their father watching them. He picked up his fork again and looked intently at his place. "I will *never* call Byka a liar again."

"That little leaper," Glynda exclaimed. "Davyd, please don't tell. I *want* to go to Datyl and Mother Nan suggested it. Please."

"What's going on?" Monar leaned forward to look around her at Davyd. "You aren't fighting, are you?" He kept his voice low too.

"No," Glynda hissed. "Just wait."

Davyd thought about it, trying to figure out what the mothers were up to. Wydon didn't want to settle down and he knew his father would oppose him going to Datyl. They knew Adlar was leaving too. It just didn't make sense.

Then in the middle of dessert the door chime sounded. Folks raised their heads and looked around as one of their household guards rose to his feet.

"Are we missing anyone?" Monar asked.

"Not a one," York answered. "I wonder who it could be."

"Maybe it's a gift from the queen," Nan suggested. "She was so busy preparing for Valdyn's wedding." She motioned for the guard to go.

"He's getting married tomorrow?" one of their guests asked. "I thought he would wait for the Harvest Court."

"No, Lyda was ready now," Nan answered, "and the queen agreed that the wedding itself could be small. She'll have enough ceremony when she's confirmed at court."

Davyd sat there, his fork still in hand, and tried not to listen to the conversation. His eyes firmly on the altar of Galton, he was the only one who didn't turn and stare when *she* entered the room. One look at his father's face told him she was there.

His blood froze in his veins and his pulse raced as everyone else scrambled to their feet. He could hear the rustle of her robes and prayed it was just another dream as it came closer. He knew when she stopped beside his chair. Adlar, across the table from him, looked like he might faint and little Aldo stared at her with wide eyes.

"Davyd, look at her," his father gruffly commanded.

Slowly, as if in a dream, he obeyed. The scarlet robes were there and he got a quick impression of two more women dressed in white before his eyes riveted on her. She'd come.

She didn't look at him but knelt at his feet like the supplicant she was. Without a word, she offered the scroll on her outstretched palms.

Chapter 25 - Scroll

17 Hoth 850

"NO!" Knocking the scroll from her hands, Davyd leapt to his feet, recoiling from what she offered. "Synda, I will *not* be hunted — not by you!"

"Davyd," York snapped. "Monar, Wydon, take him," he barked at his sons.

Wydon shot over the table to grab him.

"Into the store!" York hustled his erring son out of the dining hall and away from the robed figure on the floor.

"Priestesses, bring her to the kitchen," Nan told her attendants as calmly as if nothing unusual had happened.

"Dylla, would you please see to our guests?" She asked Monar's wife.

"Yes, Mother Nan." Dylla seemed stunned but smoothly took up the role of hostess as the manhunter and her attendants disappeared into the kitchen with Nan and Rayna trailing.

The rest of the meal was awkward as they could hear shouts coming from the store and sobs coming from the kitchen. Finally the meal was done and, since Donal had disappeared with his brothers, the guests excused themselves and made a hasty exit.

"Pitfire!" York swore at his son. "Gods," he swore again then let loose words his sons had never heard from him in a long stream of invective.

They stood grim and silent until he wore down, only Davyd looking defiant.

"Davyd, what were you thinking?" York snapped at him. "You gave your word you'd accept the hunt."

"I can't," Davyd said in a pain-filled voice. "Father, I can't. To have her then give her up. Please."

York stared at him, then motioned for his sons to let him go. They did but neither moved from his side.

"Davyd, you gave your word," York insisted then sighed. "If you hadn't given it, I would say let the gods take her, but…"

"Family honor," Wydon muttered.

"Against love?" Monar was grim. "Father, is there no way out?"

"Ask Davyd."

His son's head jerked in answer, his face miserable.

"Gods, I pity you." York looked at his son in despair. "I thought there was *nothing* worse than loving a woman you can't have but you. Davyd, you'll have to do it."

"The manhunt isn't that bad," he spoke quickly. "I've done it. They take you back to the Temple and you spend three days and nights with the woman. They'll even give you rugur if you need it."

His sons stared at him in shock but York plowed on. "When it's done, you might hear later there's a child or you might not. In any case, you'll be free to marry another."

"Father, you were hunted?" Monar asked in disbelief. "When? Does Mother know?"

"Of course she knows," York snarled. "Both of them. For all I know they told the priestess to pick me. They certainly didn't rest until I accepted."

His sons looked stunned.

"You have a sister in the Temple," York ground out. "Her name is Narys and she's three years old. Ask your mothers if you don't believe. They've seen her."

He remembered something else too. One of the attendants following the hunter was Karyn. He wanted to know why *she* was here when this girl was hunting *his* son. According to law she was forbidden to speak to him.

"Davyd," Wydon said. "I see now why Father doesn't want you in Datyl. I agree. You shouldn't go anywhere near her."

"Maybe she'll take another of us?" Monar lightly suggested and saw the flash of rage on Davyd's face. "No, I don't think Dylla is as giving as our mothers."

"Davyd, you decide," York said. "It's your choice and your honor. I'll not turn my back on you if you choose not to honor this promise but…"

"I have to," Davyd said, defeated. "Justus said it was void but I don't see it. She doesn't see it. She…" He couldn't finish.

"Is three days of love worth a lifetime without?" His voice was torn with anguish.

His brothers looked grim and his father looked ready to cry. That more than anything made up his mind. He had to do it and may the gods help him after.

SYNDA KNELT there, stunned, as her scroll was knocked from her hand and sent skittering across the floor. Davyd was yelling at her, calling her by name and shouting no and all she could do was kneel there and watch the scroll go round and round until it hit the wall.

She watched as if in a dream as his brothers grabbed her love and forced her from the room, a fierce patriarch following in a rage.

He couldn't say no. He promised. He couldn't say no.

Then she was being helped to her feet and guided into a warm, tidy kitchen by hands she couldn't see and her hood was being pushed back on her shoulders.

"She's in shock." A woman she'd seen once before looked into her eyes. "Dava, please."

"Of course." Dava was suddenly there in front of her and looking into her dry eyes. "Synda, it's all right. Everything will be all right."

"Have her drink this." The woman was back again. "It's spiced balm. I have Kural too."

"I can't." Synda tried to push the tea away.

"Davyd." She blinked, then blinked again. "He dropped the scroll. I should go get it."

"He didn't drop it!" Dava was sharp. "He threw it. Synda, he doesn't want you."

"But, but he promised." She sounded like a little girl before a sob escaped her. "He promised."

"He promised," she repeated over and over until she was crying.

"Bryndal, Mala, Byka, and, and Natra, out!" Rayna noticed her daughters and granddaughter inside the door. "Take care of our guests. Glynda, you stay."

"She should cry herself out," the woman said, "but we don't have time. If I know York, he'll change Davyd's mind and she *has* to be ready."

Synda heard Dava telling her to take deep breaths. A vial was held to her lips and she nearly gagged at the sickly sweet taste of Kural.

"That's better," the woman said when she tried to push the bottle away. "Synda, if you love Davyd, listen. We can't help you unless you do exactly what we say."

"But he rejected me. He doesn't want me."

"He wants you." The woman was grim. "Goddess, child, he *loves* you. He just doesn't want you in the hunt."

"Who are you?" Synda looked at her, trying to remember where they met. "You, you were at the Temple when they prepared me…"

"The husband's mother should always be there," Nan told her. "And I've every intention of seeing you marry my son. So does Rayna." She motioned toward a shorter, rounder woman who was watching her with concern. "We've been working for the past three days to make this happen."

Synda couldn't absorb it. "But who are you?"

The woman laughed. "Let's start at the beginning. I'm Nan York and Davyd is my son. This is my sister-wife, Rayna York." She pulled the small woman closer. "And the girl keeping watch for us is Glynda." She motioned toward a girl in her twenties.

"Is she another wife?"

"Goddess, no!" Nan burst out laughing even as the girl looked mortified. "Not even York could handle three of us. No, Glynda is Rayna's daughter. She's six months younger than Davyd."

"It was a reasonable question," Karyn pointed out. When Synda looked from her to Nan and Rayna, she spoke again. "Yes, child. Davyd's father was the one I hunted."

"Enough." Rayna turned to her daughter. "Glynda, are they out there?"

"Not yet but the guests are leaving."

"I'm not going to worry about them. Tell us when York comes back. He's not to get in here."

"Synda, listen." Nan sat in front of her and held her head so she couldn't look away. "If you hunt Davyd, you'll lose him forever. Once you take that scroll from his hands, we can't do anything to save you. You understand that? You *can't* take the scroll from him!"

"But I…"

"*Don't take the scroll.* You can marry him but not if you take that scroll."

"He won't have me," Synda weakly protested, her eyes filling with tears again. "He loves Gardon."

"He loves you more," Nan snapped. "Don't be silly. Where he lives isn't important. Would you give up Datyl if you could always have him by your side?"

"Yes! I love him."

"I know you do. Now listen. *Don't* take the scroll. Rayna and I are convincing York we need a store in Datyl. He's already agreed Glynda should go but he's still thinking Wydon instead of Davyd. If you end this manhunt now, we can get Davyd to go there."

Synda listened, not quite understanding. The woman repeated it again. Davyd in Datyl? Her Davyd in Datyl? Married to her? She looked at the woman and began to hope.

"Remember," Nan repeated again. "Don't take the scroll. Tell Davyd you'll have him in a marriage or not at all. You mustn't take the scroll or the law will force you to do the hunt. Now tell me what I just said."

"Don't take the scroll," Synda whispered, "and I won't have him…." She clung to her hand for reassurance. "Promise me this will work."

"It will," Nan promised. "One way or another Davyd will marry you. This has gone on long enough."

"Mother, they've come out," Glynda said. "Gods, I think Davyd has had it. He looks so…"

Rayna nudged her aside and looked herself. "York is taking this hard," she said to Nan. "I don't like the looks of him."

"Let me." Nan peered out then returned to Synda. "We need to get this done. Synda, if you take that scroll after all we've put our husband through, you won't be *able* to hunt. Don't forget."

Synda managed a small nod.

"Karyn, can you stand beside her and stop it?" Nan asked the woman who knew the cost. "We can't let this get fouled up."

"I will," Karyn said with a look at Dava. "But you'll have to convince your family they didn't see it."

"Agreed."

"He's found the scroll," Glynda reported. "Mother, I don't know…"

"We've gone too far," Rayna snapped at her. "Either way, York is going to sleep in the cellars tonight. We might as well deserve it."

Synda wondered why he would sleep in the cellars but had no more time to think. Someone was washing her face with a warm cloth and Dava was soothing her swollen eyes. She let them pull up her hood.

Finally the door of the kitchen was opened and the two mothers and their daughter left. Synda stepped out into the dining hall with her attendants and waited, staring at her love.

He looked haggard and drawn and her heart ached for him even as she steeled herself for what she had to do. The last few minutes had left her drained too and she couldn't force herself to move.

"Lady Synda." Davyd moved finally and he persisted in calling her by name. His voice was laden with pain. "You asked me once if I would accept your hunt and I agreed. No, I promised."

He was standing before her now and she could see him clutching that red scroll. The seal was unbroken but he was slowly crushing it in his grip.

"I'll honor that promise now." The words seemed torn from him. He held out the scroll.

Synda stepped back, her hands fluttering into her robes and away from the scroll. Then she reached up with her robed hands and laid her hood back in a move that defied manhunt tradition, letting everyone see her face.

"Davyd Yorkson, I'll take no man unwilling," she snapped. "If you won't marry me, I—I won't have you at all!"

Davyd's jaw dropped and he flushed. "Take your damned scroll!" He threw it at her but Priestess Karyn nimbly caught it and disappeared it into her robes. "And get out. You've put my family through enough grief tonight."

She obeyed. What else could she do? With her back straight and head high, she left his house.

Help me please, she prayed to Kala as Karyn stopped her from stepping out onto the street unhooded. She raised her hood. With her identity protected, she somehow made the long walk back to the Temple though afterward she could never remember it.

Chapter 26 - Turnabout

YORK watched in disbelief as the hunter stepped back from his son and flung her challenge at him, then silently cheered when Davyd ordered her out of the house. Dizzy with relief, he watched his son storm upstairs.

His wives joined him, but he didn't care. He just stood there and tried to convince himself it was over. Even when Nan took his hand in hers and covertly took his pulse, he didn't pull away.

"So what happens now?" Monar broke the awkward silence. "Can we finish dinner?"

"Only you would think of dinner," his wife scolded, hands on her hips. "I've never seen a worse birthday party and you just think of dinner."

Remembering Donal, York looked for his son and wasn't surprised to see him standing with arms folded, his eyes on the stairs. He moved when Dylla spoke, but York could see his son wanted to follow Davyd.

"Let's get the extra dishes cleared away." Rayna clapped her hands and marshaled their staff. The forgotten servants gathered the dishes and the guardsmen moved the altar back into its alcove for her. "And I want some of the honey wine." She sent Adlar down to the cellars for it.

"I'm going upstairs," York told his wife.

"Let me go with you," Nan quietly said. "Please, husband."

"No. I'll come back down."

He didn't want her. He didn't want anyone. Climbing the stairs to his room, he quietly closed the door.

"Mother?" Wydon was standing in front of her, not quite blocking her view of the stairs. "Mother Nan?"

"What?" She realized he was talking to her. "What is it?"

"Go to bed—you and Rayna both. We'll take care of this. Just go to bed."

She looked for Rayna and saw her waiting, their children in a row behind her. Monar looked as concerned as Wydon and even Glynda looked worried. The younger children seemed more uneasy at seeing their mothers ordered to bed. For them Nan pulled herself together.

"First I want some things." She gave herself a mental shake. "A bottle of that honey wine—no, get me a full bottle." She sent Adlar back to the cellar. "And some honey cakes. Vita, do we have any fresh kivak in the house?"

"Yes, ma'am," the cook confirmed. "Not a whole one though."

"A piece will do and I want a pot of hot water. Bryndal, go up to the herbs room and get me…" She rattled off an odd list of herbs. "Just a bit of each. Mix them."

She thought of other things for her children to do, sending the twins into the store to fetch a tea blend from the stock and asking Byka to get something else. Finally she had the younger children and even the servants out of the way.

Her sons were looking amused now as she asked Dylla to fetch something else they knew she wasn't going to use. When she tried to send Donal away, though, he held his ground with just a look at Monar and told her they didn't have any more in stock.

"Enough, Nan." Rayna was smiling at her. "I think you gave it away with the fly swatter. Let's just take the wine and cakes and go to bed."

Nan gave in, partly because she couldn't think of any more things to fetch and partly because her sons didn't look as if they'd budge for her. Still she'd given York time and time alone was what he needed.

"I do want the swatter," Nan said. "There's a couple of big flies upstairs and the leapers haven't caught them." As ridiculous as that sounded, she said it anyway. One more thing. Donal.

"I'm sorry your day turned out this way." She took his hands. "Tomorrow we'll finish it properly."

"It doesn't matter," Donald replied. "But I never want *anyone* to wish me a memorable birthday again!"

She gave a weak laugh.

The dining room was a mess and Donal's presents were mostly unopened and Davyd was upstairs hiding away and she just knew York was giving thanks and…

"Mother, things will be better tomorrow," Monar told her.

"If they're not, I'm going to throw Davyd over a horse and haul him away," Wydon said in his turn. He was so grim Nan wasn't sure whether he was joking or not.

"Goodnight, mothers." Glynda hugged them both. "Get drunk. I'll work tomorrow."

"Thank you." Nan wondered how many of her children knew that was what she intended to do—only it was York and not her. He rarely had more than one glass but the Datyl wine was heady and it took very little to put even York in his cups.

She hugged each of the children as they returned, even getting one of Donal's friends before she realized he wasn't one of hers. She'd forgotten he was staying.

Finally she cuddled her granddaughter—her grandson was long since in bed—and bade them all good night before following Rayna upstairs. Rayna carried the tray to her old room next to York's.

"They're getting too smart for us," Nan said as she closed the door.

Originally not connected to York's bedroom when it was Rayna's room alone, they'd put a door in so they could wander unseen between the rooms. Sometimes one of them slept here and sometimes both, but more often they shared York's bed together. Tonight, she knew, they would probably have to sleep here because York might not be welcoming.

"I know." Rayna set the tray down and went to light the lamps. "Nan, I thought he would blow up at us. Why didn't he?"

"I don't know but I checked his pulse and it was strong in spite of this. Rayna, we've got to let *Davyd* finish this mess. He's got a choice now and I'm sure he'll choose Synda."

"I agree." Her sister-wife started unlacing her and helping her shed her finery then Nan did the same for her. "I don't like to think how it hurt York to hold him to that promise."

"We knew he'd do it. And Davyd—he may not forgive us for a while."

"Probably." Rayna laid her clothes neatly over a chair then stood there in her bare skin while she let her hair down. Her raven hair was starting to gray in streaks, making her look far older than her forty years. Her body was much neater and not as plump as the clothes made it look since she regularly did the same exercises Nan did to keep her figure trim. She had a belly but that was from years of childbearing and well-earned. Nan knew York found her figure just as attractive as her own. She didn't envy her. They were partners in their marriage.

"I think we'd better wear more than perfume tonight." Nan got a pair of sturdy nightgowns out of the press. "If he's angry with us, he'll probably banish us all together."

"Probably." Rayna grimaced. "I *hate* sleeping alone. You can't get comfortable."

"I know! Even at the Temple I was wishing I had… But I don't think they even have a bed that can hold three!"

Rayne laughed but it faded quickly as Nan freed her honey-brown hair and let it hang while she brushed it.

Taking the brush from her sister's hand, Rayna brushed it for her and admired the fine texture. For the years she was Fara's ward, then York's, she had always done this. She liked the feel of Nan's brown hair, now sprinkled with gray, and sometimes wished her own was so fine but it was a vain wish. Instead she kept the nightly ritual of brushing Nan's hair as she'd once done for the queen.

"Do you want it braided tonight?" she asked and wasn't surprised when Nan said no. It would take longer to prepare in the morning but York liked it down.

After a hurried washing the two women quietly opened the door to their husband's room.

He was waiting for them. Sitting on the edge of his bed in almost total darkness, York waited.

Nan glanced toward the altar niche and wasn't surprised to see two candles lit there. Yes, he'd been giving thanks.

"Husband, may we come in?" She was careful to make no move across the threshold without his leave.

"If you are done giving me fits," York answered, his voice resigned. "At least for tonight."

"Yes, husband," she promptly answered. "No word."

"Not one," Rayna vowed behind her.

"Then come. I'm tired."

Rayna picked up the tray and followed her through the door then waited for Nan to close it with a soft click. Like white-garbed specters they moved through the room and, true to their word, said nothing as they readied their husband for bed.

DOWNSTAIRS Wydon and Monar were seeing the last of their siblings off to bed. Donal had stayed the longest of the boys, telling them about Davyd's nightmare, but Glynda was last of the girls. She was still puttering about in the kitchen, putting away forgotten things, when they settled down to finish off the honey wine.

"So what do you think is going to happen?" Wydon asked his brother with a jaundiced eye. "I've got a solari that says he rides out of here first chance he gets and forgets her."

"You're on," Monar promptly replied. "She's under his skin. He may not like giving in but I think he'll do it."

"Is that all this is to you?" Glynda said as she came out of the kitchen. "Aren't you the least bit concerned about his happiness?"

"Of course we are," Monar snapped. "But it's not something a man should interfere in. Now that that *farce* of a hunt is over with, I'll let Davyd figure it out."

"Well, you could make it easier, Wydon. You should tell Father you don't want to go to Datyl."

"But I do," Wydon retorted with an injured look. "There's nothing I would like better than setting up a store for you and maybe, just maybe, finding a husband to distract that conniving mind of yours."

"You wouldn't dare."

"That's an idea." Monar hesitated in lifting his cup to his lips. "Do you have someone in mind?" He ignored his sister's vexed look.

"Yeah. A man almost as old as Father and half as rich. He looks like he's got his health too and two sons."

"How old?" Monar's lips twitched. He could see Glynda was steaming.

"He didn't say." Wydon took a long drink before he finished. "But the son I saw looked to be Adlar's age."

"Stop it!" Glynda exploded, slapping at Wydon.

Her brother grabbed her wrist in quick reflex and twisted her around to hold her strongly against his side, all without spilling a drop from his glass.

"You stop it," Monar ordered and his sister froze. He glared at her, his usual good humor gone. "You know better than to attack a swordsman."

"It's all right," Wydon said. "I was ready."

"But you might not be next time. Let her go."

Their playfulness was gone when he released Glynda. She stepped away to smooth her skirts and looked ready to cry.

"Wydon, please. We never meant you to go to Datyl. Tell Father you won't."

"I'll think about it."

Glynda gave him a tremulous smile. "That's all I ask."

She fled up the stairs.

"Definitely a plot," Monar commented. "Glynda, Mother, and Rayna too, I bet."

"I wish they'd leave him alone. Davyd should make his own choices without *them* interfering."

Monar studied him, surprised by his vehemence. "I think all they did was give *him* the choice. He didn't have one with the hunt or with that promise hanging over him. Now he does."

Wydon brooded and Monar wondered why he was opposing the match. Or was he opposing it? It was hard to say. Even though they were close in age Wydon wasn't quick to share his feelings — not when it really mattered.

"Wydon, let Davyd choose," he finally spoke again. "He'll have to live with her in the end. If he decides to go his own way, that's his affair."

"Right." Wydon suddenly relaxed. "But it would serve Glynda right if she were to marry."

"You were serious? This man does exist?"

"Oh, he's real but I don't see why he'd want such a meddlesome woman," Wydon said. "I only thought of Jarol because he works out of Datyl."

Their good humor restored, the two brothers poured the last of the wine into their cups and debated the future of their family.

Chapter 27 - Synda

18 Hoth 850

BREAKFAST the next morning was a subdued affair. The younger children looked to their elders for guidance and, seeing them quiet, followed their lead. Only two-year-old Natra seemed unworried that her grandparents hadn't appeared yet or her Uncle Davyd.

Stifling a moan, Monar drank more water to ease his headache. He should get some of his mother's brew but hesitated to ask for it. Everyone would know he'd drank too much if he did and his sisters—even his wife—would tease him for not knowing his limits. He suspected now that Wydon had let him drink most of the bottle. He certainly looked cheerful enough.

"Here they come," Mala declared.

They all looked up as first York then the mothers descended the stairs.

"Father." Monar was on his feet with the rest. "Mothers."

"Good morning," York said without a smile. "Let's have a better day than yesterday."

"Yes sir," they chorused.

York sat down with his wives then began dishing up his plate with the food the younger children insisted on passing. Cook brought out fresh platters of pan-fried tubers and rykas eggs too, presenting them to York as the master of the house.

"Donal, you're free to do what you please today. You no longer work in the store but are a guardsman as far as this family is concerned. Have fun."

Donal looked surprised and not too pleased to be cut free of the family business. He looked at this friend though and smiled. "Thank you sir."

The younger children looked envious but Monar knew it wasn't really a treat. If Donal wasn't going to the barracks in two days, he'd be at a loss for things to do. He found it hard not to work when he was visiting and he actually owned the store in Sefron in partnership with his parents and his wife's kin.

"Monar, Wydon, I'd like you two to manage the store today," York continued. "I'm going to the Temple for a rest day and I think your mothers have other plans. Since it's only open half a day, you can handle it."

"Yes sir," Monar responded. Like most businesses, York's stayed open only until noon on Sixth Day. Since a lot of employers gave their people both the sixth and seventh day off, many people did their shopping on Sixth Day and kept their Rest Day for renewal. It would be busy but nothing like Woman's Day.

"I'm going to have a day of peace," York announced. "And I don't want messengers sent after me unless the store burns. I don't care who fights who or who gets married today. It can wait until I get back. Is that clear?"

"Yes sir," the children chorused.

Monar wasn't surprised by the edict. With the mothers and Glynda plotting against Davyd, it just made sense to get away from the whole mess. Now he regretted taking on the store. He looked at his brother and saw he was having second thoughts too. Mala was already arguing with Aldo over the last piece of bread.

Donal settled it before he could. Taking the piece of bread from their grip, he laid it on his plate and cut it neatly into threes. Picking a piece for himself, he let the twins have the others.

It was neatly done and a familiar lesson. Fighting over food was stupid when you could and should share. If you did fight, it was the right of the judge to take an equal portion and leave you with less than you would have had if you shared in the first place.

His father had seen the little drama too and seemed pleased by the outcome. Except for a whine from Mala and a sharp protest from Aldo, the twins didn't say anything as their brother dispensed justice. Monar doubted they would have been so quiet for him. They looked to Donal more.

Donal put a thick coating of jam on his piece and passed it to two-year-old Natra. She ate it with a bright smile and sticky hands.

"The first bells will ring soon." Monar rose from his seat. "Bryndal, will you help?"

"Yes brother." His fifteen-year-old sister promptly rose. "If I may?" She looked to Mother Nan for permission.

"Go on. I'm not working on teas today."

Bryndal smiled and left her place.

"Aldo, you're with me too." Monar saw the twin he picked smile while his sister looked disappointed. He wouldn't take both. They tended to compete with each other.

"I'll close," Wydon announced. "And I'd like Mala, Byka, and Adlar." Neither one of them named Glynda nor the brother who was missing.

Monar led his crew out to the store. Helping Bryndal take the shutters down, he prepared for the day. Too short to handle the shutters, Aldo counted the money in the money box. Like all of them he had learned to count using real money.

The bells rang out just as the last shutter came down and Monar grinned at the timing. Walking over to the hour glass, he flipped it as the last of the notes sounded and set the sands to marking the time.

It would be a short day.

DONAL climbed the last few steps up to the roof of York's and tried to push open the trap door. Locked. Thumping on it, he hoped this time his brother would let him through. Finally there was a grating sound and the bolts were drawn back.

"Who is it?" The trap opened just a little way. "I don't want company."

"It's Donal and I brought you breakfast. I'm alone."

"Oh."

The trap door fell back against the roof then his brother offered him a hand up.

"Who else knows I'm up here?"

"Wydon asked when you weren't in your room last night. I haven't told anyone else."

"Good." Davyd ran his hands through his hair but it did no good. The stubble on his chin and red eyes spoke of a sleepless night. "You're a good man."

Donal grinned.

"I've got bread, meat, cheese and some eggs left over from last night. Cook saved a roll for you too and some sweet roots."

"Sweet roots?" Davyd exploded, then managed a watery grin. "I need more than sweet roots to cure this. How's Father?"

"He's going to the Temple for a rest day. I think he's tired of all this. Monar and Wydon are managing the store."

"I'll see them later. Don't shoot the bolts." Donal took the carrysack from his brother. "I'll be down when I'm ready."

"Don't take too long," Donal cautioned. "The little ones might lock you out."

"I know!"

They'd both been locked up on the roof before by their antics and had even done it to Glynda and Nathan while they were courting. There were bolts on both sides of the trap so it could be secured either way. The little rooftop hideaway was something the queen had requested early in the planning of York's but never used. Since there were no buildings flanking theirs — only streets and their own yard — it was completely private and screened from curious eyes.

Donal retreated down the flight of steps and looked around the tea room. No one there. The pots of herbs were put away and sealed against moisture and the shutters were closed against most of the light.

Taking a deep breath, he inhaled the fragrant smells but didn't touch anything. This room was his mother's domain and only Bryndal worked with her here. Some days the two of them were up here for hours to make a new supply of a popular tea.

He had to go. Checking once more that he hadn't accidentally thrown the bolts on the trap, he went on his way.

FOLDING a piece of cloth over a knife blade, Monar demonstrated its sharpness with a clean cut and saw his customer smile.

"Five sols," the holder offered and Monar nodded, giving his hand on the deal. They'd been haggling over the price for a while and Wydon was already at work with another customer. The shift was changing.

"Come back again Holder Londo." Monar took his money and watched the holder leave then jotted down the price, the knife, and the holder's name in his notes for the day.

Looking around to see if all customers were being waited on, he was surprised to see Davyd at work. His brother was at the tea counter and opening canisters of tea for a Sunborn lady to sniff.

He looked all right. Dressed in a long tunic of dark brown and black hose, he would have looked grim save for the brown and gold tabard he wore belted over it—a sign that he worked in the store. His hair was combed and he was clean-shaven but there were still signs of a sleepless night to those who knew him well.

"I'll take a two-pound package of Starry Night, a half-pound of the Children's Blend, and one of this new one," the lady was saying. "What did you call it?"

"Spring Rain," Davyd answered and listed the primary herbs.

"Spring Rain," the lady repeated. "How much for all?"

Davyd set out the teas on the counter. "One solari and two sols."

She didn't blink at the price. "Done." Turning to her guardsman, she motioned. "Please pay him."

"Yes, my lady." The guardsman fished the price out of his pouch while Davyd put the purchases into a cloth sack. The lady's maid stepped forward to take it as three coins were dropped into Davyd's hand.

"Thank you, Lady Barbara." Davyd bowed to her with a genuine smile. "York's appreciates your business."

"And I appreciate York's. Tell Nan she really must come to court and let us know all the details."

"Yes ma'am." Davyd's smile didn't slip. "I'm sure she'll do that." He waited till the lady had taken her leave before heading to the cash box.

"You heard?" He muttered to Monar. "It's all over Gardon."

"I heard. Not just that but I've had two men come courting Glynda this morning. This town is full of gossip about York's."

"Yes, but Lady Barbara lives at the Citadel. If she's heard…"

"So the queen knows." Monar shrugged. "Let's get out of here. Wydon can handle it."

He nudged his brother to the dining hall, saw there were others there, and kept him going till they reached the yard.

"Gods, I can't even work without people reminding me of *her*." Davyd shed his tabard.

"Then maybe you should get away," Monar suggested. "We've got three horses we don't need here plus mine. There's no reason you can't take them to the hold."

Davyd didn't seem to hear. "Monar, what should I do. She shouldn't marry me."

"Shouldn't marry you?" Monar repeated in disbelief. "Why not? You aren't exactly a pauper."

"She's Sunborn." Davyd looked at him like he was daft. "A full-blood. She shouldn't marry Kalryn."

"Mother did and so did her mother. If it's good enough for them."

"They weren't full-bloods. And they weren't acknowledged."

"Mother was," Monar retorted. "And Beatta could have married Sunborn. Mother could have too. Davyd, blood is no barrier. Synda wants you and she's kept the door open so you can ask."

His brother had it bad if he was bringing up blood. Monar decided it was time for a new argument.

It was true that Lord Platon hadn't married their great-grandmother, being already married to another, but that was no stain on *them*. Only the old lord could be censured for his deeds and there were plenty who did censure him for his treatment of his favorite and her youngest child. Even so their grandmother had to run away to marry Kalryn instead of Sunborn and his mother had had her own battles with the old man before she gained her freedom.

No, that was no barrier. If Synda had a father or brother to fight her choice, it would be different but he didn't think she did. Who she married was her choice and Davyd's.

"That Sunborn lady wants you," Monar was blunt. "But the decision is yours. No man can be forced to marry a woman he's not touched. You haven't touched her, have you?"

Davyd's growl was answer enough.

"I didn't think so. You'd better marry her so you can."

"She should marry Sunborn."

"Would you be happy if she did?" Monar demanded. "Could you quit thinking about it if she left you for another?"

"No." Davyd sat down heavily on a mounting block. "Gods!"

"Gods." Monar hid his smile. "I think you've got it worse than I ever did. I nearly fought a man who paid court to Dylla but I think you'll kill one."

"Mother said Lord Edan was courting her then I saw him in the Flowing Cup. I wanted to challenge him but Father was there."

"I'm glad!" Monar was startled by that admission. "Challenging him—Davyd, you don't challenge a Sunlord!"

"I know but I almost did it. If he had looked at me...."

"Davyd, get her wed. You aren't thinking straight and that's dangerous. She's chosen you. Choose her and be done with it."

His brother was silent and he knew there was something else worrying him. "Why not tell Wydon you want the Datyl store?"

Davyd's head shot up and he knew he had it.

"Wydon doesn't want to be tied down. Last night he told Glynda that he'd stay just long enough to see her set up with good men. He even has a husband in mind for her."

"He wouldn't! Glynda can't be forced."

"She's a woman." Monar hardened his heart. "It's custom that the men of the family choose her husband. If Wydon speaks for the family in Datyl, he can do it."

"Mother wouldn't allow it. *I* won't allow it. And I don't think Wydon would try it."

"You're right," Monar said. "He was joking but he's serious about not staying in Datyl. Ask him if you don't believe me."

He waited for his brother to say something.

"Well, if you *can't* force yourself to marry the girl, you wouldn't be interested in Datyl either. I don't think you're ready for a store." He turned for the door then stopped. "Davyd, leave the horses. In the state you're in, I wouldn't trust you without a pair of guards and you'd just have to bring them back anyway." With those harsh words, he left him.

Davyd swore. Not trust him? He'd never had that from his oldest brother but he knew it was true. He hadn't slept more than an hour last night and he was tired but thoughts of that girl and her challenge infuriated him. She'd hunted him only to reject him. She was nothing more than a harlot who showed her wares then demanded a price beyond what a man could pay.

Gods, he wanted her. Remembering what it felt like to hold her, to kiss her, to spend the day with her, he ached. And he wanted to feel that hair of hers against him. She'd worn it loose last night and he'd wanted to wrap it around his hands and feel its softness. Now he wondered if she wore anything under those robes and despaired of ever knowing.

Sitting on the mounting block, he tried to think what he should do. If Wydon would give up Datyl—but why would his brother do that? To have a store! He looked at the yard around him and tried to imagine owning something like this. He couldn't but it would be such a dream.

Synda was the wrong wife though. He couldn't see her as a merchant. He couldn't even see her as someone like his mother. She'd be no good at marshalling a household and he doubted she could sell a flask of water to someone dying of thirst. No, she was the wrong wife.

Sunborn and a painter too. He couldn't see her surrounded by practical things. No, her household would be full of color and servants who never ate in the same room and she'd have someone like Lady Alva to cushion her from the hard facts of life. No doubt, she'd let her child be raised by another. With a start, he remembered what she'd said about her mother—the mother who hadn't cared she was going on a manhunt.

Gods, he cared! He cared so much it hurt. Thinking of what his life would be like with her and then without her, he let the hours roll by, sunk in his misery.

WYDON finished with his last customer and looked up as the noon bells began to ring. His brother was already pulling out the shutters and starting to hang them when three new customers walked into the store. Adlar froze.

Wydon stared too, just as surprised as his brother to see the hunter. Of course, she didn't look like a hunter now. Dressed in a sensible green gown with a gold sash, Synda of Datyl was the perfect image of a Sunborn lady out for a shopping day.

"Lady Synda," Wydon greeted her with careful politeness. "And Lady Alva and…" he looked at the third woman.

"Karyn." She supplied her name with a smile. "Is your father at home?"

"No." Wydon wondered if he should send for him in spite of his orders. He noted the Temple braid she wore and wasn't surprised to see it had the gold bead of a sworn priestess.

"Good. We came to see Lady Nan."

"Of course." Wydon motioned to Adlar to finish hanging the shutters. Where was Davyd? If he found out Synda was here..."

"I'll get her!" Byka popped up from behind a counter, startling the ladies with her sudden appearance, and made a dash for the door before Wydon could say anything. He hadn't even known she was there.

"Which one was that?" Karyn asked. "The youngest?"

"Yes, lady. That was Byka the sneak."

"You're not serious." Synda looked at him in shock. "Surely she's not."

"Lady, you haven't had her spying on you yet," Wydon said, though he did it without heat. "If you want to keep a secret in this house, you find out where she is before you tell."

The priestess smiled but the ladies from Datyl looked uncomfortable. He didn't care. Remembering Davyd's anguish, he thought it just that this Sunborn lady was uncomfortable for a change.

"That's Adlar." He motioned toward his brother. "Excuse me." He went to help him hang a stubborn shutter and left them standing alone.

"This is so different from what I expected." Synda looked at the wares she could see in the partly shuttered store. "I thought they'd sell just a few things but it looks like—"

"Like they've got everything? Yes, York's is unique that way. More than three lots full of wares you need and some you just want when you see them. Rayna told me her father's store in Sefron offered only pans and dishes and the women who shopped there would go elsewhere for cloth and three blocks away for tea and even further away for other items. When they opened this store, she was delighted to be able to sell all those things under one roof."

"And it's successful?" Alva looked awed. "I would think other merchants would protest this."

"We buy from them and others outside Gardon." Wydon was listening. "And, since we can't carry everything, we're always willing to direct customers to the merchants who *do* have what they want."

"You give business away?" Synda looked surprised.

"If we don't carry it, yes. They usually buy something else from us and they know they can stop here for other things or ask us if we don't carry it. We're the first place holders stop in Gardon."

He finished hanging shutters and rejoined them.

"I traded for these pots only after Rayna told me she'd had a lot of requests." He pulled two pots from a display and showed how it nested into another. "I was told the bottom pot keeps the top one from getting too hot but I've also heard women say they can cook two dishes stacked like this."

They looked interested, especially the artist, and he couldn't believe she'd even seen a pot before. Davyd was going to marry her? He couldn't pick a more pampered child.

"I hope you know what you're doing," he muttered to the girl and saw her startled look and the grim face of her guardian.

"Why? I thought you liked me."

"I like you well enough, lady, but I wasn't thinking of you married with children on your lap and a store like this to run. And Davyd won't let his children be raised by servants. None of us would."

"You think that's what I want?" Synda looked like she'd just been slapped. "I *want* my children to know *me*. As for this," she motioned to the store, "I may not know anything about it, but I'm willing to learn. If it's what Davyd wants…"

"That's enough, Wydon."

He snapped his head around to see Mother Nan in the doorway, Byka behind her. His mother's look—the one she reserved for erring children—was warning enough.

"Mother Nan." He gave her a bow.

"I'm sure Synda will make as fair a merchant as I have," Nan said. "And I am sure Davyd will be as pleased with her as York is with me. You will *not* judge her."

"Yes, Mother." He refrained from pointing out that she never worked in the store and, as far as he knew, never had.

"Where did Davyd go?"

Wydon hesitated.

"Did he go out, I hope? Or is he still on the roof?"

"He came down. He was working this morning but he left with Monar."

"Let me know if you see him. I don't think Synda should see him today. We'll be in the solar."

"Yes, Mother."

The third floor room was the favorite retreat of the girls and where his mothers occasionally entertained. The men preferred the dining hall or the arms room on the second floor. They privately considered the second floor to be their territory—all except their mothers' rooms—and the third floor to be women only. Even the female servants had their quarters up there—all except Cook who slept near her precious kitchen.

He waited until his mother escorted the Sunborn ladies out then helped Adlar with the day's receipts.

"DO they all hate me?" Synda waited till she was settled in a stuffed chair to ask that timid question. "I thought he'd ask me to leave."

"He doesn't hate you. It's just that he's worried about Davyd and he's probably concerned about his father too. York took this all very hard and I had a time convincing him he should leave."

"Where did he go?" Karyn asked.

"To the Temple. I suggested he spend the day there. Byka, bring Natra here."

She scooped up the suddenly shy two-year-old and balanced her on her knee.

"This is my granddaughter. She's two and still needs a lot of watching. If you marry Davyd, this little one will be going with her mother to Datyl to make *your* life interesting."

"She will?" Synda looked gravely at the little girl and smiled. She got a smile back. "Natra? I like that name."

"She looks just like her mother did at this age. Your children will probably look more like you and Davyd. Glynda is one of Rayna's daughters."

"Glynda is the one I met?"

"Yes. Byka, here, is our youngest daughter and the quickest on her feet. When you want a message run, she takes it."

The six-year-old was beaming at the praise.

"Byka, go ask the twins here."

She took off before her mother finished.

"Now you haven't met Bryndal." Nan introduced her herbalist daughter as the fifteen-year-old set cups and a teapot before them. "And there's so many others."

Synda and Alva looked overwhelmed and Karyn interested as they met all the children of York. Not allowed in the house before because of the restrictions of the hunt, Karyn had kept up on who was who and how they were doing through visits Nan made to the Temple. She'd met all but Aldo of the boys but only in the course of her duties. Even now she didn't explain who she was but was just here to satisfy her curiosity while she chaperoned Synda.

"Are there more?" Synda had lost count by the time she met Donal and his friend. He didn't look pleased to see her but was solemnly polite. She knew he was Davyd's favorite from things her guardsman had said on the trail.

It was strange. All the girls seemed happy to meet her but the boys were hostile. Ten-year-old Aldo had been the worst, bluntly accusing her of hurting Davyd before his mother shushed him up, but even those she met before were hostile. Only Monar told her she'd be a fool to let Davyd go—and that was after she snapped at him for telling a blatant lie about Davyd and an innkeeper's daughter.

"Do you want Davyd next?" Byka looked ready to fetch him.

"Is he in the house?" Nan demanded.

"No, not in the house." Byka shook her black curls. "He's out in the yard. He's been there for hours."

"In the yard?" Nan walked over to the window and peered down, her face changing as she caught sight of her son. "Synda, come here and see your future husband."

She obeyed, looking out the big window with trepidation. The yard seemed a long way down and she got an impression of stalled horses and parked wagons before she saw him and gasped.

He was sitting on a stump with his head bent and his shoulders slumped, looking more defeated that any man she'd ever seen. Her heart went out to him and his misery. Was this her Davyd? Remembering the fire in his eyes when the raiders had him pinned and helpless, she could hardly believe he was the same.

How could she do this to him? Tears welled up in her eyes and she wanted to rush down and tell him it was all right. She wanted to soothe his misery away and see him happy again—or at least angry. Anything was better than the forlorn defeat she saw.

"It's all right." Nan turned her away from the window and looked in her eyes. "He *will* survive this and so will you but I want you to remember him like that. If you *ever* make him this miserable again, be sure that this whole family will come to Datyl and see your days are just as miserable!"

Synda laughed through her tears but she knew it was no empty threat. Lady Nan was so different. She wasn't like her mother at all but cared for all the children in her house even though more than half weren't hers.

"Mother," Glynda burst into the room. "Father's coming. Rayna is delaying him, but..." She gestured, nearly breathless.

"Where is he?" Karyn demanded in a panic. "Nan, if he should see me..."

"I know." Nan reacted quickly. "Bryndal, take Karyn up to the tea room. York never goes up there." The words were barely out of her mouth before the two were gone.

"I'm afraid you'll meet York too," Nan hurriedly warned. "But be assured he won't bite *you*."

Synda had no time to panic as a larger, older version of her Davyd strode into the room and stopped, his eyebrows shooting up as he saw her standing there with his wife.

She wanted to disappear when his shock turned to disapproval but he was already turning away to make a courtly bow to Lady Alva as Nan introduced her. It was only when his wife presented her that he looked at her again and made the same bow.

"Lady Synda," his voice rumbled. "I'm sorry we didn't meet under other circumstances."

"So am I." Synda's voice quavered. "I've heard so much about you."

"Oh?"

"Davyd told me you traveled into the mountains and met a whole race of women," she said in a rush, then flushed when she knew she didn't have it right. "I mean a city run by women."

"That I did but I didn't know he'd told that story. That was a *long* time ago."

"Not so long," Synda corrected him. "He said it was just before he was born—" Then she remembered her love's age and blushed.

This man didn't look that old! If she'd met him on the street, she would have him forty instead of somewhere in his fifties. He looked fit and his color was good and he seemed accustomed to the sword at his side — just like Davyd.

"It was a long time ago," York repeated more gently. "I've fathered eight children since then and earned every gray hair on my head — and in my beard." He rubbed the growth on his chin. "I'm still glad he told you about it."

"I am too."

"Where's the other one?" York turned to his wife. "I heard there were three ladies?"

"The other you may not see, husband." Nan answered him. "I invited Karyn as well."

"Nan, you risk a lot," York snapped at her then stopped and sighed. "Well, I think I should go somewhere so you can get her out of the tea room. Just to keep you happy, I'll get Davyd away as well." He turned to look at Synda. "But the next time I see this lovely lady in the house, I would like to see her with Davyd and *not* hiding from him."

Synda was stunned by his abrupt change but glowed in his approval.

"And you will *not* hunt my son again," York warned her, his smile gone. "I want to see you trade vows and raise a family in the proper way."

"Yes sir," Synda stammered. "I just didn't think — "

"Women never think," York interrupted her. "At least, not until they are certain they have the man where they want him. You've won Davyd and you'd better make him happy."

"Yes sir," Synda managed to say, feeling like a bad little girl. "But I've not won."

"You will." York was blunt. "He just doesn't know it yet."

Chapter 28 - Drunk

18 Hoth 850

DAVYD managed to avoid speaking to all but his father for the rest of the day and even left the house to eat at the Flowing Cup. It was late when he finally said goodnight to the guardsmen who insisted on seeing him home and staggered up the stairs to his room.

"You're back." Wydon was waiting for him.

"Yesh, I'm back."

"How much did you drink?"

"Not enough." Davyd decided with an effort. "Are you going to demand I marry her too?"

"Gods, no. I think she'd be a poor wife for you."

"What?" Davyd flared. "She's mine!"

"Davyd, listen. She's *not* a merchant any more than Mother is. Do you really want a wife who can't work in the store?"

"*Won't* have a store," Davyd denied. "Thash yours. Monar says I'm not ready for one."

"I'm not taking that store. I told Father tonight I'm not interested and Monar is not the head of this family. If you want it, it'll happen. If not… Wydon shrugged. "I'm not doing it."

"You can't throw it away!"

"And you're drunk," Wydon said with disgust. "Go to bed."

Davyd didn't move and Wydon pushed him toward the bed then had to duck when Davyd swung at him. The next thing he knew his brother was on top of him and he was struggling to keep him away from his knife.

"Stop it!" Using his greater strength, Wydon wrested his knife from him then hit him. Feeling Davyd go slack, he pushed him to one side.

"Gods." Monar was there in the doorway, one of the household guards behind him. "How much did he drink?"

"Too much. He jumped me."

"Let's get him to the water closet and make him give it up. If Mother finds out—"

"Forget Mother. Father might kill him for being such a fool."

They were taught from an early age that you didn't get drunk in public and you didn't drink enough to lose control. Davyd had done both.

Between the two of them they got him to the water closet and back again without waking any family. Hushing him up when he started to complain about their treatment, they stripped him and put him to bed.

DAVYD sputtered when water his face and filled his mouth then tried to get away from it. Falling off his bed with a thud, he looked up to see Wydon over him and wondered for a wild instant what he was doing in his dream. It should have been Synda with her long legs…

"Get up."

His brother's voice was cold as he set down the water bucket. "Breakfast is waiting and Father wants to see you."

"Father?" Davyd vaguely remembered coming home and a fight. "Gods, did I get drunk?"

"You did. Get dressed and try not to look the fool."

Davyd winced, his head pounding, as got off the floor and took the tunic Wydon threw at him. Seeing it was his good tunic in the house colors, he nearly threw it back. He didn't deserve to wear those. One look at his brother's grim face made him wear it anyway and add the dark brown hose. They were his best clothes.

Wydon yanked a comb through his hair then shoved him out the door.

"Stop it." He turned on him. "I'm not your kid brother."

"Then start acting like a man. You could have been killed last night. If the city guard hadn't brought you home—"

Davyd paled. "Does Father know?" he asked, his voice barely audible. Turning green at Wydon's nod, he gasped. "Let me…" He headed for the water closet in a rush.

A few minutes later, pale but feeling better, he joined his brother at the stairs.

"I didn't tell him." Wydon was grim when they stopped on the landing. "I think he heard."

With that warning Davyd stepped into the dining hall and braced himself for his father's justice.

No one seemed to notice. Food was being passed around the table and the younger children were already eating.

Davyd followed Wydon to his seat. His head felt huge and pounded every time his siblings clanked their spoons against glasses or plates. Gulping down a glass of water, he willed the pain to subside.

His father looked at him then turned back to his meal. Davyd wondered if he knew after all but then Cook set one of his mother's brews down in front of him. They knew.

Drinking the brew down, he waited for them to bring justice. It didn't come. He ignored his plate, the very thought of food making him queasy. Only when his father finished eating did he look at him again.

"Have you decided?"

"Sir?" Davyd couldn't believe the question. Did he mean punishment? When they were children they had to set their own punishments for the worst misdeeds.

"Are you going to marry the girl or not?" York demanded and a hush fell over the table. "If you aren't, I want to know today."

"Why?" Davyd shot back, angry his father was putting him on the spot. "Why today?"

"Because I have another commission from the queen waiting and if you're too idle to stay sober, I want you to take it."

"I'll take it," Davyd promptly said. "If it's not escorting her."

His sibs looked disappointed but he didn't care. Anything was better than the thoughts he'd been thinking this last day.

"York, surely…" Nan started but subsided at a look from her husband.

"I doubt the lady wants to see him either," York said. "And Fara specifically asked for Davyd. She was at the Temple yesterday for her son's wedding."

"Did you see it, Father?" Mala asked. "Was Lyda really beautiful?"

"Yes, she asked me to witness and Lyda was radiant. Even that dour brother of hers smiled when she kissed him. I didn't think *he* would come."

"Lord Mowyt?" Nan asked. "Well, he had a right to be there."

"He has a right to a lot of things but he doesn't exercise them," York said. "Davyd, you have the store in Datyl. If you're not ready to open it, we'll wait until Glynda has a husband."

"Yes sir." Davyd glanced at his sister. She looked ready to cry. The other girls looked unhappy too. He knew he could make them happy with just a few words but he couldn't do it—not yet.

"You have an appointment with the queen this morning," York said. "If you're done eating, you'd better get ready. Wydon, you go with him and take two guards but let him see the queen alone."

Davyd flushed, knowing he was being punished for last night but was glad it was only that. The one time Monar had come home tipsy his father had made an example of him and stripped him of his weapons for nearly a week. His punishment was light by comparison. He was even getting another royal commission.

Hoping to avoid his decision for a while, he left the table.

An hour later he was freshly washed and joining his brother for the walk to the Citadel.

"I think it's good Father is sending you away," Wydon commented as they strode down the street and Davyd knew he wasn't done needling him. He gritted his teeth and bore it but was unprepared for his next words. "If that girl decides to hunt again…"

Davyd stopped in his tracks and spun around to face him. "You think she'll hunt again?"

"I would if I wanted a child like she does. You don't want to be here if she tries it. You'd better keep some distance between you until she forgets you—that is, if you really don't want her."

Davyd paled. She could hunt again. She could come after him or, worse yet, choose another. He didn't want her choosing anyone else. Now that she'd challenged him to marry her, he didn't want to lose her.

"You're too young to get married," Wydon flatly stated. "Only twenty-one. Father didn't marry until he was twenty-five and even Monar waited that long. You shouldn't rush into a marriage you aren't sure of."

"I know," Davyd answered automatically. "I didn't plan to marry until—" he broke off, staring at his brother. "You don't want me to get married."

Wydon was twenty-five and hadn't courted anyone yet. By all rights, he should have been the next to marry.

"Or do you want Synda?" he demanded, suddenly seeing his brother's opposition in a new light.

"Gods no," Wydon exploded, stopping in his tracks. "Davyd, you can't think that. I would never—" His horror looked genuine.

"Never? Then why are you pushing me away from her?" His voice rose and passersby stopped to watch. "You've been telling me she's not a merchant's wife. You've been throwing my age at me. You *don't* want me to marry her!"

"No, I don't." Wydon lowered his voice as a pair of city guards noted them. "Everyone in the family has been pushing you together and that's wrong. If you can't make up your own mind, you've got no business getting married."

"And if I want her?" Davyd demanded, his temper cooling to an icy calm. "What then?"

"Then marry her," Wydon quickly retorted. "It's your life. I just don't want you to ruin it."

Davyd stared at him, confused. He wanted Synda but it was true she'd never make a merchant and he couldn't even ask her to try. She was Sunborn and an artist and probably couldn't even manage her own household. The match made no sense but did it have to? She wanted him and he wanted her.

There would be talk though and he was sure she wouldn't be able to handle that. There was always talk when a Sunborn took a Kalryn mate. It was understood if a man did it to get a son outside his fruitless marriage but the comments were sharper, more barbed when a woman did it. He'd heard some pretty rough jokes about how one lady couldn't find a Sunlord strong enough to share her bed. There'd even been speculation on how many men did before she married—all of it crude and undeserved. Synda couldn't handle that.

Gods, he could almost hear them speculating whether something had happened on the journey to Gardon. He cringed at the thought, knowing it was very close to being true.

"Davyd, it's your decision. Just don't let the mothers push you into it before you're ready. If you do want her for a wife, I'll be behind you."

"You said it yourself," Davyd retorted. "She'll never make a merchant's wife."

"Does she have to?" Wydon unexpectedly changed course. "Mother Nan isn't a merchant and you'll have Glynda to back you."

"I can't see her living over a store either," Davyd said, his expression bleak. "She has a villa."

"You could always live with her and walk to work," Wydon jokingly suggested. "Others have done it. Gods, I've done it. You know I don't stay in the store at Sefron."

Davyd glared at him and started walking again but the words stuck in his mind. Datyl was so peaceful he might be able to split a household. Glynda and a few guardsmen at the store with a housekeeper and some servants to support her. Yes, he could leave Synda's household as it was and walk to the store. That was a possibility.

His pulse quickened as he put that problem behind him but the thought of the gossip chilled him. She wouldn't be able to handle that and she probably wouldn't keep quiet about their marriage — and he wouldn't want her to. Maybe if they waited until people forgot he'd escorted her to Gardon.

They paused at the Citadel gates and talked to the black-uniformed guards. They were let through but their household guards were turned back.

Davyd and Wydon continued on, being stopped twice more by guardsmen and finally being given a guide who led them up to the royal level of the building and to the queen's own chamber.

"I'll stay here," Wydon said in the last guardroom. "She didn't send for me." He greeted a guard he knew and waited for Davyd to shed his weapons.

Davyd handed him his sword belt and dagger. This routine he knew, having done it just a few months ago. Was it really just a few months? It seemed like ages to him. He wondered what his commission would be.

The doors opened and two of the queen's guards followed him into a warm salon which served the queen as an informal audience room. Glancing at the desk, he saw it still stacked with papers. His second glance was for the massive tea cabinet his mother told him came from Datyl. He knew the queen created some of the teas his mother sold in the store but he'd never seen the inside of that black-lacquered cabinet.

His eyes went to the chairs by the stone fireplace next but the woman standing beside them was not the queen. He turned to look at another door just as the queen appeared.

"Enough now," the queen said to someone inside that room then shut the door. She was smiling when she turned to him.

"It's good to see you again," she said and took his hands before he could bow to her, surprising both him and the guards. "Lyda was quite pleased with her crystal and so was Valdyn. I gave the third to Tarus."

Davyd found her informality disturbing and drew back his hands to give her a formal bow. "My queen."

"Davyd Yorkson," Fara replied, smiling as she turned to her guards and servant. "You may go. Davyd is a son of York."

"Yes ma'am," a guard responded but gave him a look that promised the worst if he harmed her.

The queen waited while they left, hands clasped in front of her.

Davyd felt like he was being examined. He squirmed, uncomfortable with her close study.

Fara was beautiful. As tall and slender as his mother, she could easily have passed for her twin in dim light but there the resemblance ended. The queen commanded those around her while his mother was more diffident to those outside family. He couldn't imagine Fara being second to any, not even the husband she'd lost over ten years ago.

"She did capture you," Fara said. "Although I like the smile she gave you better than the one you wear now."

"Pardon?"

"Come here." Fara beckoned. "Look at this."

She stopped before a painting he couldn't see when he entered the room.

It was him! He knew in a flash this was Synda's work. Staring at the ready grin and the too-handsome face, he knew it was flawed. He wasn't that good looking. Knowing what he must have been thinking when she saw him smile like that, he stole a glance at the queen. Her eyes were on the painting.

He hadn't known she was so good. Remembering the countless sketches she'd done, he guessed that was when she planned this painting. Maybe she'd got her sketch book back after all. He thought it was lost overboard with her.

"It isn't finished and I want to see it done," Fara said. "It's such a fine work. I've already asked if I could buy it, but she said no."

Davyd couldn't imagine anyone telling the queen no or her accepting it.

"Now I want you to see Lyda's." Fara motioned him toward another painting next to his. "She hasn't finished it either."

Davyd stared, thinking it was the lady herself. A blue gown that matched blue eyes and golden hair not quite the shade of his lady's filled the canvas so cleanly it looked like a window. He didn't know paint could be so alive. Looking to the queen for permission, he lightly touched the edge of the dress to reassure himself it was just paint.

"It looks done," he finally said. "And a real masterpiece."

"It almost is," Fara acknowledged, "but she hasn't signed it yet and I'll not have it unsigned. When she went to the Temple, I had them moved here to protect them."

"Why didn't she finish?"

"That manhunt got in the way. Now she swears she won't paint at all. I don't have to guess why."

Davyd stiffened.

"Why are you refusing her?" Fara demanded. "If you think she's not virtuous…"

"Gods no," Davyd burst out. "She can't. I mean. And I wouldn't care anyway."

"Then why?" the queen snapped. "You've had more than enough time to walk over to the Temple and ask her. It's clear she's not going to settle for anyone but you or let any other man give her a child."

He glared at her, almost saying what he thought but choked in back. She was the queen.

"Davyd, if you let her talent go to waste, you'd do Gardon and Datyl a great disservice. And if she doesn't pass on her talent, it would be a shame. She's the best artist I've ever had at this court."

"She shouldn't marry Kalryn. As much as I want her, she shouldn't marry below her—"

"That?" Fara cut him off. "You fool. I didn't think any son of York's could be so…"

"If your father hadn't married Nan, but he did and all the Sunborn women in Gardon envy her. It's not the color of a man's eyes or hair that counts but what's in here." She rapped him on the chest.

"Why do you think the women in Nan's family have consistently married Kalryn?" She wasn't through, her eyes flashing angrily. "Nan could have been Sunborn. She could have married Sunborn. She was *raised* to be Sunborn but she threw that away when York asked her and never looked back."

"I'm not saying Synda will throw away *her* birthright or even that she should but I think it far more likely that you'll do what your father did and earn a Council right yourself."

"I know you'll be welcome in Datyl. I've seen their Sunborn men. I even married one." She stopped for a breath and glared at him. "And Alden left Datyl because of the politics—he couldn't stand it. They count politics more important than people."

"Synda has too many brains to get involved at court and she's done right to seek a man who has no interest in it. I just wish she'd chosen someone who could make up his mind before her fertility ends."

"Ends?" Davyd seized on that, dazed by her unexpected attack.

"Ends! Oh, get out of here. If I want to give your family a commission, I'll pick someone else. You've got to get your life in order first."

Davyd started toward the door but turned back. "What do you mean—her fertility ending?"

"Ask Synda. She doesn't have forever and it's about time you talked to *her*."

Davyd opened the door. Wydon was on his feet and so were the guards. They looked uneasy and he knew they'd heard the queen if not what she said.

Then he started to get mad. Guessing his mother had put her up to this, he was embarrassed and irritated all at once that the *queen* knew what was going on in his life. She had no right.

"Let's get out of here."

"What about the commission?" Wydon asked.

"There wasn't one. She's been plotting with Mother. I bet Mother came to see her yesterday."

"She didn't." Wydon caught up with him. "She was home all day. She even spent the afternoon with…" His eyes widened. "Father!"

"Pitfire!" Davyd knew too and knew he was lost. His father was pushing this? And that comment about her fertility…

His steps slowed. Could she be? He hesitated as they crossed the court then stopped.

Remembering his mother's grief when she lost a child — the only girl she would ever bear — he tried to imagine what it would be like to have no children at all. Then he was thinking of that wondrous painting of Lyda. It was better, so much better, than the one of him. She couldn't quit painting — not for him.

"What is it?" Wydon realized he wasn't following. "Davyd?"

"I've got to see Synda."

His brother's face changed and slowly he smiled. "She's at the Temple. I asked."

"I know."

They parted company at the Temple. He knew this time he would settle it. If Synda wouldn't have him, this would be the end.

Chapter 29 - Choice

19 Hoth 850

DAVYD strode up and down the room where they put him and glared at the door, willing Synda to appear so he could get this over with. Finding out she was in the Women's Court, he had to wait for her to come to him. Men weren't allowed there.

What if she didn't come? He faced that bleak possibility. Everyone thought she wanted him but he'd hurt her feelings not once but twice during the hunt. Then he'd waited and made her suffer. She just might be contrary again and tell him no but he wouldn't take it this time. If he couldn't get her to say yes now, today, he swore he'd walk away and forget her. This had to be it.

Half convinced she'd refuse to see him, he was still bracing for it when he heard a soft click and spun around to see her just inside the closed door.

"Synda." His tongue suddenly felt thick and dry in his mouth. He couldn't move. Now that she was here, his feet seemed rooted to the floor and his face felt wooden. His stomach tensed and he wished he'd eaten. Gods she was so beautiful. Her hair was hanging loose and he wanted to wrap its soft strands around his hands.

"Davyd." She looked as scared as he felt.

"I'm sorry about the hunt," he said, the words sounding lame. "I didn't mean to hurt you."

She blinked, her eyes shiny with tears. She gave a tiny shrug. "I shouldn't have asked you to accept it. I was wrong."

"That's it?" Davyd couldn't believe what he was hearing. "You didn't think you should ask me?" he exploded. "Maybe you should have asked Lord Edan?"

"Him?" Synda stared at him. "Why would I want *him?* He'd never leave the court. Goddess, he isn't even good-looking."

"And I am?" Davyd's lips twitched and some of his fear drained away.

"You're beautiful." Synda looked at him with such a look of admiration that he felt the blood rushing to his face.

"Tell me," he invited, never thinking she would.

She hesitated but it wasn't long. "From the first time I saw you I itched to paint you. I sketched you every chance I got and I *tried* to get that damn tunic off you. I *dreamed* about you and when you kissed me…" She looked dreamy and hungry all at once.

"I remember the sketching." Davyd folded his arms and looked at her. "But I remember there were others—including the captain."

Her lips hardened and her eyes sparked with anger. "You *know* that was because you *wouldn't* sit for me. And he was nice while you were—"

"—guarding you," Davyd finished. "Synda, why do you want me? Marrying a Kalryn will only get you snide comments and insults. I've seen it happen."

"I know." Synda spoke quietly, looking a little daunted by the prospect. "But I still want you and I don't care what *those* people say. It doesn't matter either. There aren't any stores in Datyl like York's."

Davyd sucked in his breath, wondering how she could be so confident about a store she'd never seen.

"Will you keep painting? I don't want you if you won't paint."

"Want me?" Synda flushed. "You want me for my painting?" She bristled and advanced on him. "Davyd Yorkson, if that's all you want."

Pulling her close, he shut her mouth with his own. Her resistance was brief. She melted into him as he deepened the kiss. Holding her against him, he pressed her hips against his throbbing manhood.

"You think that's all I want?" He finally broke the kiss, his breath ragged.

She wiggled.

He gasped and hurriedly put some space between their hips.

"Don't," he begged. "Synda, not yet."

Smiling up at him with a knowing smile, she tried to get closer.

"Synda, no." He abruptly let her go and retreated. Catching his breath, he studied her with a mixture of surprise and lust. "Where did you learn that?"

"They prepared me." She folded her hands and answered him with a pleased expression. "And I paid attention."

Davyd gave a wordless laugh and looked at her with new respect. She wasn't innocent anymore.

"They told me what rugur does." Synda lost her smile. "I'm glad you didn't tell me. Those raiders — they were going to use it."

Davyd remembered. Drugged with rugur, she would have had no chance against the needs of her body. Men were also held in its grasp but not as fiercely as women. "You'll never need rugur. I promise you that."

"Oh, I don't know." She gave him a timid smile that still managed to be wicked. "If you won't have me…"

"Will you paint?" Davyd repeated his question. "I don't want you leaving that to be a merchant's wife. I don't think you should even work in the store."

She looked disappointed. "If you don't want me there, I won't go." Her lip trembled. "But I'll paint," she finished with a rush. "And you can sell some of those."

"Agreed." Davyd wondered who could afford work like hers.

"And *I* want to hang them. I've always arranged my own work so it's in the best light."

"Agreed." He thought that was reasonable.

"And Glynda said I could talk to other artists and see if they'll sell to York's. I know a sculptor and there's a potter and…"

"Do you know everyone in Datyl?" Davyd shot back, realizing she had no intention of staying out of his business and Glynda was leading her on. *When had she met Glynda?*

"Not everyone — just the artists and those who stay away from court and do something with their lives."

"And how will they feel when they see your half-blood children?" Davyd demanded. His heart went cold when she had no answer for that.

"I'll go," he said, resigned. "I'd not wish that on anyone."

"Davyd, no!" Synda made an abortive gesture. "I was trying to think of the words. Please."

"If you can't say it —" he was grim.

"I can!" She was blocking his retreat. "When they see my healthy, *happy,* half-blood children," She looked at him with such warmth he couldn't move. "And see the man I call husband…" She didn't finish but encircled his neck and drew his lips down to hers.

Davyd took the kiss she offered and knew no amount of talk was going to make her ashamed of him or the children she bore. Still he couldn't leave it. As they finished their intense pledge, he looked into her wondrous green eyes. "And what? Will you keep the hunters from my door?"

"They won't dare!" Her look promised dire consequences for any woman who tried. "And I won't share your bed with another wife."

"Good!" Davyd lifted a lock of that wonderful hair to his lips. "And you will leave off tempting men."

"As long as you make me happy," Synda replied with an arch smile. "I still want my three days and nights."

"You'll get them." Davyd rubbed the bodice of her dress and she gasped as his hand found a nipple through the fabric. "Again and again."

"You promise?"

"Always," Davyd muttered and sealed his vow with a kiss.

Epilogue

19 Hoth 850

NERVOUS, yet exhilarated, Davyd stood beside his love and waited to exchange his vows in the Temple of the Flame. His family had come, every one of them, to witness the rite along with Synda's new friends. Anxious to get it over with, he mentally rehearsed his lines and knew his love must be doing the same.

Finally the Black Priest arrived, stepping up to the altar to conduct the rites. A priestess Davyd vaguely recognized as one of Synda's attendants stood with him.

Justus gazed fondly at them then smiled at the assembled company. "In the service of the gods and goddess, I am glad to be here to guide these rites. Let us begin."

"In the beginning there was but one spark of creation. From this spark sprang the Flame to light the void of the universe. The Flame is eternal, crossing all time and space to be part of each of us and everything that is. Within us we each carry a spark of it that grows as we grow and glows most brightly when we share it or have another share with us."

"Through the union of this man and this woman two small embers of the Eternal Flame are shared and will grow to a brighter fire. Soon they will be three and a child will come from their joining to be sheltered by their love and respect for each other."

He smiled at them. "Let the sharing begin."

Synda took the candle the priestess held out to her as Justus stepped aside. With a trembling hand, she lit it from the altar flame and offered it to Davyd.

"Davyd Yorkson, I give thee the flame of my soul. Let it warm your nights and bring light to your days."

Davyd took the candle she offered and solemnly made his first vow. "I accept this light of your soul and will guard it always and feed it well with my love and the fruits of my labor. I swear to keep it close and let no other spark separate my light from yours."

With those words said, he turned and handed the lit candle to Wydon, his choice for protector, and accepted another candle from Justus.

Lighting his own candle, he offered it to his bride. "Synda Verasdatter, I give thee the light of my soul that it may fill you and bring you happiness."

Synda took the candle, protecting the flame with her cupped hand and letting the light shine on her radiant face. "I accept this light of your soul with gladness and swear it does not shine on barren ground. The field is ready for your seed." She reddened as she said the words.

Davyd smiled, more confident now as he took her candle back from his brother.

They faced the altar and spoke the next vow together. "By the Flame, we pledge our love and join our souls that we might form another."

Working together they lit a solitary candle waiting on the altar, a symbol of the child to be.

Justus stepped forward again. "Do you pledge to protect the children of your union, sharing equally in their lives?"

"We do."

"Then let the gods bless this union for all to see." Justus picked up the altar candle and held it high. "May it be long and fruitful!"

"May it be long and fruitful," the witnesses chorused.

Davyd carefully gave the lit candles back to Wydon then turned back to his bride. Mindful of the witnesses, he gave her a light, chaste kiss before the altar.

"Davyd, surely you can do better than that," Monar said, disgusted. "Or maybe we should show you how." He pulled Dylla close and started to kiss her.

"He knows how." Synda looked up at Davyd with daring in her eyes. "And so do I!"

Pulling his head down to hers, she kissed him back with passion and let all the world know that *this* guardsman was hers forever more!

The Author

Ellen Anthony is the creator of two science fiction universes and the winner of the 2001 Epic Award for Best Mystery. She can be found on Facebook and she regularly responds to readers and reviewers.

Her plans for 2024 include a re-release of SEARCH FOR THE SUN (the sequel to MANHUNTER and winner of the Epic Award) and TOO YOUNG A KING. These will be published under her own label to keep them from going out of print a third time.

Below is a list of her published works. You can find out more by visiting The Jasper Stone Mysteries Group on Facebook.

THE SYRAN NOVELS

The Manhunter (2000 Epic Award finalist)

Search for the Sun (2001 Epic Award winner, Publisher's Nominee for the International Ebook Award, Finalist for the Reviewer's Choice Award). *Publication pending*

Too Young a King (2002 Epic Award finalist). *Publication pending*

The Blood Circle (2003 Epic Award finalist) *Available now*

THE JASPER STONE NOVELS

Murder is Bliss
To Marry and Suspect
Coral Crosses
Between Heaven and Hell
Shadow Mars
Shadow Earth
Webs of Deceit
Rebel Circuits
For the Future

Light & Shadows
Shipwrecked *In progress*
The Future Comes *Pending*

LETTERS THROUGH TIME

Lura's Oregon Trail Adventure (2002 Epic Award Finalist)
Jacob's Oregon Trail Adventure
Mr. Harding's Oregon Trail Adventure
Mrs. Harding's Oregon Trail Adventure (pending)